Madness Heart Press
2006 Idlewilde Run Dr.
Austin, Texas 78744

Bone Factory and other Tales of the Supernatural by Christopher Reed is a work of fiction. Names, characters, places, and incidents either are the product of the author's imagination or are used fictitiously. Any resemblance to actual persons, living or dead, events, or locales is entirely coincidental.

First Edition October 2019

Cover by John Baltisberger

www.madnessheart.press

The Bone Factory
&
Other Tales of the Supernatural

Very special thanks to Ron Grimm, for his invaluable assistance guiding a closet science geek through the quantum world. And to my wife, Cynthia Carle, for her inspiration, brilliant editing, and allowing me continued access to her amazing mind.

Inmate 10742

John,

It's been a long time. I recently read your excellent and fascinating article in The Psychologist about alien abduction belief and felt compelled to pass this on to you. Of course, this must remain in the strictest confidence and not be shared with anyone. I would, however, value your professional opinion on this individual.

A little explanation. In April of last year, I took the job as Chief Psychiatrist at Oracle State Prison, Special Psychiatric Unit. Over the next year, I interviewed each of the inmates, familiarizing myself with their cases. This is a transcript of my interview with Inmate 10742. I think you might find it interesting and would welcome the opportunity to discuss at a time which might be convenient for you. I've omitted my own questions and comments so as to not distract from the patient's train of thought.

Best,

Robert

AUGUST 17

Interview with Inmate 10742

Why am I in here? Says right there in my file, doesn't it? I attacked a guy, hurt him bad. So they locked me up.

Oh, well, there's always more to it, isn't there?

NOTE: AT THIS POINT, the inmate looked over at the small window high on the cinder block wall. He stared at it for a long time, not saying anything. I didn't interrupt his silence. After several minutes had passed, I noticed tears welling up in his eyes. He started speaking again, still focused on the window, without looking at me. After a few moments, whatever emotion he was feeling seemed to disappear. He spoke, on the whole, in a reasonable manner. At times he exhibited an attitude of resentment typical, in my experience, of most incarcerated individuals.

THERE ARE THINGS OUT there. Things we don't know about. No, that's not exactly right. Things we don't want to know about. Most people, hell, almost everyone, thinks it's nonsense. Just an overactive imagination or some crap like that. But I've seen them. Well, I've seen some of them. I know I'm not gonna get out of this place for a long time, so it doesn't make any difference whether I talk about it or not. But I know I'm not the only one. Other people have seen them. A lot of them are probably locked up, like me. Others, they just don't say anything. They're smart. I'm not so smart. I should have kept my mouth shut, like them, and I probably wouldn't be in here.

They say I'm pretty crazy. Maybe I am. They say my brain doesn't work like other people's brains. I have no problem with that. I'm glad it doesn't. I'm not exactly in awe of the way other people's brains work. In fact, I think that's why I lost it, why I attacked that son of a bitch. See, people always love to quote that line from Hamlet: "There are more things in heaven and earth, Horatio, than are dreamt of in your philosophy." It makes them feel so cool. Like they accept the big mysteries of the universe. Bullshit. Tell them a story about how you saw something for real, something nobody else has ever seen, and all of a sudden you're a whack job. They laugh at you. Or, they say you're delusional and lock you up. Then they write articles about you in the paper supposedly just reporting the story you told but, in fact, their real story is how this crazy guy is going around claiming to have seen a monster. The story turns out to be about you and how much of a flake you are. Oh, yeah, everyone loves that. Makes them feel so fucking superior.

Yeah, I've read a lot of Shakespeare. I like to read. I'm a lot smarter than you think. Just not smart enough to keep my mouth shut.

So, Dr...what was your name again? Is that what you want? I mean, I'm guessing that's why I'm here, right? Because you want to hear the crazy guy's crazy story?

What do you mean do I want to tell you the story? I don't give a fuck whether I tell you the story or not. You're the one who set up this appointment. What is it with you guys, anyway? It's all questions. You're the ones with the damn degrees. You're supposed to have the answers. So how come you're always throwing the questions back at me? What the fuck is that?

The pictures? What about them? I've drawn a hundred of them. You've seen them. You've got them right there in that file, right? It's what it looked like, what can I say? You guys ask me to draw pictures of it. So I do. Then you try to figure out what they mean. I love that. Oooo, this is what the crazy guy thinks he saw so it must be the inside of his fucked-up brain, right? Let's see if we can analyze them and figure out if it represents some childhood trauma or something. Maybe he hated his father. Spoiler alert, Doc. I did hate my father. He was an abusive drunk and treated my mother like shit. So, is that what that thing represents? Hey, why not. I really don't give a fuck what you decide is wrong with me.

Yeah, the story. Okay. Okay, Doctor...what was it again? Right. You know, I'm pretty fucking tired of telling this story. So this is the last time. Ever. You got your little tape recorder on, right? Good. You can analyze it, maybe come up with some really cool theory about my delusions and write it up for Psychology Today. You might even end up on the talk shows.

Okay, well, excuse my cynicism. You know, I don't care that they busted me for fucking that guy up. Fine. It was wrong. So I'm guilty of assault. Lock me up for that. I get it. But they put me in the psych unit. They branded me a mental case. Because I told the truth. And, you know what, I'm going to be a good guy, a good inmate. In four or five years they might let me out of here. But I won't be the same guy. They've changed my identity. To the rest of the world, for the rest of my life, I'll be a crazy guy. How would you feel, Doc?

How did it begin? It didn't...begin. It just happened. Someone's in a car crash you don't ask how did it begin. Jesus.

All right. I was working for this tree service company. It's a rural area and limbs blow down, trees fall across roads, people build a new house they need to clear some trees. That sort of thing. So we'd been contracted to brush the phone lines feeding this little tiny town...well, it wasn't really a town, just a gas station and a grocery store with a little lunch counter...Henson. But the phone line went over the mountain to Gruber. Bigger town, but not much. Long job. We could do about a thousand yards a day. Me and this other guy. Kenny. It was gonna take us about a month. I loved it. It's why I took the job. I like being outside.

What do you mean do I have a problem with being indoors? Another stupid fucking question. I didn't say I had a problem being indoors. I said I like to be outdoors. You turned it into a problem. Christ, you guys...Look, you want to hear the story or not?

Okay. Fine. Anyway, I like climbing trees. I've always liked climbing trees. When I was a kid, I saw a tree, I had to climb it. I read this book about the first guys to climb to the top of the redwoods. 300 feet up there. I'd love to do that sometime. Anyway, brushing the phone lines was great. During the winter storms branches would fall on the lines, sometimes trees would go over onto them. So we'd go up there and clear the branches off the lines, splice them back together. You get it.

We had what you call climbing spurs that strap onto your calf and foot. You throw a strap around the tree to hang onto, then you dig the spike into the bark of the tree and just climb it. I loved climbing those big bastards. Just sit up there a hundred and fifty feet off the ground, stare out at the mountains and eat my lunch.

So this one morning, the day it happened, we're having breakfast in Ella's before we head up the mountain. The little place in Henson I talked about with the lunch counter? It was run by this old Native American guy, Melvin, and his wife, Ella. She's white. They're both about 80. He's cool, real laid back. But Ella is, what's the word, cantankerous. Sucks on a toothpick and snarls at everybody. But once you get to know her, you realize she's okay. She loves animals. Feeds a couple of foxes out in the back and some deer. So Ella asks us where we're going today, and we tell her we're going about halfway up the draw along Ray's Creek. Ella's pouring me some more coffee, and she says, "Dead Man's Creek."

We ask her what she means.

"What they used to call it."

"Why'd they call it that, Ella?" I ask.

"Folks died up there. Two at least, maybe more. Folks stopped talking about it. Stopped going up there, too. Didn't want to remember any of that, so they changed the name."

So I ask how they died and she just shrugs.

Yeah, well, the mountain people up there have all kinds of stories. It's just part of their world. Melvin says he saw Bigfoot twice. Anyway, we didn't think much about it. You just sort of chalk it up to local folklore.

So, we finished our breakfast, and we're heading out the door, and Ella says, "Take a couple of extra waters from the case there. Don't go down by the creek."

Well, that sort of rocked me. Not just what she said about not going down by the creek, but the fact that she didn't charge us. Ella was notoriously tight. For her to give anything away was unheard of. So I knew she had to be pretty serious.

I grabbed a couple of bottles of water and thanked her. "Why not go down by the creek, Ella?" I had to ask, right?

She was cleaning the counter after our breakfast. She didn't look up. She just said. "Somethin' down there."

On our way up the hill, I told Kenny what she said. He just laughed it off. I didn't say anything, but I was thinking about it. There was just something in her voice. One thing I learned from my time up there was that the mountain people have instincts about certain things, and it's a good idea to listen to them. If they tell you you won't catch fish a certain day...you won't catch fish. Or if they tell you, there'll be nine inches of snow in the morning you can count on it. They know that world. Ella and Melvin had been there their whole lives, and nobody knew those mountains better than them.

Anyway, so we head up the main road for a few miles then turn off onto this forest service access road that heads up the draw toward Ray's Creek. We've got a four-wheel-drive SUV 'cause otherwise you'd never make it. The road runs about a hundred feet above the creek most of the way. We pulled over almost to the summit. It takes a while to get up there. Once we stopped, we had to gear up and then hike another three hundred feet or so before we reached the phone line. As we're working our way up the line, I keep looking down to the bottom of the draw where the creek runs. Kenny's kind of raggin' me for taking Ella seriously. But, damn, I couldn't stop thinking about it.

So we work for about three hours. There were a lot of repairs on the line in that section. It snows hard up there and a lot of branches go down. So we didn't make much progress as far as linear feet go.

Kenny? He was okay, I guess. We had some good laughs together every so often but damn, the guy just never stopped talking. And all he ever wanted to talk about was football or hunting and how many deer he killed. Or, as he put it, "boogered." "Boogered me a four-point buck up in that canyon." He was a real hillbilly. But mostly it was football. He was a crazy fan and played that fantasy game. He had to tell me about every damn trade or whatever, even if it wasn't football season. Some days I just wanted to stuff something in his damn mouth. His wife had left him and took their kid, and I thought, well, no shit. He probably drove her nuts talking about football.

Yeah, yeah, I know, Doc. They tried to make a case against me, saying maybe that day I'd just had too much of Kenny. Complete bullshit and they had no evidence. And, as you can see, I never got charged, so don't even start, okay? The truth is I felt kind of sorry for him, which is why I never told him to shut up. But it was one of the reasons I liked to climb a tree and eat my lunch, just to get away from his yammering for a bit.

So, that day we broke for lunch, and I picked out this beautiful Ponderosa pine and headed up for the top. Kenny always liked to sit in the truck and look at his football charts or whatever they were. So, I climb up as high as I can go in this tree. I'm up there a good hundred feet. It was a beautiful view. I'd never been up that high in those mountains before. I could see forever. I kind of stretch out on this big old branch with my back against the trunk. I can see the truck down the hill below and all the way down into the canyon. And while I'm eating my sandwich, I see Kenny get out of the truck and head down the slope toward the creek. And, I mean, if it wasn't for what Ella had said earlier I wouldn't have thought anything about it. But now I'm thinking this might not be a good idea. I holler down at him, like, where the hell are you going? And he just waves back up and holds up a water bottle. Well, we'd always fill up our water bottles from the creeks up there because the water was so good. So, usually, it was no big deal.

Kenny disappears into the trees, and I go back to my lunch. I'm thinking that he's probably right to just laugh the whole thing off. I mean I'm trying to talk myself into it, but I just don't have a good feeling. And now I'm getting nervous. So I keep staring down there, waiting for Kenny to come back up. I'm sort of timing it, thinking how long it would take him to fill up that water bottle. But he's not coming back up. And I'm staring down trying to see if I can see him. Then suddenly I hear this short scream. And, way down in the middle of the trees by the creek, I catch a glimpse of Kenny's red shirt. But I see something else. Some other shape that I can't make out. It's too far away, and it's dark and shadowy under those trees way down there. Then I hear another scream, and I fucking panic and start climbing down as fast as I can.

I'm calling down at Kenny, but I know there's no way he can hear me. It's too far away, and I know the creek down there is going to be making a lot of noise. It takes me about ten minutes to get down the tree. You can't move too fast with climbers and a strap. But damn, my heart is racing and I finally get down, unbuckle the climbers and run down to the truck. I grab the rifle we always have with us, and I move as fast as I can down the hill toward the creek. And as I get close, I stop. Shit, I realize that - I mean, I saw somebody else, or something besides Kenny. Then I remember what Ella said. "Somethin' down there." And that word...somethin'. That doesn't mean a person. I mean, you don't know what it means exactly. So now I'm just fucking freaked. And what I really want to do is get my ass back to the truck and get out of there as fast as I can. But I can't just leave Kenny there. I have to see if he's okay, what the hell happened, right?

I call to him a couple of times, but there's no answer. So I make my way really slow down the slope, I can hear the creek now. It's steep in this area, so the water is falling fast over rocks into some pretty big pools. I cross a sort of open area until I get to where the trees begin at the edge of the creek. My hands are sweating, and my grip on the gun is slippery. I wipe my hands on my pants. Shit, I can hear my own damn heart beating.

Now I'm trying to figure out what I could have seen. What was down there. And I figure the only logical explanation is that it's gotta be some kind of big animal. Maybe a bear or a big cat. Most likely it's a black bear. They don't usually want to bother people. Mostly they'll just run off. But if you surprise one, they'll attack, especially if it's a female with a cub. And this is the time of year when that's a real possibility. Christ, I'm thinking it got Kenny and he's either dead or hurt really bad. And if it is a bear and it's still there, then it's not going to be too happy to see me, and I might have to shoot it. And, damn, you better be a real good shot to take down a bear before it gets to you. And I'm no big game hunter like Kenny. And the thing is, as much as it seems to make sense that it has to be an animal like that, I tell ya Doc, I know damn well I'm wrong. I can just feel it.

So, I'm in the shadows of the tree canopy, moving down the bank real slow, and suddenly I realize something feels strange. The air is different. It's thicker and warmer, and there's a weird smell. And I realize...I know the smell. It's the smell from right after a thunderstorm. Ozone. I always liked that smell. You know what I'm talking about, right? It's always fresh and clean. But out there it just smelled wrong. Why the hell would it smell like ozone there by this creek? There weren't any thunderstorms. It was a warm sunny day.

So I climbed over a few big rocks and moved down closer to the creek. Right in front of me, the water fell down a pretty steep drop, you know, like steep rapids. But just above me, up a little further was a big pool, I don't know, maybe thirty feet across. It was formed by a pretty high waterfall, about ten feet high. Ray's Creek isn't some little babbling brook. It's a big strong creek, a lot of water pouring over the falls and making a lot of noise. I scanned the whole area with the gun ready. But I didn't see anything. There was no sign of Kenny. So I called his name, but there was no answer.

The air was feeling even heavier, and it was kind of darker than it should be, and now I know something definitely wasn't right. The ozone smell was even thicker. I started to get kind of dizzy. I saw these little flashy things in the air, like electrical sparks. Just random, all over the place. And I'm thinking I should get the fuck out of there fast. Then the sparks get faster and there's a lot more of them. Pew pew pew pew pew. In the air. It's like the whole place is electrified. I really wanna run, but I'm getting dizzier like I'm looking at these sparkles and it's kind of hypnotizing me or something. And I can feel my body going numb. The gun slips out of my hands and falls onto the rocks. I hear it fall, but I can't even react to it.

And then I look over across the pool, and I see something sticking out through the waterfall, just above where it hits the pool. It kinda looks like a really big head. I have no idea what I'm seeing. I'm feeling kind of queasy, and I rub my eyes, and when I look back, it's gone. I just thought I was imagining it. I figured it was just some kind of hallucination. Like there's so much ozone that it's messing with my brain.

Then I see something else. There are ripples in the pool like something is swimming toward me. Then it starts to rise up out of the water in the middle of the pool. This time I know, it's no hallucination. And God almighty, Doc, I see that it's Kenny. And I can see he's dead. His eyes are open but kind of milky. His whole body's just rising up out of the water. And I didn't even see it at first. What's behind him, I mean. It's that thing. That thing in the drawings you've got there, Doc. I'm not much of an artist, but that's what it looked like. That head that kind of looks like some giant salamander but a whole helluva lot scarier. I think I didn't notice it at first because it's so much like the color of the rocks. But it's lifting Kenny out of the pool. It's huge. Its whole body looks kind of like a lizard, and it has to have long legs, because I see it's a pretty deep pool and it's standing upright, holding Kenny by the neck. And suddenly it just throws him. Heaves him like forty, fifty feet up the bank, like Kenny's just a toy or something. I watch his body go flying and drop onto the side of the hill. The sound of his body hitting the ground...God, it was just horrible.

I look back at the pool, and the thing is standing there staring at me. I can see it clearly now. It's got this ridge that sticks out in the middle of its head, like between its eyes and then goes down its back. And there are all these tiny electrical sparkles crackling right along that ridge. And those eyes. I couldn't draw the eyes very well. I'm not much of an artist like I said. But its eyes were slits with this almost glowing green inside and this black horizontal slit in the middle.

Then it starts coming toward me. And I can't even move. I remember, at least I think I do that I wanted to turn and run but I couldn't. My body just didn't work. And it's about three feet from me, and I can feel this electricity like my skin starts buzzing as it gets close to me. I know I'm going to die. That what happened to Kenny is about to happen to me. And there's nothing I can do about it. Then suddenly I hear this high pitched sort of crazy squealing noise. I can't tell where it's coming from, but the creature turns its head and looks back at the far side of the pool. I look over, and I see three more heads, same kind of creature, but they're a lot smaller. They're sticking out from out of the base of the waterfall, and their mouths are open, and I can see this is where the sound is coming from. They're making a kind of pulsating screaming sound, really hard to describe. And the big creature opens its mouth and lets out this crazy weird gurgling sound. Maybe it's some kind of language, I don't know. But the three smaller heads disappear back behind the waterfall.

The creature looks back at me. It sticks its head forward right at my face, so it's just a couple of inches away. I'm just frozen there, just staring at the face of this monster. There are all these tiny sparks flashing all over the surface of its skin. And I can smell it. Like it's got some sort of smell that isn't even animal. It's more like some kind of chemical or something. And those green slit eyes, the pupils are getting bigger, then smaller. And then this tongue comes out its mouth, this flat black tongue that's kind of forked, except there's a bunch of little pointy forks sticking out the end, and it flicks all over my face like it's tasting me. And I can feel this tingly sensation where it touches me, like little electric shocks. Then it opens its mouth really wide, and I see all these, not teeth, but like ridges of really sharp bone, and I know I'm about to die. Except that it just makes more of those sounds. More gurgling, with what sound almost like really high musical notes mixed in and it gets louder and louder, and my ears start hurting, and my whole body is shaking, and everything gets blurry and...that's it. I guess I just passed out.

Okay, so, you read the rest of my file there, Doc, and you can see they found me that night walking down the road out in the middle of nowhere. I don't have any memory of what happened after that thing stuck its head in my face and I woke up in the hospital three days later. The cops came and started asking me questions about Kenny. So I told them the truth. I told them what happened. What I saw. Big mistake.

That asshole? It was his attitude. That's why I went after him. Shit, that weasly little son of a bitch...what do they call him, some kind of profiler or something? First, he starts treating me like a hick, like I'm from the hills like Kenny. Which is bullshit to begin with. I didn't finish college, but I went for three years. I just decided I wanted to live differently, be out in nature. But I read everything. Like Shakespeare. And I read science magazines. Christ, the guy's sitting there just inventing this whole story as if he knows better than I do what happened, how it went. You know what he asked me, Doc? He asked me if I read a lot of monster stories, if I played fantasy video games, shit like that. I'd had it.

No, of course not. There's no justification. I didn't plan on hurting him that bad. Just the way we fell, he hit his head, and it messed him up. I don't feel good about that. After what I'd seen, what happened to Kenny, to be treated like that...I just lost it. Read the rest of the history there, Doc. You can see how nice and neat they made it all. Just call the guy crazy, and it's all wrapped up.

You know how many times I asked for a polygraph? So, how come they never allowed me to take one? Huh?

Yeah, I had an attorney. She was okay, I guess. I just fucked up. So, what's your angle on this, Doctor? You have any say about my future, or are you just curious about the nut case with the monster story?

Really? Well, that would be very satisfying. I don't really care if anyone believes me anymore, but if you can get me a polygraph...

Yeah, I know they're not considered evidence. I don't care. I also know that they use them a lot and if they didn't mean something they wouldn't, right?

What? I thought you weren't going to ask me any more stupid questions. Jesus Christ. How can there be some other possible explanation? It happened just the way I said. Just...get the fuck out of here. You're no different than the rest of them. You want me to confess to being crazy. Shit, it's unbelievable. Or not. Maybe it's the most believable thing there is. There are things out there, Doc. And the truth that they really exist, man, it's so perfectly protected.

Oh, come on, Doc. You know damn well how. It's protected by all the nice neat little fairy tales we invent to make us feel so secure. Because we can't stand the idea that there are things we don't know. That's just way too scary. So when something comes along, like what I saw, we just sweep it under the rug. Don't want to hear about it. Just can't fit a story like mine into your tight little concept of reality. You remember that movie, A

Few Good Men? Yeah. Remember, when Jack Nicholson says to Tom Cruise, "You can't handle the truth?" That's it. That's why I'm really in here, Doc. Because nobody can handle the truth.

Bullshit. I don't have to admit anything. That's fucking sad, Doctor. You want to know about reality? Then get in your nice comfy Lexus and go up to Ray's Creek. Dead Man's Creek. About three and a half miles from the main road, up that fire road. There's a diagram there in the file that describes where they found Kenny's body. Go up to Dead Man's Creek, Doc. Go meet the truth.

PERSONAL NOTE:

I received permission from the Board of Prisons to administer a polygraph test to the inmate in question. There were, for reasons that were never explained, very strenuous objections raised by the County Sheriff's Department that had investigated the case. However, the State Prison System had assumed legal authority over the prisoner and, with my urging, they overruled the Sheriff's Department protests. The test results indicated that the inmate answered all questions about the incident at Ray's Creek truthfully. I reviewed the police files related to the death of Kenneth Porter. His body was found approximately fifty-five feet from the banks of the creek. The body had been recovered two days following his death and had been partially consumed by coyotes and vultures. It was determined by autopsy, however, that he had died of drowning. The suggestion by the prosecution in the case that the inmate had drowned the deceased and then dragged or carried his friend's body up the bank to the place it was found was highly questionable. The defense had called several experts who testified that the forensic evidence didn't support this theory. There were serious contusions on the body, indicating that he had probably fallen and hit the ground with substantial and inexplicable force not reasonably attributable to another human. Nevertheless, a jury found the accused guilty of second-degree murder.

On a subsequent weekend, my own curiosity got the better of me and I drove to the remote area where the incident occurred. Using the diagram from the police report, I found the access road that led up the mountain to the spot on Ray's Creek, aka Dead Man's Creek, where Kenneth Porter's body was recovered. There was a thick chain across the road. A sign hanging from it read:

Restricted Area – No Entry
Trespassers Will be Prosecuted
U.S. Forest Service

I HAD PLANNED TO REQUEST special permission to investigate the scene of the incident. My schedule, however, has not permitted me the time to pursue the matter further.

The Bone Factory

PART ONE

Katherine Mann cowered in a dark corner of the break room in Building C. She was waiting for death. She was waiting for the clattering sound of its footsteps in the hall outside. She knew exactly how it would take her. She'd seen what it did to the others. The anticipation of the agony she was about to suffer was an icy poison coursing through her veins. Shivering and barely able to breathe, numb with fear, her mind flashed back to an incident from her childhood.

Her cat, Midnight, had chased a skinny half-grown stray into the back of her yard. The big strong alpha male was preparing to pounce for the kill when Katherine caught up. She grabbed Midnight, locked him in the house, and ran back out to find the kitten hunched in a corner in a state of shock, frozen, completely unresponsive. No words of comfort or gentle stroking could rouse it from its death trance. It had given itself over to its terrible fate and was simply waiting to die.

The image of that poor kitten stayed with her all her life. Maybe because somewhere deep in her subconscious, she knew she was seeing a glimpse of her own ultimate end. The only difference was that, in her case, there would be no one to save her at the last minute. It was too late. It was on its way, and it would find her very soon. Her only hope was that her end wouldn't be as torturous as what Brad had suffered. Brad Weller, owner, and CEO of Vargo Chemical Corporation. Her boss. The man who would, very soon, be to blame for her death. No. That was a cop out. For years she'd been an enabler, allowing Brad to use her, and everyone else, for his own selfish, childish motives. Her impending fate was her own doing, and she knew it.

FIVE MONTHS PREVIOUSLY she'd almost quit, almost unwittingly saved her own life. Brad had fired Susan, one of her best friends and head of executive personnel. A woman, of course. Katherine knew how powerful it made him feel to fire a woman. Susan made the mistake of standing up to Brad in defense of a young exec. The poor naive kid made a minor blunder during a face-to-face with a representative of the Indian Government. Brad wanted him transferred to a meaningless job in the California office. Susan told him it was an overreaction and a big mistake. The guy was talented and a big asset to the company where he was. Brad couldn't stand being confronted, especially by a woman. So he canned her.

Katherine turned her resignation in the next day. *Find yourself a new Executive Assistant, and this time I mean it.* If only. He plied her with more perks, another raise, another dose of humility and hyperbolic waxing on about her indispensability. Like all the times before, she eventually caved. She'd known since she started working for him why he valued her so much. She made him look good. At five foot seven inches tall, a little too fat and not particularly good looking, Brad needed all the help he could get. She stood about four inches taller, a former beauty queen who hadn't put on an ounce since her reign as Miss Minnesota. She had a master's in public relations and could walk the talk. Whenever they entered a room full of his peers, she inspired envy. She always made him look like not only the luckiest guy in the room but the smartest.

Then came Delhi.

The plant opening was not only a milestone for the company but had international political and economic impact on relationships between the US and India. It was a very big deal. Katherine flawlessly escorted Brad through the myriad of meetings and dinners and parties and finally the ribbon-cutting ceremony. Every so often she'd pull him aside and whisper little tidbits about some celebrity or politician that would set him up for the perfect introduction.

The US Ambassador was particularly smitten by her. During a lavish dinner at the embassy, he'd informed her of a high-level opening on his staff. His instinct told him it was a perfect fit for her if she wanted to move on from the corporate world and, as he put it, "have some real fun." She'd had plenty of such offers. The diplomatic world actually did intrigue her. She'd already decided it was going to be her next move. But not with this guy. He was oily and intolerably condescending to the Indian staff at the embassy. She'd had enough of that. The only real reason she'd hung in as long as she had with Brad was the generous paycheck, which allowed her to pad her savings. She wanted to have plenty of cushion once she did finally bolt.

The Delhi facility was a shiny state of the art sodium hydroxide production facility. The stuff was more commonly known as caustic soda. The streamlined plant was also designed to make use of its most predominant by-product, hydrogen peroxide. By using the hydrogen peroxide in production, and selling any excess, the company would be saving millions in operating costs. And the India facility would triple the output of caustic soda produced by its lone American plant in Ohio.

On the day following the Ambassador's dinner was the dignitary and press tour of the gleaming new factory. The upbeat tenor that the Vargo P.R. department had hoped for was annoyingly compromised by an ominous out-of-season monsoon sky looming over Delhi. It was hot and sticky. Fidgety reporters and dignitaries kept glancing up at the dark clouds that were about to unleash a torrent on the city. Street vendors were closing up early, and a sweating populace was scrambling to get home early lest they be caught in a deluge.

The tour of the factory was just wrapping up. On a stage under the beautifully landscaped entrance gate, with its life-sized gold-leaf elephants holding up the enormous V that was Vargo Chemical's company logo, Brad was following the script that Katherine had prepared for him to the letter. She knew the wrap-up needed to be a carefully phrased tribute to India and her people. He declared India the shining jewel of Asia, the guiding light to a brighter future for all peoples. He praised the ingenuity of her citizens, who were setting a standard for the rest of the world to follow. In spite of his less than alluring looks, Brad consistently pulled it off. Katherine always thought he would have made a very good character actor, one who would be consistently cast as a greasy corrupt senator or a crooked small-town sheriff.

As usual, he disappeared quickly after his final remarks, leaving Katherine to answer questions and bestow pleasantries on the guests as they left. Brad may have been a first-class jerk, but he was no dummy. He knew he could leave them with no better final impression of Vargo Chemical than Katherine.

The press always hung around the longest, doing their best to impress this beautiful corporate spokesperson with their pithy, intelligent questions. Katherine was constantly amused. Reporters always seemed to think theirs was such a sexy profession that they were somehow irresistible. The last news hound finally sulked off, disappointed that Katherine wasn't wowed enough with his credentials or his knowledge of the best clubs in Delhi to accept his dinner invite. As she started back toward the company offices, she glanced up at the ghost gray clouds, wondering what they were waiting for. She noticed there were three bajaj, the open auto-rickshaws that were the main taxis in Delhi, parked at the curb of the circular entrance driveway. Their drivers stood together chatting, glancing at the gate.

She was about to ask a security officer to find out who they were intended for when she heard Brad's voice. She turned to see him and four others heading toward her. Oh, God. Katherine knew what was coming. Whenever there was a milestone of any sort for the company, Brad would conjure up some sort of annoying spontaneous celebration. He loved being the big spender with a sense of adventure. During her first few years, Katherine had a good time at such company fetes. But the new party smell had worn off. Now it was pretty much just business to her. Nobody else knew that, of course. Not even Brad. She could fake it with the best of them.

Accompanying Brad was Larry Cordiss, the Delhi plant's head of production, who was reading aloud the rave reviews of the day's tour on his cell phone. He was one of Brad's favorite party dogs and no doubt partly responsible for whatever was about to take place. Stephen Morris, the British-born beer and soccer-obsessed COO, was arguing the off-sides rule with Akram Gupta, head of HR. Akram was a Delhi native but had attended college in England. He wasn't a partier and he knew Brad only wanted him along to interpret. But he was a good company guy and always did a commendable job of hiding his discomfort. Both Larry and Stephen had been stationed in India for a long time and spoke some Hindi, but interpreter was below their pay grade. The fifth member of the group was Vargo's head lawyer, Mick Scarborough, who had very little time to talk about anything but himself or single malt scotch. Brad also liked single malt and, in fact, had met Mick during a tour of distilleries in Scotland. He loves to tell the story of how he hired Mick over a couple of three hundred dollar shots of The Dalmore, 1968.

Brad excitedly announced to Katherine that Akram had let slip knowledge of the best outdoor cafe in Delhi. After a quick stop at the hotel to change clothes, they were going to celebrate the day by checking out the real India. The cafe was on the northern edge of Shahjahanabad, also known as Old Delhi. It was an obscure neighborhood not usually frequented by Westerners.

On the way to the hotel, Katherine grilled Akram about his old hood. She was familiar enough with India to know that there were areas where outsiders simply weren't welcome and was surprised that Akram, who was born here, would suggest an excursion to old Delhi. Akram explained that he hadn't offered up the restaurant as a destination for dinner. It had simply come up in a good-natured argument about the best food in Delhi. But Brad jumped on it and insisted that they had to try it. Akram tried to talk him out of it, explaining that the neighborhood wasn't really a destination for foreigners. But Brad had his mind made up. And Brad was the boss. Akram tried to reassure Katherine, explaining that his family was very well known there and nobody would dare bother them. Katherine wasn't buying it. It was obvious that Akram was uncomfortable with the idea. She called Charlie Dellums, head of Vargo's security and asked him to meet them at the hotel.

Charlie was an ex-Philadelphia police detective who got sick of the politics and corruption of public service and went private. He was the most honest guy Katherine knew. He was six two with sandy blond hair going gray and a rock-solid body that never went near a donut. He was a hunk. And smart. His blue-grey eyes saw through the tiniest bit of bullshit. They'd become close friends and confidants. Katherine's favorite photo, which she kept on her refrigerator, was a shot of her and Charlie sipping Mai Tais on a beach in Maui. They looked good together. If Charlie hadn't been twenty years older...

After a quick shower and change of clothes, she met the merry band of adventurers in the lobby of the hotel. They were staying at the Maurya Sheraton, a popular destination for American corporate types. As she walked up to the group, a waiter was passing out tall icy drinks. Everyone was already in a pumped-up party mood. Charlie was in the process of trying to talk Brad into getting them all a table at Bukhara, the world-famous restaurant right there in the hotel. Bukhara was the usual go-to choice for company dinners and proclaimed by some of the sexiest food critics in the world to be the best restaurant in India. Charlie pointed out that it had started to rain, and just the trip to Akram's neighborhood was going to be messy. But he and Katherine both knew it was useless. The more you tried to talk Brad out of something, the more determined he became. The higher the risk, the more attractive it was to his macho inner explorer.

They piled back into the three bajaj. The drivers had expressed extreme discomfort at the idea of braving the coming storm, but Brad plied them with a generous wad of American dollars, and they finally caved. She would never mention it, of course, but Katherine knew enough about Delhi to know that the monsoons were a way of life here and that Brad had been played. Once loaded, in more ways than one, they headed north in the rain toward Old Delhi. Fortunately, the route didn't require them to traverse the muddy side streets where a bajaj could easily get stuck. Katherine rode with Charlie, and they talked hockey all the way. Her father had played for the Detroit Red Wings. She and her brothers were fitted with skates before they could walk and she herself became a fairly good defenseman. She even played for her college team until a spiral fracture of her fifth metatarsal ended her hockey career. She had, however, remained a rabid fan. Brad gave her Red Wings season tickets every year for her birthday, and since their offices were just outside of Toledo, Detroit was an easy commute. Charlie was born Canadian and a diehard Maple Leafs fan. Friendly wagers on games had become a routine for them.

As they neared their destination, they turned onto a narrow side street packed with vendors scrambling to keep their merchandise dry and soaking wet shoppers grabbing a few last supplies before heading for cover. The little motorcade brought suspicious stares from the locals as it wove slowly through the chaos of the market. Bare-footed kids in ragged t-shirts ran alongside the bajaj with open hands thrust inside, pleading for a coin.

Brad's spontaneous excursions into what he condescendingly referred to as "the real world" often made Katherine uncomfortable. She looked at the grubby kids running alongside the taxi and wondered how she got so lucky as to be born into her so comfortable, unchallenged life. She wanted to reach into her bag for some change, but she knew it would attract an even larger crowd and, besides, anything she handed over would ultimately end up in the pocket of one of the snake-eyed pimps the street urchins worked for.

The bajaj pulled over in front of an open-air restaurant. A crude assortment of tables and chairs were arranged beneath a rusty metal roof. Each table had its own decorative thatched umbrella which also served as an extra layer of protection from the inevitable rains. Akram had called the owner in advance, notifying him of their impending arrival. Several employees rushed out to the curb with umbrellas to usher them inside. A pleasant man with a clean white shirt, who Katherine assumed to be the proprietor, bestowed enthusiastic welcomes in broken English. He ushered them to a table next to the sidewalk that had been prepared especially for them.

Considering the lousy weather, the restaurant was surprisingly busy. The all-Indian clientele consisted of businessmen in animated conversations, colorfully attired families, and couples happily indulging in ample portions of butter chicken, a tandoori variation which Akram explained was the house specialty. There was a large smoky outdoor kitchen at one side of the restaurant spewing out tantalizing aromas that reminded Katherine how hungry she was.

The meal began with a powerful spiced sweet rum, and fruit juice concoction served in coconut shells. As drink after drink was downed, Brad and his buddies constructed an embarrassing tower of upside-down coconut shells, a phallic tribute to their drinking prowess. Night descended. Lanterns hanging from the rafters now illuminated the restaurant. The Monsoon finally abated. Plates of steaming succulent fare came and went. The stack of coconut shells grew. A sitar player in one corner serenaded the patrons with mysterious strains of traditional music.

Brad was his usual semi-obnoxious self, loudly holding forth without concern for the comfort zone of the other customers. Except for the occasional glance at some outburst of laughter, most of the other patrons patiently ignored the foreign invaders. But Katherine noticed one group of potential customers move on when they saw the table full of noisy, inebriated Westerners.

Brad stood and held up his drink. "A toast. To India. To its people and all the glories of this bounteous land."

The others all chimed in semi-enthusiastically. "India! Hear hear!"

Katherine leaned into Charlie and said quietly, "Remind me why I came?"

He didn't have an answer.

"I'm sick of it, Charlie."

"Yeah, I know. You've been sick of it for a long time."

"I'm such a coward. I should have moved on a long time ago."

"You're loyal. I get it."

The rain stopped. In the steamy, dimly lit streets outside the restaurant, life took on a more sinister aura. Katherine was distracted from the boisterous conversation by one particular group of young men who stopped nearby and seemed a bit too interested in their table. They kept glancing in their direction, whispering amongst themselves. She nudged Charlie with her knee.

"Yeah, I see them."

He was about to get up and alert the owner when the two uniformed Delhi cops who'd been hanging out in front of the restaurant intervened and persuaded the group to move along. Katherine suspected that the police presence was arranged by the owner to ensure that her group would not be bothered. It was, after all, going to be a very profitable evening for him. Katherine turned her attention to a small, bent, hollow-cheeked older man standing in the shadows across the street. Like the thugs, he'd been staring at their table for quite a while. But, considering his physical condition, he didn't look like much of a threat. He started to move off several times, then returned, as if he was trying to make up his mind about something. He seemed to be focused on Brad, but every so often he would look directly at Katherine and smile. His sunken eyes were dark and sickly. The streets of Delhi were full of desperate souls like him, but there was something about this guy that affected her more than most. He finally made a decision. He limped out of the shadows and started across the street, straight toward their table.

Katherine noticed as he approached that his skin had a greyish hue, and one of his eyes was cloudy. He greeted them with a toothless smile and several bows. He spoke in Hindi and gestured with wasted arms. He focused his entreaties directly at Brad. Akram, looking unusually annoyed, sternly reproached the intruder and told him to move on. A couple of restaurant employees were on their way to assist in his removal, but Brad stopped them. He insisted that Akram translate what the man was saying. It was obvious that Akram was not happy about this, but when Brad got into one of his "I want to connect with the natives" moods, there was no denying him. Especially if he was drunk. Every once in a while during the conversation that followed, the emaciated beggar would smile and bow to Katherine.

"Thank you, miss lady." They were the only words in English he uttered.

"What's he saying, Akram?" Brad was playing the magnanimous Raj.

"His name, sir, is Ranjit Malhotra. He says he recognized you from your picture in the paper. With the Prime Minister, in front of the plant."

Akram hesitated. He obviously resented being forced to translate for a person he didn't think should be allowed anywhere near this gathering. Mr. Malhotra was undoubtedly one of the Dalit, the lowest class in the Hindu caste system, formerly known as Untouchables. Even for someone as educated as Akram, ancient religious beliefs die hard, and such an intrusion was not just unwelcome, but an insult.

Brad was getting impatient. "Come on, Akram. What's he want?"

Akram reluctantly continued. "He wants to express his appreciation to you. His two daughters have both recently been hired by Vargo Chemical. They are to be working in the plant's cafeteria, one of them as a manager."

Mr. Malhotra, sensing that his comments were being received kindly, continued enthusiastically. He spoke quickly, waving his atrophied arms and smiling broadly. Katherine found it remarkable that a man in his condition could still find pleasure in anything.

Brad was smiling himself, enjoying the encounter with this poor broken man in his own twisted way.

"God, I love this guy. What's he saying now?"

"He says he's going to die soon and his dream was to see his daughters with good jobs so he could move on to his next life in peace. And now, with his old eyes, he sees them so happy. He implores you please, Mr. Kind American sir, to protect them, as he has very little to leave them."

"Ask him what their names are?" said Brad.

Mr. Malhotra said they were Adhira and Sunita.

"Tell him I will take very good care of Adhira and Sunita."

Akram translated. Mr. Malhotra put his hands together and bowed to Brad. He then said something that made Akram react angrily. He gestured for him to leave, causing Mr. Malhotra to back up a step, bow again, and start to leave.

Brad was having none of it. "What the hell, Akram? Let the man speak. What's he saying?"

Akram was very irritated now. "Sir, this is unimportant, I assure you."

"Really. Well, how about if I be the judge of that."

Akram paused for a moment, humiliated by being upbraided by Brad in front of the others. He decided, however, that defying his boss might not be the best idea, in spite of how upset he was.

"Mr. Malhotra says that he is so poor that he recently sold his skeleton to the bone traders so his daughters could buy new clothes for their job interviews."

They were all dumbstruck. It sounded completely outrageous.

"What the hell does he mean he just sold his skeleton?" asked Brad.

Akram tried to change the subject, suggesting they move on to a very good bar he knew. Brad was getting irritated with Akram and reminded him coldly that he had just asked a question.

Akram, very reluctantly, told them about the age-old trade in human bones. India, he explained, was the foremost source of skeletons for research and medical institutions. It was a shadowy underworld that once relied primarily on grave-robbing as a source of bodies. Now, however, if you had the right connections, you could sell your own remains to the bone traders while you were still alive. After you died, the bone traders had the rights to your corpse. The sale price, for a poor person, was a quite decent sum of money.

Katherine was as fascinated by these revelations as everyone else. But she had a bad feeling about where this conversation was going. She could see Brad getting more and more excited. She interrupted to remind everyone that they had an early flight back to the states in the morning and maybe they should call it a night.

Brad acted as if he didn't even hear her. He pressed the poor sick old man for more information. Where did these bone traders work? Did Mr. Malhotra know the bone traders personally or did he go through an intermediary? Akram was getting more and more uncomfortable with the subject matter. But he begrudgingly explained that the old man knew someone who worked at the bone factory. It was just north of the city on the bank of the Yamuna River. Katherine knew what was coming next, and her stomach turned.

"We're going there, right now, gotta see this. You can take us there, right, Mr. Malhotra?"

It wasn't really a question. It was pretty much a directive from the boss. Akram had finally had enough. He stood up, angry. He didn't care what Brad thought of him. This was too much. It was an outrageous request. This kind of thing was indecent. He would have nothing to do with it.

Brad told him to calm down. He understood and respected his beliefs. All he was asking was for Akram to go with them so he could interpret Mr. Malhotra's directions. He didn't have to go inside if he didn't want to. But Akram further protested that the bone trade had been illegal in India for years. Just by associating with those people the whole party could be subject to arrest. Mr. Malhotra probably won't want to risk taking them there anyway.

Brad whipped out his wallet and pulled out two hundred dollars. He held it out to Mr. Malhotra. Akram stared at Brad with deep contempt.

"Sir, you are inviting the most terrible karma." He walked out of the restaurant and disappeared down the street.

Like a good soldier, albeit a fairly drunken one, Steven, the Brit COO, stepped up and took over the translation. He explained to Mr. Malhotra that the money was for his daughters if he'd take them to the bone factory. Mr. Malhotra was stunned. He smiled and took the money, glancing at the street to make sure no one saw him pocket such an amount of cash.

Charlie sensed Katherine's disgust with yet another one of Brad's absurd plans. He leaned over to her and quietly suggested they head back to the hotel. She found herself in a bit of a quandary. The idea of visiting such a place sounded pretty repulsive. Growing up a hockey player, Katherine was tough and could take a hit, so she wasn't one to shy away from the extremes. But she knew wherever this bone factory was, it was very likely going to make this neighborhood feel like Beverly Hills. If she went back with Charlie, Brad would be without any kind of sober protection heading into what sounded for all the world like hell on earth. She knew that the logical, safe choice would be to say screw Brad. If they skin him and sell his skeleton to some medical school in China, it's his own damn fault. But Katherine didn't work like that. In spite of the fact that Brad was so much older, she'd come to feel in a lot of ways like he was an unruly little brother for whom she was responsible. Besides, she was with Charlie. As long as he was close, she felt like she could handle pretty much anything.

Brad paid the proprietor of the restaurant handsomely and, as they were piling back into the auto-rickshaws, the entire staff came out to thank the generous foreigners. Mr. Malhotra got into the front of Brad's bajaj next to the driver. Mick, Mr. Single Malt Scotch, had, of course, brought along a silver flask of rare whiskey. He procured some glasses from the restaurant so they could all relish its smoky sweetness as they headed for the bone factory. Mick offered glasses to Katherine and Charlie. Charlie declined. Katherine thought that considering their destination, some fortification might be a good idea but then realized that her keenest wits might come in handy and opted for sobriety.

The auto-rickshaws buzzed through the sticky storm-splashed Delhi night. The streets were getting darker and more deserted the further north they headed. They crossed the Wazirabad Bridge over the Yamuna river and proceeded up the eastern bank. The stench of the river was almost unbearable. Tons of sewage poured into its waters daily, leaving the Yamuna with the dubious distinction of being perhaps the most polluted river on the planet. Thankfully, the godawful odor gradually subsided the further north they traveled. But the humidity this close to the river was especially oppressive and the slightly more breathable air did nothing to make Katherine feel any more sanguine about their purpose.

They were traversing sparsely populated areas of crumbling deserted buildings and shantytowns. Insect-infested thickets of jungle crowded up to the roadside in patches. Open fires glowed here and there where groups of homeless had gathered to cook whatever meager pickings they had scrounged that day. The Dalit eyed the rickshaws suspiciously as they passed. At one point, two men jumped onto a motorbike and followed them closely. Not good. Katherine could see that even Charlie was concerned, but the bike finally veered off toward a small settlement.

They turned onto a dark muddy road which wound past oily ponds and abandoned roofless shacks and finally into a cluster of very old sagging wooden factory buildings close to the riverbank. A few low wattage electric bulbs burned here and there casting bottomless shadows through the dreary, desolate complex. Rats skittered across the ground, and strange insect sounds conjured up images of very unpleasant multi-legged creatures looking for someone to chew on. Katherine thought that it would actually be less scary if it were completely dark and silent. If there was ever a place where evil could find the perfect corner to lurk in, this was it. The three rickshaws stopped outside a moldy three-story structure. There were two fairly new trucks and one very old hearse parked in front. Dim amber light filtered through several filthy windows of the building. Katherine was now hoping Mick had some of that scotch left.

A man in a dark suit suddenly came quickly around the corner of the building. He had a cloth wrapped around his head, covering his nose and mouth. He ripped it off and threw it onto the ground. He stopped for a moment, took several deep breaths, and got into the hearse. He started the engine and sped away. He paid no attention at all to their group.

Katherine could see that Brad and Mr. Malhotra had gotten out of their bajaj and, with Steven still interpreting, were talking quietly. Mr. Malhotra was no longer smiling. As he talked, he kept glancing at the building. He had his hands clasped and was bowing to Brad as if embarrassed about whatever he was saying. Brad gave him another handful of cash, which Katherine assumed was a bribe for admittance. Mr. Malhotra climbed awkwardly up onto a rickety loading dock and knocked on a rusty metal door. When the door opened, Katherine saw the shadowy form of a man even smaller than

Mr. Malhotra. They exchanged a few words then both disappeared inside.

Katherine swatted a bloodthirsty mosquito away from her face. She took in the reality of their isolation in this grim godforsaken landscape. A haunting distant screech echoed through the night. Her logical mind told her it was just a bird. But in these surroundings, it sounded like some sort of demonic warning. A sudden wave of foreboding enveloped her.

She turned to Charlie. "Remember how you once told me that, after so many years as a cop, you could sense situations where you knew death was close by?"

"I remember."

"So, are we all going to die here?"

"Well, it's pretty grim, but no, I don't think so."

"You don't think so. Great."

They joined the others near the loading dock. Brad was fidgeting with anticipation like a kid on Christmas morning. You would have thought he was about to open the Ark of the Covenant. He'd already decided this was his greatest adventure of all and was blathering on about how he should write a book about his exploits in foreign lands. No one else had ever had adventures equal to his. Before he could embarrass himself further, the door opened, and Mr. Malhotra and the small person came out and down the steps. Katherine was flabbergasted to see that the person accompanying Mr. Malhotra was a boy, 12 years old at the most. He had a big smile on his face and, most surprising of all, he spoke very passable English.

The boy introduced himself as Bobby Patel and, on behalf of his father and brothers, he welcomed them to Patel and Sons International Medical Supply Company. Katherine was so relieved she almost burst out laughing. This happy, seemingly carefree child instantly neutralized the looming threat Katherine was feeling.

Bobby said he was informed by Mr. Malhotra that his good friend Mr. Weller, a good friend of India, and his good friends, requested a tour of their factory. Everybody was good friends. This was good, thought Katherine. Bobby looked at Katherine. The smile disappeared for a moment. He explained that it would perhaps be best if the lady waited, as there were not happy things to be seen.

"Wait? Wait where? Out here? Not a chance in hell, pal."

Bobby's smile returned. "Then please to all follow me."

They all climbed up onto the loading dock and moved to the rusty door. As soon as Bobby opened it, the smell hit them.

It was a vile, ghastly fetor like nothing any of them had ever experienced, a heavy stench of sulfurous rot mixed with an intense chemical odor that cursed the olfactory senses and stung their lungs. They were enveloped by such a foulness that they didn't dare breathe through their mouths for fear of ingesting some mortiferous airborne plague. Katherine felt as if it was actually sticking to her skin, that she would never be clean again.

Bobby led them into a small anteroom with a cluttered desk at one side. Still smiling, he reached into a basket and produced a handful of colorful scarves. He casually remarked that some people found the smell to be too difficult and perhaps the visitors would care to make use of a complimentary mask for the nose. Everyone grabbed at the scarves like passengers on the Titanic lunging for life jackets. They quickly tied them around their mouths and noses. The scarves had been treated with a strong perfume of something akin to a spicy incense. Although the feculent odor was still there, the scarves actually went a long way to making breathing possible.

Bobby welcomed them again to Patel and Sons, where only the most modern, legal and expert methods were used. He led them through some double doors. And into hell.

It was a large warehouse space perhaps a hundred feet square, lit by a series of high wattage bare bulbs hanging from the ceiling. Sunken into the concrete floor were rows of vats about eight feet square. Some were filled with a murky steaming liquid. A brownish roiling foam covered the surface of others. The spaces between the vats were covered with wooden pallets to create a walkway that was about four inches above the concrete. They had entered a gaseous realm devoted to the processing of the human corpse.

Along one wall, what looked like fishing nets were suspended about six feet above the floor, their contents dripping into a concrete drain. The netting was fairly tight, so it was hard to clearly see the odious remains they held. But you only had to look a little further along to see a row of skeletal shapes laid out on the floor. The bones were covered with a putrid, pinkish gelatinous mush. Against the back wall, three men in rubber boots and aprons, wearing filthy surgical masks, were using stiff brushes to clean the hideous mush off the bones. The images conjured out of the twisted imaginations of Bosch, Dante, and Poe didn't come close to the obscene realities of this foul necropolis. Those guys were pikers.

Katherine's brain went into some sort of state of shock, perhaps a self-protective response to override the horror and help make survival possible. From then on, she functioned as if in a semi-trance, a zombie-like observer disconnected from any emotional reality. She heard Bobby's voice as he launched into a description of the process the company employed to produce their final product. She understood what he was saying, She heard the others commenting and asking questions. But the voices were distant and dreamlike.

In a friendly, matter-of-fact tour guide voice, Bobby took them through the production process as they walked carefully on the pallets. He explained that the company would purchase bodies, very legally, from the families of the dead, or from morgues if a person went unidentified for a long period of time. The corpse would then be wrapped in a fishing net and put into the river, with a concrete weight anchoring it to the bottom. It would be left in the river for two weeks where scores of small fish picked at the flesh until there was nothing left but a mass of slimy bones and connective tissue. About ten feet from them were several of these abominable fish-eaten corpses lying on the floor.

Katherine watched as a worker jabbed his fingers into the eye-sockets of a skeleton and dragged it onto a sheet of plastic.

Even in her disconnected state this was overwhelming. Her knees gave out. Brad had to grab her to hold her upright.

Two more workers lifted the plastic with the corpse and slid it onto a table where other's began scrubbing the offal from the bones, removing as much of the decomposed flesh as possible. The skeleton was then lowered into a vat of diluted caustic soda which dissolved whatever bits of flesh remained. He pointed to some workers who were using long poles to lift skeletons partially out of the steaming baths to see if they were ready to be removed. Katherine saw a skull with a tortured grimace break the surface and seemingly beg for mercy before being plunged back into the roiling tub of death.

She noticed Larry tap Brad on the shoulder and point to a far wall. Against the wall was a stack of 55-gallon drums of caustic soda. The label on the drums said Vargo Chemical. The grotesque irony wasn't lost on Katherine. She made a somewhat strangled sound.

Charlie gently shook her and asked if she was all right. Sensing everyone looking at her, she somehow found a way to say she was fine, although it felt like someone else was speaking. She had reconnected with reality enough to see Mr. Malhotra looking down at one of the vats. She wondered what he could possibly be thinking, knowing that his own bones would soon be subjected to this same macabre unnatural treatment.

Bobby pointed out a row of skeletons laid out on racks, fresh out of the caustic soda baths. They had a dark yellowish tinge to them. It was necessary at this point, he explained, to lay them out on the roof of the factory, where the sun would bleach them to the pure white that was required by their customers. After they were sun-bleached, they were then submerged in yet another vat, this one containing hydrochloric acid, which was the final purification of the bones. Bobby pointed out the acid vats on the other side of the room. It would be advisable not to go any nearer to them. The guests were not wearing rubber boots, and any small amount of hydrochloric acid could be harmful to their very pretty shoes. He then asked them to please follow and, to Katherine's immeasurable relief, ushered them out of the sickening horrors of the processing plant and up a flight of stairs.

The second floor of the bone factory was where the skeletons were assembled and readied for shipment. Six men were laboring at a row of workbenches in the middle of the room, engaged in casual conversation. They glanced up at the visitors, seemingly unconcerned. But the talking suddenly ceased. Some of them were drilling and wiring the bones together. Others were using surgical saws to separate skulls into pieces. Bobby explained that skulls needed to be shipped in sections, the interiors being as important for study as the outside.

The walls were lined with maybe a hundred gleaming white skeletons, and at one end of the room were stacks of shipping boxes. Compared to the barbarity one floor below, there was something almost beautiful about this space.

Katherine had, some years before, visited the catacombs of Paris, the underground ossuary that now housed the bones of over six million people. She remembered thinking, as she walked past altars of skulls and bone chandeliers, that the sight of a single skeleton can be frightening, but millions of them somehow inspired a profound connection to the simple natural process of life and death. There was a certain peacefulness to it.

Now, looking at the assembled skeletons in the bone factory, she might have felt something similar, if it weren't for the repugnant odor that was still clinging to her like a wet rotten burial shroud.

And then, just as she was thinking the worst was behind her, the nightmare slipped into a whole new dimension.

Brad asked Bobby how much they were paid for a skeleton. He answered that for a top-quality skeleton, where all of the bones were from the same body, they were paid sixty-five dollars. Brad took out his wallet and, as if he were casually shopping at a neighborhood flea market, offered to buy Mr. Malhotra's skeleton from Patel and Sons.

No one could believe what they had just heard. Even Bobby was taken aback, and his ever-present smile vanished for a moment. Larry laughed, figuring it was a joke. The others got on board. Good one, Brad. But Brad assured them he was serious. Everyone looked at Mr. Malhotra, who didn't understand. He asked Bobby to translate. When Bobby explained what Mr. Weller's request was, Mr. Malhotra looked at Brad and muttered some words in Hindi. Bobby said he wanted to know why Brad would want his skeleton. Brad explained that he meant it as a compliment. He said he thought it would just be great to own the skeleton of a good man like Mr. Malhotra, whom he actually knew.

Katherine was pulled completely out of her stupor by Brad's outrageous request. She told him to stop this absurdity and take her back to the hotel. Brad ignored her. He said that he respected Mr. Malhotra and thought his skeleton was worth a lot more than sixty-five dollars. He told Bobby he would pay Patel and Sons three hundred dollars for it. He counted out the money and handed it to Bobby. Bobby looked at the money and asked them to wait, please. He needed to speak to his father. He left the room through a door beyond the shipping boxes.

A queasy embarrassment had descended on the group. Mr. Malhotra was still looking a bit stunned.

Katherine was done. Nothing she had witnessed in the bone factory had disgusted her more than Brad's unconscionable request. She walked up to Mr. Malhotra, took one of his wasted boney hands in hers and simply said, "I'm sorry," hoping he understood what she meant.

Mr. Malhotra looked right at her, bowed, and with what sounded like a peaceful resignation said, "No worry, nice lady. Thank you, nice lady."

Katherine bowed to him respectfully. She turned her back on the group and headed for the door. She didn't even look at Brad as she left. Charlie went with her, of course, and they headed back the way they came. Katherine kept her eyes on the floor, trying to block out the vileness of the bone factory as much as she could. But as she passed the steaming vats of caustic soda, eating at the remnants of human flesh, she had a sickening premonition that something terrible would come out of this.

When they finally made it through the door and back outside it was like awakening from some morbid drug-induced hallucination. They threw the now disgustingly sticky face scarves onto the ground, climbed into their auto-rickshaw, and sputtered off toward their hotel through the cursed and putrid night.

Part Two

THE EXPLOSION AT THE Delhi plant occurred almost two months after the day of the ribbon-cutting ceremony. Nobody knew exactly what happened, nor was it likely they would ever know. The destruction was so enormous the authorities speculated that any evidence of the specific cause would probably have been vaporized. But it seemed to investigators that it was probably triggered in the hydrogen peroxide distillation area. H2O2 is a substance so volatile that it was once used for rocket fuel.

The blast ripped into the fabric of Indian society at 4:03 pm, just before the end of the workday. There were over seven hundred employees still on site. Most of them died within seconds. Others were not so lucky. The ones who survived, as well as thousands of residents of the surrounding neighborhoods, were being treated in an array of hospitals for horrific burns inflicted by fire laced with caustic soda. The early estimates were that over two thousand people were dead and tens of thousands had suffered injuries ranging from severe burns to inhalation of highly toxic smoke. Foreign countries were sending emergency medical response teams to help with the massive number of casualties. It was an unimaginable disaster.

Katherine was awakened at 5:30 in the morning by a call from Charlie. She lay on her bed in the dim light of dawn, her throat tightening as Charlie broke the news. Charlie said that Brad was on his way to Delhi. He wanted her to stay in Toledo and handle the press. Handle the press. It sounded absurd. Thousands of people dead or suffering horribly, and she was supposed to handle the press.

The day after they had returned from Delhi she'd given Brad her ninety-day notice. This time she was really through. The Delhi experience had pushed her over the edge. She didn't blame Brad. He was who he was, and he wasn't going to change. It had been her own choice to go to the bone factory, and she was adult enough to accept responsibility for her own actions. But the morbid memories of that night still haunted her. She knew she'd never be rid of them until she had left Vargo Chemical far behind. She made it very clear to Brad that there was no talking her out of it this time. He didn't try. On the other hand, neither did he apologize or seem regretful in any way. His only request was that she find her own replacement. As much as she disliked the idea of subjecting someone else to Brad Weller's conscienceless world, she agreed. Right now, her priority had to be herself, and whoever took over would have to deal just like she had.

As she drove to her office to begin "handling the press," Katherine remembered that about two weeks before the explosion Brad had a meeting in his office with company executives and a man she knew only slightly, Oliver Petterson. Nice guy. He was a safety engineer from the Delhi plant. She never attended those kinds of technical meetings, but she'd seen a confidential memo alerting the participants to the subject for discussion. It was about a safety report, something to do with the cost of venting in the hydrogen peroxide distillation area. She also knew that the meeting didn't end well. She had heard raised voices through the door. Oliver burst angrily out of Brad's office. He stopped for a moment to catch his breath and compose himself. He told Katherine it was nice to have known her, and he hoped she had a great life.

Later, when she asked Brad if everything was all right, he assured her that things couldn't be better. It was all he offered, and she knew it was a lie. And she knew he knew she knew that he was lying. And she knew he didn't care. In the wake of the disaster, the memory of that meeting took on a haunting significance.

The three weeks following the explosion were the worst of her life. As stories of the massive disaster poured in through the media, the images of ultimate misery were interspersed with clips of the Vargo Chemical plant in India, before and after the explosion, the Ohio plant and, of course, Brad. And Katherine. She was frequently there, right next to him, mostly trying to deflect the questions being hurled by ravenous reporters. They were dogged everywhere. Media vans were parked outside her apartment when she got home and were there when she left in the morning.

The worst part was poring over the lists of victims, identifying company employees. Each name represented an excruciating death, and never-ending grief for the family left behind. One day she saw the names of the two Malhotra sisters. Adhira. Sunita. She cried for an hour. Their father had imagined that the jobs at Vargo would lead to a better life for them. Instead, it ripped them from the world in a cataclysm of caustic fire. The whole thing would have been unbearable if Charlie hadn't been right there, by her side, through it all. Together they closed innumerable obscure bars he knew of, joints in parts of town where they wouldn't be recognized or bothered.

Because of all the mayhem, Brad panicked at the thought of Katherine's impending departure. One night, drunk and desperate, he came to her apartment with a bouquet of flowers and VIP tickets to the Stanley cup playoffs, pleading for her not to desert him in his hour of need. She didn't bite. He finally gave up, telling her to keep the tickets as a farewell gift. She thanked him, and he sulked away like the damaged little boy he was.

Two days left. She was almost out from under it. She'd soon be heading for a peaceful, remote cabin in the Maine Woods that a friend had offered her for as long as she wanted. Thick dark clouds had moved over Toledo. The view of the city out of her office window resembled the unearthly El Greco painting of the Spanish city bearing the same name.

She was starting to pack up personal stuff when she got a call from Molly, the receptionist at the front desk. A large box had just been delivered for Brad. The receptionist asked if she should have someone bring it up to his office. Katherine was focused on her own last-minute details. She had no interest in dealing with anything of Brad's. She told the receptionist to leave a message on Brad's voicemail informing him that it had arrived and just have someone put the box in the supply room.

The day seemed to drag on interminably as Katherine tied up a loose end here and there, packed several boxes out to her car and took a long lunch with Charlie at the commissary. They talked about hockey and reminisced about their early days at the company. Charlie was the only person who could get Katherine to smile anymore. He kept reminding her that this maelstrom of shit that she had been unwittingly sucked into would soon be behind her and that she'd find a new life. He knew that the next day was going to be her last, and as they headed back toward the offices he suddenly stopped, took her by the shoulders and said,

"Skip it. Just go. Now. And don't look back."

It was exactly what she needed to hear. She felt a huge weight lifted off of her. She hugged him, and they made plans to meet for a drink later. She had one more box to load out from her office, and then Vargo Chemical would be history.

Charlie's cell rang. He was needed in Building C, right away. He hurried off, and Katherine headed for her office.

The clouds had grown even darker. A cold, dreary gloom settled over the late afternoon. It started to rain. Katherine got a chill as she walked quickly to the front door of the main office building. When she entered the lobby, she found that all the lights were out. People were scrambling for flashlights or using their cell phones to light their way. Katherine figured it must be the storm. She didn't really care. She just wanted to get her things and leave.

Since the elevator was out, she used her cell phone's light to find her way to the stairwell. She was reaching for the doorknob when she was struck by a faint but alarming odor. She froze. It was a smell that would be forever implanted in her memory. It was the smell of the bone factory. But how...? Then it hit her. A large box had just been delivered for Brad. No. Not possible. It had to be some kind of weird sensory flashback brought on by the stress.

She stood there, stunned, trying to shake away the loathsome images that had crawled into her mind again. She wanted desperately to just run to her office, grab her things, and drive away. But she couldn't not know. She went back to the dark lobby and down a hall toward the first floor supply room. The door was partially open. Using her phone to light her way, she found the box lying on the floor. It was about five feet long and two feet wide, made of heavyweight cardboard. It had been opened. Who would have opened it? It could only have been Brad. He must have been told it was here and removed the contents. Inside was a large black plastic bag. The bag had been ripped open. It was empty. There was some kind of moist residue on the inside of the plastic. She noticed the bag had a zipper. Why would you have to rip it open if there was a zipper? Her hand was shaking as she turned over the top of the box to look at the shipping label. Shipped from Patel and Sons, New Delhi.

But where were the contents? Why would Brad have removed, God almighty, the skeleton of Mr. Malhotra? The morbid stench of the bone factory was making Katherine dizzy. She felt her legs start to give out under her. She staggered out the door of the supply room and moved as quickly as she could back to the lobby and toward the stairs. The power was still out, and the darkness had become even more intense. She heard the rumble of thunder outside. The storm was finding its power. People were still scrambling back and forth with flashlights, but she was so dazed she couldn't make out what they were saying. Then she saw Brad come hurrying out of the door to the stairwell talking on his cell phone, obviously upset. When he saw Katherine, he took the phone away from his ear and hollered across the lobby at her.

"Something's going on in Building C. They say someone was killed." He turned and rushed out the door.

Katherine stood for a moment, dazed, trying to process at she had just heard. She heard Charlie's voice in her head saying, "Just go, now." Yeah. It was the only choice that made sense. She headed for the stairs. Three steps up, she stopped. Charlie. He'd been called to Building C. Brad just said someone had been killed. She turned and ran out the front doors, through the pouring rain, toward the factory.

Building C was the main control center for the plant and was just adjacent to the enormous diaphragm cells where the caustic soda was processed via electrolysis. Katherine was soaking wet and out of breath by the time she got there. She fumbled with her security card, cursing, finally swiping it. It didn't work. The power was out here, too. A terrified looking technician came blasting out the door. She grabbed him and the door. She asked him what was going on, where was Charlie? He shook his head, pulled her hands off, and bolted. She went into the lobby of Building C and called for Charlie. There was no answer. She didn't see anybody.

She knew that if there was ever a sudden loss of power in the control room, it could cause major problems and there was an enormous backup generator designed to immediately kick into operation in such a circumstance. It had obviously failed. But there should be very loud alarms going off. None. She was alone and scared. She just needed to find Charlie.

She cautiously moved through the lobby and into the main control room. Her cell phone was the only light. Rows of dead computer monitors and video screens filled the space, which was normally staffed by at least a dozen technicians. It was deserted. What she was able to see with the light from her phone was not good. Chairs had been knocked over, papers and manuals strewn about the floor. It looked like there had been a huge fight. But most disturbing of all was the smell of the bone factory, hanging in the air. She moved carefully toward the far end of the room. She was looking for the stairway she knew led to an outside door, beyond which was the exterior manufacturing area of the plant. Just outside the door was a catwalk where technicians could observe various machinery and processes going on below. She was almost to the stairway when her foot kicked something soft. The beam from her phone illuminated a body lying on the floor. She gasped and jumped, slamming her thigh hard into a desk. Reeling in pain now, she focused her light on the body and saw that it was Larry Cordiss, the head of production. He was on his back, his head lying in a pool of blood. His throat had been horribly lacerated, and there were two bloody sockets where his eyes should be. She spun away from the sight, barely catching herself before she fell. She yelled out in horror.

"What's happening? Charlie?"

Then she gathered all the strength she could muster and stumbled up the stairs, pushed open the door to outside and collapsed onto the catwalk.

She grabbed onto the steel pipe rail and slowly pulled herself upright. She gazed down at the caustic soda production facility and the mass of decomposers, diaphragm cells, evaporators, filters, holding tanks and miles of piping that connected them all. A series of battery-operated emergency lights cast a dim greenish glow through the plant. A steady rain was falling. She saw three more bodies lying on the ground in different places, all of them with gouged-out eyes like Larry. Blood was flowing through rainwater. She called for Charlie again. Her voice was muffled by the sound of the rainstorm. She heard a distant voice call to her and looked down to see Brad coming from around a holding tank. He yelled at her to call the police, to get help.

She fumbled with her cell phone. Her hands were trembling so much that she dropped it. It fell off the catwalk and shattered on the wet concrete fifteen feet below. She heard a sound coming from another part of the plant, a strange clacking sound, like someone pounding sticks against something hard. Clack, clack, clack, clack, clack. And then it appeared.

A skeleton came running down a passageway between machines. But this was not the gleaming white sun-bleached skeleton of the medical supply variety. These were the hideous semi-processed fish-eaten bones that had yet to bathe in the final caustic solution. Bits of putrefied flesh still clung to it, and its skeleton hands were covered with blood. Frozen in disbelief, Katherine watched as this abomination that was once Mr. Malhotra stopped, looked one way, then another, then right up at her. It knew who she was. She could feel it. She sank to her knees, barely able to hold onto a railing. She heard Brad call her name again. The skeleton looked in the direction of his voice and started toward him. Brad didn't know it. He was behind a tank, unaware of the demon he was about to encounter. Katherine wanted to yell, to warn him, but she didn't have the breath to even whisper.

Brad rounded the tank and came face to face with the impossible thing. He fell back against a large pipe. It stood there and stared at him for a moment. He was pleading, no, no, no. Please no. A slimy yellowish skeleton hand shot out, and two bone fingers stabbed his eyes. Katherine covered her ears to try to block out Brad's screams. The entity, with its fingers hooked into Brad's skull through his eye sockets, dragged him to the base of a holding tank and dropped him onto the wet ground. Brad was holding his face, wailing and pleading incoherently. The skeleton of Mr. Malhotra, whose daughters had died so horribly at the Vargo Chemical plant in Delhi, pierced the tank with its bloody bone fingers, releasing a blast of caustic liquid hell onto Brad.

Brad's pleading turned into torturous wails of suffering. A sickening brownish smoke billowed upwards as the concentrated caustic soda dissolved his clothing in seconds and then started eating through his skin. The screams stopped. Brad had passed out from the unbearable pain. The entity stared down, clenching its bone fingers into a fist then opening them over and over as Brad's body was transformed into a gelatinous mass of smoldering tissue.

The monstrous specter looked up at Katherine. It started moving in her direction. Clack, clack, clack. It was coming for her. She lunged for the door. She dove back inside and down the stairway that led back to the control room. She fell on the pitch-black stairs, hurting her knee. She no longer had her cell phone to light her way, but she managed to find the lobby door. It was locked. She pounded on the glass and called for help. But there was nobody there, inside or outside.

She ran down a short hallway. At the end was a red battery-operated exit light over an emergency fire door at the end. It was locked, too. Which made no sense. It was one of those doors that would always open from the inside. That was the idea. But it wouldn't budge. Hide. She had to hide. She tried several more doors and finally found one that was unlocked. It was the break room. As soon as she entered, she fell over something. She felt around in the dark and realized it was another body. She jumped back, her brain spinning from the relentless horror of it all. Out of nowhere, an actual rational thought came to her. She went back to the corpse and searched its pockets. Yes, a cell phone. She turned its light on and saw that the body was Stephen Morris, Vargo's COO. His eyes had been gouged out like the rest.

Katherine made her way to the end of the room and curled up in a corner, on the floor. She tried dialing Charlie's cell number. There was nothing but a crackle of interference. She tried other numbers. The same. The truth came to her simple and clear. She was going to die. Right there. Very soon.

With her arms wrapped around her legs and her heart pounding out its last beats, Katherine heard an echo of Akram's words that night in the Delhi restaurant, his warning to Brad. "The most terrible karma." She had never believed in karma. To her, the concept was another one of those woo-woo ideas that people invented just to make them feel like they knew how it all worked. But karma had come to wreak havoc and inflict carnage on her world. It had come in a fiendish form, and it could not be stopped. As she waited to die, Katherine realized that karma was simply the consequence of choice, the price you pay for the things you sign onto. She had chosen to be an enabler for a greedy loathsome man whose disregard for proper safety procedures had wrought death and destruction on the very people who were making him rich. How could she have possibly justified it all those years? It hadn't really been all that difficult. Everyone pays their dues to get ahead, right? Then there was the money, of course. And if she didn't do it, someone, else would, so what difference would it make? Justification after justification. But now her karma had caught up with her, and she was about to pay the ultimate price.

Clack, clack, clack, clack. The rhythmic footsteps of death got louder and louder as they approached down the hallway. They stopped at the door to the break room. Katherine realized she hadn't even thought of locking the door. Not that it would have mattered. She had seen clearly that the accursed thing possessed powers far beyond the rules of her world. The door swung open. A faint red glow from the exit sign in the hall back-lit the preternatural executioner as it stood there in the doorway, gazing into the room. She was overcome again by the vile odor, and images of the bone factory flashed through her mind. She saw her own fish-eaten body hanging in a dripping net.

It was coming toward her. Clack, clack, clack. She could see it clearly now as if it carried with it some sort of otherworldly light. The demonic morbid face, rotted flesh still clinging to it, dripping with hatred, was focused on her. It got closer and closer. It was standing right over her with a death grimace and blood-soaked skeleton hands. She closed her eyes, and like that little kitten so many years before, she gave herself over to the truth of her fate.

And then the most unexpected thing of all happened. Nothing.

There was an immeasurable amount of time when there was nothing but silence. But as she was floating in the vast emptiness of what was surely the last moment of life, she heard a voice.

"You go, Miss lady. Thank you, nice lady."

She heard the clack, clack, clack of the skeleton feat, moving away from her. It stopped at the other end of the room by the door. It spoke again, the voice echoing back through the darkness.

"Please, Miss lady. Go fast. Now, Miss Lady."

She couldn't wrap her brain around what was happening. She opened her eyes. She could see the thing, there at the door, looking back at her. She stared at it, numb with wonder.

"Thank you, Miss lady."

The skeleton of Mr. Malhotra turned and walked quickly back out the door. Clack, clack, clack, clack. The boney footsteps faded into the distance. She was alone again in the darkness of the break room. She was alive.

Katherine lowered her face onto her arms and gasped for breath, sobbing, choking. Overwhelming fear had turned into impossible relief. She thought she heard her name being called from somewhere in the darkness.

"Katherine."

Two hands grabbed her arms. In a state of delirium, she screamed and fought, but the hands didn't let go.

"Katherine, it's me. It's all right now. I've got you."

It was Charlie. She collapsed into his arms.

"You're okay. Gotta pull yourself together now. Okay?"

Only half-conscious, she mumbled into his shoulder. "Gotta go fast. He said...go fast."

"Yeah. We're going. Just hold onto me. You'll be okay."

Nobody else in the world could have brought her around to where she could even move at that point. But holding onto him, she was able to regain at least some awareness of reality and make her body function. He guided her quickly out of the break room, down the hall and out the emergency exit door and into a pouring rain.

Katherine stopped outside and looked back.

"It opened. The door opened. It wouldn't open before."

Charlie nodded his head. "No."

Katherine grabbed his jacket and looked at him, desperate.

"He was here, Charlie. That thing...it was Mr. Malhotra. I swear it was!"

"I know. I know. It's okay. You're not crazy, Katherine. I saw it, too."

"But...how? I don't understand."

"Neither do I."

"He said, "go fast."

And they did. They ran through the raging storm while, behind them, in the depths of the factory, an entity from another realm was carrying out its final act of vengeance.

THE VARGO CHEMICAL facility in Toledo, Ohio, was destroyed by a massive explosion at 6:32 pm. The majority of employees who were still on site had been safely evacuated before the explosion. Thirteen people died at the factory, including CEO Brad Weller and COO Steven Morris. The people of Toledo were lucky. The heavy rains that were hitting at the time kept the potentially toxic effects of the explosion at a minimum. The cause was never determined. Some speculated that Brad Weller himself had instigated a suicidal sabotage of his own plant, born of unbearable guilt for the horrible disaster in India.

THE GRUESOME AFTERMATH of the explosion in Delhi produced a plentiful source of new product for the bone factory.

PLUSH

Does fear create horror, or does horror create fear? This was the kind of question that, had he been able to think philosophically, Jerome Woodman might have considered that hot sticky night in a ninth-floor apartment in New York City.

It wasn't his apartment. It belonged to his friend Debbie. Jerome's apartment was being fumigated for bedbugs that his train wreck of a roommate had carelessly invited in. Debbie was out of town visiting her parents in D.C. and offered her place as an escape. Jerome was hoping that one of his male friends would offer him a couch, but bad timing scuttled that idea. So, against his better judgment, Jerome accepted Debbie's offer.

Jerome didn't have anything against women. He liked women. They didn't like him as much as he liked them, but he didn't resent that. It was just that he'd never been in Debbie's place before and, well, a lot of women, even when they were grown, tended to have stuffed animals.

The thing was, Jerome had a deeply embedded, wrenching horror of stuffed animals. Plushies, in any form, had qualified as his greatest fear since he was a small child. He blamed his twisted older sister, Mindy, for this phobia. Mindy always felt Jerome was the favorite child, babied and coddled by both parents, so she took extreme pleasure in tormenting him in every way possible. When Jerome was only three, Mindy had planted the idea that the stuffed beasties were out to get him. She was constantly terrorizing him by hiding one in a closet or backpack or anywhere Jerome would suddenly and unexpectedly come upon it. Mindy would heighten the effect by smearing ketchup on their mouths as if they had just fed on some other innocent child.

Jerome was now 29, but his fear of plushies hadn't subsided. He would still do everything in his power to stay away from toy stores and Christmas displays. There were times, however, where he might be distracted and suddenly find himself in trouble. One night, for example, he and some friends were walking on Fifth Avenue. It was Christmas time, and they were approaching a department store. The window displays feature colorful, expensive clothing. But, to Jerome's horror, the store had also populated the displays with cute fuzzy stuffed animals. Before panic fully kicked in, Jerome managed to fake an irresistible hunger for roasted chestnuts and dashed for a vendor across the street.

Although he'd become fairly successful at avoiding them in his daily life, he could never drive them from his dreams. He was still stalked in his slumbers by malevolent stuffed puppies, ravenous drooling teddy bears or plush ponies with only one thing on their evil minds, Jerome's death. He never told anyone, of course. Such a revelation would curse him to a lifetime of shame and embarrassment. He had already lost two potential girlfriends by freaking them out in the middle of the night when he woke up screaming. The alpha state was not a safe place for Jerome.

Jerome had considered finding help, but revealing his embarrassing condition, even to a professional therapist, was too much contemplate. Push came to shove, however. Angry and frustrated at the loss of one girlfriend he particularly liked, he decided to go to a hypnotist. He'd read about how hypnotherapy could help you get rid of fears. He just had to make sure no one found him out. Jerome and most of his friends lived in the East Village, so he made an appointment with a guy he found online who had an office on the upper east side. He was fairly confident that he wouldn't run into anyone he knew up there.

Unfortunately, the visit to the hypnotherapist proved to be a disaster. When Jerome bravely confessed his phobia, the therapist stared at him for a minute then took out his cell phone and made a call.

"Good one, Jerry. Better than last year, you son-of-a-bitch."

Jerome listened to the conversation completely confused.

"The guy. The guy you sent in. Come on, man, I am so onto you. You know you can't fuck with me. I've known you way too long. Uh huh. Uh huh. Sure. Hey, man, it was good. Scared of stuffed animals. I love it. You da man. What? What? Oh, bullshit. Come on. Wait, is this like a second part to it? Holy shit. No. Really? You swear. Oh shit. Okay. Yeah."

The therapist hung up and did his best to look remorseful. He said he was so very very sorry. That his friend was in the habit of pulling sophisticated April Fool's pranks on him every year, and he was just so sure that this was one of them. Jerome hadn't even considered the date. Yes, it was April first. But so what? He didn't even know that people still did April Fool tricks like that.

The therapist kept apologizing and assuring Jerome that he really could help him, that his fear was truly valid as anyone's. Jerome was considering whether he could chalk it up to something as simple as an honest mistake when, suddenly, the guy just burst out laughing. Jerome was flabbergasted. It was the most unprofessional and unbelievable thing imaginable. Through his laughter, the therapist kept trying to say he was sorry, so sorry. But he couldn't control himself. He laughed even harder.

Jerome just got up and left without saying anything. As he walked down the street back to his apartment, he felt an ironic satisfaction, knowing that he'd been right all along. That not even a professional could take him seriously, let alone help him. But he also felt more alone than ever.

Debbie had given Jerome a key several days before he had to vacate his place. With an overnight bag in tow, he took the elevator to the ninth floor and nervously entered her apartment. The door opened directly into the living room. He switched on an overhead light and looked around. The coast was clear. So far. Debbie, it seemed, was a very tidy woman with simple taste in home décor. There was a small couch and a glass-topped coffee table sitting on top of a fuzzy white rug. The floors were old wood, fairly recently re-sanded and varnished. Debbie seemed to be fond of antique china teacups. A small but classy collection of them graced different tables and shelves here and there. He guessed that they were probably inherited.

He set his bag on the couch and took a look at the kitchen. Nice. Clean and neat. There was a note on the counter. "Jerome. Hi. There's some chicken salad in the fridge from the deli down the street. It's great. Eat it. The AC doesn't work very well, but if you open the kitchen window, it usually helps. See you soon. Debbie." Okay, this was maybe going to work out fine. He liked chicken salad.

Jerome didn't mind the heat so much, but it was humid, and the apartment was stuffy and damp. The kitchen had one large double-hung window, like a lot of older New York apartments, with a sill that sat only a couple of feet from the floor. He pulled the window up all the way, and some cooler air rushed in. Much better. The window had a screen in it so you couldn't lean out, but by putting his forehead right against the screen, Jerome could see some of the streets below. It was cool to look down onto the people on the sidewalk and see the businesses all lit up. He wished his own apartment had a window overlooking the street. He walked back into the living room and stopped, gazing over at the bedroom door.

Bedrooms.

Bedrooms were the real threat. They were always in the bedrooms. The pleasant feeling Jerome felt momentarily in the kitchen vanished. He was suddenly queasy. The same old cold nauseating fear crept up his spine and wrapped an icy hand around his psyche. He stared at the bedroom door. It was in there. He just knew it. He could feel it. And it was waiting for him. He tried to get ahold of himself. Come on, Jerome, you don't know that. Get it together, man. You have no proof whatsoever. But the door to the bedroom was closed. That was bad. If Debbie had left it open, he would have just glanced inside and would have known. But he had to open it himself. And what if it was dark? Then he'd have to find the willpower to turn the light on. If there was one of them there, shit.

Jerome was starting to sweat. He thought about just saying fuck it, grabbing his bag and leaving. He could sleep on a park bench. His fear of being mugged didn't even compare to this. Or he could go further into debt and get a hotel room. His heart was racing now, and he was breathing hard and fast. He slapped his own psyche and told himself to get his shit together.

He went back into the kitchen, found a glass, and had a drink of water. He took some deep breaths. He'd always known, objectively, that it was crazy, that his paranoia was completely irrational. Paranoia is always irrational. Nobody in the history of the world had ever been harmed by a stuffed animal. Little children slept with them every night, for Christ's sake. Didn't matter. He'd tried a thousand times to hold onto this kind of logic, to convince himself that they couldn't possibly ever hurt him. But it was useless. Deep down in the darkest part of his being, he knew they were just waiting for their moment, waiting to make their move. They had something in store for him. Something dreadful.

He gathered as much willpower as he could and went back into the living room. He stared at the bedroom. Fuck. He paced for a while, drank some more water, then finally made his decision. He slowly crossed to the door, grabbed the knob. He was shaking, sweating, hardly able now to catch a breath. With a trembling hand, he turned the knob and pushed, slowly. The door squeaked open, sending a chill through his whole body. Christ, why did the fucking door have to squeak like that? And goddamn it, it was dark in the bedroom.

With the door halfway open Jerome froze. He wanted to just slam it and run. But something kept pulling him further in. Was it them? They had power over him. They'd always had the control. Or could it possibly be his own will to finally face his fear, to suck it up and confront it? He wanted so badly to believe this. He'd fantasized about the day when he could walk up to that huge toy store window and laugh at all the plushies and just flip them off. Fuck you. You don't scare me.

But no. He knew that was a fantasy that would never come true. They were in control, now and forever.

He ran his hand on the wall inside the door, feeling for a light switch. He glanced into the darkness and saw two little gleaming specks in the darkness. Eyes. He jumped. The motion made his hand jerk and flip the switch, lighting up the room.

It was on the bed. A large plush puppy with floppy ears, staring right at him.

Jerome let out an anguished cry and fell backward. His momentum carried him back into the living room. He tripped over the rug and fell against a small end table, knocking a teacup and saucer onto the floor. It shattered. In trying to break his fall, his hand came down onto a sharp chunk of porcelain, slicing into his palm. A hip and elbow hit the floor hard. The pain immobilized him for a moment. Some weird strangulated sounds of fear and desperation escaped his throat. When he was finally able to move, he saw that blood was gushing from the wound on his hand. It was bleeding so profusely that it quickly formed a small puddle on the hardwood.

Jerome pulled himself up, painfully, and staggered toward the bathroom, blood dripping across the floor. He slammed the bathroom door behind him, lunged for the sink and held his hand under cold running water. The cut was bad, a jagged slice from the base of his little finger almost all the way to his wrist.

He wrapped a copious amount of toilet paper around his hand as he searched for some kind of bandage. He found a small box of Bandaids but nothing substantial enough to deal with a gash that long. In a lower drawer, he finally found an ace bandage, the kind you use on a sprain. He wadded up a bunch of toilet paper, pressed it against the wound and then wrapped his hand, securing the bandage with two little metal clips.

He leaned on the sink and tried to catch his breath. He'd dealt with the wound. Good. He had to gather himself now and figure his next move. He looked behind at the floor and saw a trail of blood leading under the door out into the living room. The extent of the damage he'd just done to Debbie's apartment hit him. He sat down on the toilet and put his head into his hands. He might be able to get the blood cleaned up, as long as it hadn't gotten onto any furniture. But the teacup, god. How was he going to explain that? Your stuffed puppy freaked me out so much...yeah, right. He'd have to lie, again. Tripped on the rug. Fuck it. It would have to do. The rug. Oh, Christ, what if there was blood on that fucking fuzzy white rug? His brain was a scramble of worst-case scenarios.

While he sat there on the toilet disgusted, embarrassed, trashing himself from every direction, Jerome heard a sound. At first, he thought he was hearing was the water running in the sink. But no. It was a strange slurping sound, and it was coming from the living room, outside the bathroom door. He listened carefully. It happened for a few moments, then stopped. Then it started again. What the hell is that?

"Hello? Is someone there? Debbie?"

He didn't really expect an answer. There was no way anyone else could possibly be in the apartment. He would have heard the outside door open and close if someone had come in. Unless someone had been hiding in a closet. Ridiculous. But something was making that noise.

He looked at the blood on the floor and in the sink. He grabbed several handfuls of toilet paper and started to wipe it up. God, there was so much blood. He threw the paper in the toilet and flushed. As he pushed the handle down, he heard and felt something snap inside the toilet tank. The handle slipped and just dangled loosely. Something had broken in the flushing mechanism. The bloody toilet paper just floated there, swirls of blood now mixing with the water. Jerome was stunned. How could this be happening?

He wiped his face in frustration. He felt something moist. He looked in the mirror and saw a huge swath of red across his cheek. Blood had seeped through the ace bandage on his hand, and he had smeared it on his face. He freaked. With manic a fury, he hit the mirror with his hand. It shattered. Glass reigned down onto the sink and splintered into hundreds of pieces. A large shard caught his un-bandaged hand and embedded itself just behind his thumb. He grabbed it and pulled it. In the process, he cut one of the fingers he used to grasp the shard. Blood gushed from the two new nasty cuts.

"Jesus Christ, no. No, no, no, no, no. Fuck." He grabbed furiously at the toilet paper, pulled off a long length, and carelessly wrapped it around his finger and the newly cut hand. It was a total rat fuck. The bleeding was so profuse that the toilet paper was pretty much useless. More blood was now dripping onto the floor and sink. He grabbed for a towel to wipe his face and blot his hand. Are you kidding me? White towels. Why the fuck would anyone have white towels in a white bathroom?

Why didn't she have red towels? Red towels would be a colorful accent. The room needed it for Christ's sake. He threw the gruesome, bloody towel onto the floor in anger.

"God, what's going on? This is..." He didn't have words. He was just caught up in a surreal maelstrom of bloody horror. Then he heard the sound again. The slurping from the other side of the door.

"Who the fuck is out there?" He yelled it at the top of his lungs. He realized that if a neighbor was home, they certainly would have heard him. He didn't care. He had to do something. He couldn't take this anymore. He had to get out of Debbie's apartment and away from the evil plush puppy. Gotta go. Gotta go. Gotta go. He didn't have any other option now. Even if he could somehow overcome his terror of the fucking plushie, which was highly unlikely, he'd never get this mess cleaned up, not with two cut up hands.

He decided to just go right to an emergency room. He'd tell Debbie everything. The truth. It didn't matter anymore if she thought he was crazy. He'd pay for everything. Fuck debt. Fuck everything. He just needed it to end. He didn't even care now if she told his other friends. Fuck them too. He'd move. He'd move to Seattle. His brother lived in Seattle. His crazy brother, Nathan, who started all this and still laughed at his terror of stuffed animals. Fuck fucking Nathan. At least he wouldn't have to pretend.

He reached for the bathroom doorknob. He stopped. He listened. He didn't hear the noise now, but he'd heard something he shouldn't have been hearing. He felt blood dripping down his hands. He looked at them, looked at the bathroom. It was like a fucking slaughterhouse. He thought of what it would be like for Debbie to come home and discover this gruesome disaster. He felt terrible. But there was nothing for it now. The damage was done.

The ace bandage on his hand was now soaked in blood and dripping, as was the toilet paper on the other hand. He pulled the paper off and threw it in the toilet, adding to the horrible crimson soup. The wounds kept pouring forth. His pants and shirt were now splattered with blood as well. He grabbed another towel from a rack, another fucking white towel, and wrapped it around the unbandaged hand. This was it. He had to go.

He grabbed the doorknob and twisted it, pulling the door inward. It was all he could do to keep breathing. He looked out into the living room. Nobody visible.

He looked toward the kitchen. Nothing. He took a step out of the bathroom. He looked down at the floor. There were blood splatters all over the white rug in front of the couch. Shit. Then he saw the spot where the blood from his initial cut on the teacup had formed a small pool. The pool was gone. And so were most of the drips that had trailed toward the bathroom door. There were little moist smears. It was as if someone had wiped it up, but not exactly. He couldn't figure out what he was seeing. But right now he didn't care. He just needed to get out. He turned and began to move toward the front door. He winced as he took a step. He'd been so distracted by the bathroom bloodbath that he'd forgotten about his hip, which stabbed at him when he put weight on it. He limped on a bit more then froze for a moment. The plush puppy was sitting by the front door, blood smeared all around its mouth. Jerome screamed and threw himself backward, falling once more onto the floor.

In those few brief moments of this unending agony, as he was falling backward, things became suddenly horrifyingly clear. Jerome saw the truth. This was their plan all along. This is what they wanted. His blood. The sound he heard from the bathroom was the plush puppy lapping up his blood from the floor. And now it was blocking his escape from this indescribable hell.

When he fell, he slammed his head hard against the bathroom door frame. There was a blazing flash of light. He was dizzy, his vision blurry. He felt a stream of warm liquid flowing down the back of his head and neck. He looked across the room. Things were hazy, swimming. Was it was coming toward him? He tried to focus. It was. It was coming.

Jerome grabbed at a table that sat against the wall and tried to pull himself up. His foot slipped on the bloody floor, and he stumbled. He pulled the table over. It crashed to the hardwood, and he went down again. A small lamp bulb exploded and two more teacups shattered on the floor. He was on his side. He glanced over toward the door. God, it was coming.

"Help me!" His desperate cry went unanswered.

He scrambled clumsily to getaway. Every part of his body was screaming in pain, and he had little control over his movements. He twisted awkwardly, knelt on one of the broken teacups and slashed his knee open. More blood gushed. He tried to crawl over the broken table, falling yet again. His face slammed down onto some more broken shards of teacups, ripping into his cheek and forehead. He was now oblivious to the pain and the mass of blood that was splashing everywhere. He just needed to get away from that stuffed hellhound.

He thought he heard knocking, maybe someone calling. Too late. Too late. He somehow managed to pull himself up. Wobbly and crying in terror, his feet slipping on the blood-drenched hardwood, he lunged for the kitchen. He couldn't control his momentum, and he crashed hard into the refrigerator, splattering the white surface with blood. He bounced hard off of it and stumbled sideways across the room. He tried to stop himself, but his bloody, slippery shoes flew out from under him. Jerome hit the window screen hard. It popped like tissue paper, and he sailed helplessly out into the New York night. He made a desperate grab for the window sill, but his hand was soaked in blood. Life simply slipped out of his grasp.

As Jerome fell the nine stories, he caught a glimpse of the evil stuffed puppy looking down at him from Debbie's window sill, a bloody grin on its demonic face. Jerome didn't care. The air that rushed by him as he plunged to his doom was the cool wind of freedom.

Whether fear creates horror or horror creates fear was irrelevant to Jerome now. He was finally free from both.

His body slammed through an awning hanging over the sidewalk in front of a greengrocer. He landed face down in a waist-high display cart of fruit and vegetables. His head was twisted unnaturally, facing the street. The passers-by that happened to be on the sidewalk at that moment stood frozen, stunned by what they just witnessed. They stared at the blood-drenched mangled body that fell from the sky. In his last moments of life, Jerome saw a woman clutching her little girl, shielding the child's eyes from the gruesome sight. The little girl was holding a pink teddy bear. The plushy bear was staring at Jerome, smiling.

Jerome smiled back. He raised a bloody middle finger at the bear and exhaled his final breath on a pile of crushed cantaloupes.

Porcupine Hill

"What is that?"

Allison Cote studied the video for a long time. She adjusted the brightness, trying to get it as clear as possible. The images were taken the previous night by a heat-sensitive infrared wildlife camera in a swampy wooded area called Porcupine Hill. The motion-activated camera had recorded a porcupine, sniffing around a baited cage trap that Allison had set out two days previously.

In spite of her fondness for the spiny critters, her interest in the porcupine was tangential. She was studying the population density of fishers, the second-largest member of the weasel family, outsized only by the wolverine. The area had gotten its name because of an unusually dense porcupine population, making it an ideal hunting ground for fishers, one of the porcupines' only natural predators. Fishers are extremely powerful predators with a very slick and certainly brutal method of killing a porcupine. They'd tear at its face to disable it, then flip it over onto its back and rip into its throat.

The video Allison was studying had, so far, revealed nothing of importance relevant to her study. She would have moved on from the porcupine, except that something peculiar in the footage had caught her eye.

She turned to her colleague, Sammy Tanaka, who was scanning DNA samples.

"Hey, Sammy. Come here and tell me what the hell I'm looking at."

Sammy got up from his work station. He leaned over her shoulder to check out the footage.

"What?"

"There. Right there. What is that?" She'd paused the recording and pointed at a dark shape in a corner of the image.

Sammy looked closer. "I don't see anything."

"Oh, come on. Right there. That doesn't look like a person to you?"

Sammy tilted her screen up a bit. "Nah. It's just a trick of the lens. The infrared does stuff like that." He went back to his own computer.

Allison said, "Yeah, okay. I guess.," But she wasn't really convinced. To her, it looked like the dark shape of a person, partially hidden by some small trees, staring right at the camera. She isolated that corner of the photo and zoomed in on it. The image became pixilated and blurry, but she could swear that there were two little bright spots where a person's eyes would be. If it was a person.

Sammy looked over at her, seeing that she was still semi-obsessing over it.

"What time was the shot taken?" he asked

"3:07 am."

"Uh, huh. Lot of foot traffic out there that time of the morning."

"Right. Moving on."

She scanned through the rest of the video. The porcupine had come back a couple of times, probably thinking it had just missed some trick by which it could get to the apples inside the bait cage. Then a raccoon showed up, and the two creatures got into a brief spat. No fishers, though. She decided she'd give this location a few more nights. If there was still no sign of a fisher, she'd try a new location.

ALLISON WOKE THE EARLY the next morning soaked in sweat. Another short drug-induced sleep. Two years since Linny had died and the nights were still torture. Being alone in the dark with her memories was excruciating. She was continually playing out Linny's last days, imagining different scenarios that didn't end with her death.

Craig had kept telling her she needed to move on. They could have another child. It made her crazy. How the hell do you move on? What an absurd idea. Finally, he moved on without her, to a small town outside Ottawa. After a couple more months of even lonelier rage and unrelenting grief, she realized that, as many times as she'd considered it, she was not going to escape the nightmare by taking her own life. She was going to have to live it out. So she buried herself in her work, seldom leaving the lab before three am. Couple of Ambien, three or four hours of haunted sleep and she'd be back at work.

She found a way to limit her still frequent bouts of weeping and cursing the universe to times when she was alone. Her job as a mammal research specialist for the Ministry of Natural Resources allowed her this modicum of control since she spent so much time in the field. The natural world became a friend whose shoulder she could cry on. A friend who, whenever she'd break down in an isolated woodland or on the shore of a lonely lake, would never tell her she had to move on.

As the pickup bounced along the dirt road on the way to Porcupine Hill, Allison thought again about the last words Linny had spoken to her. She was barely conscious, a shell of the beautiful little girl that had filled her life with love and joy. Her eyes were closed, her breathing shallow and fading. She stirred a bit, and a thin, dry little voice said, "You need to help her, mommy."

Allison, gently holding her daughter's weak cold hand, asked, "Who do I need to help, honey?"

There was no reply. But Linny smiled as if she'd seen something that made her happy. Moments later, she was gone.

The mystery of Linny's words had haunted her every day since. But today, driving slowly through the lush Southern Ontario woods, Allison realized that it had been that final smile that had kept her alive. She saw the whole incident as a kind of gift Linny had given her to keep her going.

As she reached Porcupine Hill and pulled the truck off the road into a flat grassy turnout, it dawned on her that, for the first time, she was thinking objectively about what she'd been through the last two years. She turned the engine off and stared out the windshield. Images of her ordeal flashed through her mind. She saw herself crumpled on the bathroom floor. She saw herself raging at Craig, resentful that he didn't seem to be sharing her level of grief. She saw herself sitting at the kitchen table, weak and useless, like a broken chair. She snapped out of the flashback and looked in the rearview mirror. She hadn't really taken notice of her own face for so long, her own appearance surprised her. Right, that's what she looked like. Out loud, she said to herself, "You need a haircut."

Allison grabbed an equipment bag from the seat and got out of the truck. She looked around at the thick woods in front of her and was surprisingly moved by what a beautiful spot it was. She'd been there several times previously, but never consciously considered the surroundings. She had simply trod through the woods in a kind of a trance, changed out the SD card in the camera, put new bait in the cage, taken some notes and left.

As she made her way through the woods, she became aware of her hands gripping the worn handles of the equipment bag. She felt her left foot being irritated by a drooping sock. She felt the warmth of the sun on her cheek. She didn't know what was happening, but she had an odd feeling that things were suddenly different. It was as if she had awakened from a dream and somehow regained an awareness of the physical reality of her own life. She looked down and saw a large beetle that had flipped over onto its back. Its legs were flailing helplessly. Allison bent down and gently turned it over. The beetle crawled off into the weeds. She was touched by a strange empathy for the beetle as if she understood the writhing helplessness and then the sudden sense of finding yourself upright again.

It irritated her. She wasn't looking for entomological metaphors or some sort of psychic transformation. She didn't have any interest in thinking about ridiculous things like her own appearance or an uncomfortable foot. She'd found a kind of security in her detached world of hurt. What was she supposed to do now? Care? Caring required a kind of responsibility that she didn't feel capable of anymore. In spite of the unceasing nightmares, grief was a safe haven.

The hell with all of it. She focused again on her purpose for being here. Retrieve the camera and bait trap and install them in a new location. Leaving the beetle and her annoying revelations behind, she pulled her wrinkled sock up and headed further into the forest.

Porcupine Hill was dominated by a lush mixture of deciduous trees, with a few stands of conifers here and there. Black ash, maple, ironwood, and poplar dominated, broken up by scattered clumps of hemlock and the occasional eastern cypress. Most impressive, though, were the giant ancient white oaks. Perhaps out of reverence for their sheer magnificence, they'd been spared by the loggers who ripped through the area a century ago, harvesting millions of board feet of timber that would become the bridges and railroad ties and cities of Southern Ontario. It was under one such oak that Allison had placed the cage trap two weeks previously. She'd anchored it in a shallow depression between two large roots that twisted outward from the base of the massive trunk. For some reason, this spot of forest floor was bare of the wispy grass that grew profusely over the surrounding area. Just a thin layer of leaf mulch covered the moist earth.

The camera was set up about twenty feet away, mounted three feet from the ground on a sturdy ironwood tree. Allison went to the camera, approaching it from behind. The motion-sensitive infrared worked in daylight as well as darkness. Any movement within the scope of the viewfinder would activate it.

She switched the camera off, pulled out the SD card, and put it in her pocket. She was about to remove the camera but hesitated. Something didn't feel quite right. She was overcome by the feeling that she wasn't alone. It didn't make any sense. The chances of there being anyone else in this part of the woods were virtually nil. Maybe in the fall when deer season was in swing, maybe then a hunter. But in June? Not likely.

About forty feet from where she was standing, there was a drop-off in the forest floor, beyond which was a fairly large marshy area with about six inches of water in it. It was clogged with sumac and buckthorn bushes. It had been a rainy spring, and there was an abundance of water everywhere in the region. Allison's attention was pulled toward the marsh. A few bushes in the middle of the swamp were wavering, as if something had jostled them. She had no idea what. She didn't see anything. She did a complete 360, scanning the surrounding forest.

"Hello?" There was no reply, of course. Because there was nobody there. She shook off the illusion. She put a new SD card into the camera and headed for the cage trap under the oak. She knelt down, opened the trap, and pulled out the apples that were intended to attract any resident fishers. She stuffed the shriveled apples into her bag and pulled out a couple of fresh ones. She heard a very faint sound. It was the sound of someone crying. A girl. It was a little girl crying. Allison bolted upright. She couldn't tell where it was coming from.

"Hello? Where are you?"

She looked toward the marsh again. Nothing. There was a small knoll a ways away, from the top of which she could see more of the forest. She climbed the knoll quickly. There was plenty of sunlight penetrating the canopy, so the visibility was good.

"Hello? It's okay. Do you need help?"

She heard the crying again. Now it seemed to be coming from somewhere close to the giant oak tree. It had an unusual echoey quality, which seemed incongruous since the thick forest usually dampened sounds.

She saw a shadow move. There was someone behind the tree. She trod as quietly as possible back down the knoll and approached the oak, slowly.

She spoke softly. "I'm right here. Are you okay?"

She moved very carefully. She didn't want to frighten a child.

A little bit further and she'd be in full view of the backside of the oak. As she took another careful step, a ruffed grouse exploded out of the grass and flapped off through the trees. Allison jumped, and a short yelp escaped her throat. Her heart was pounding.

"Goddamn it."

It took her a bit to catch her breath. She finally looked around to the other side of the tree. There was no one. Of course, there wasn't. If there had been, the grouse certainly wouldn't have been hiding there.

Then it struck her what she was actually hearing. A fisher. Fishers are notorious for making sounds that can be mistaken for a child crying. In regions where they're plentiful, it's not unusual for the authorities to get calls from locals claiming to have heard someone crying in the woods. She also knew that sound can do weird things out in the forest, so maybe it wasn't nearly as close as it seemed.

She was encouraged again about the potential of this location. She returned to the trap and put the bait apples in place. As she was carefully setting the trap door, she heard something running through the woods behind her. Running towards her. Coming fast. She jumped up and spun around. And saw nothing. But the sound got louder. It was right on top of her. She felt a chill shoot through her as if she'd been hit by an icy wind. She fell back against the trunk of the oak, hitting her shoulder hard. She yelled at the forest.

"What the hell is going on?"

The forest didn't answer. She scanned the area. Nothing unusual at all. Her heart was pumping. She shook her head like an animal throwing off water as if jostling her brain might make something make sense. Was she losing her mind? Hallucinating? First, the annoying feelings of uninvited emotional transformation and now this. She had no idea what to think. The drugs? Maybe she'd been overdosing and didn't realize it. She'd been prescribed Lexapro for her depression. One of the side effects is hallucinations. Or maybe this was all some kind of major psychotic break.

She pulled herself to her feet, rubbed her bruised shoulder, and looked around at the forest once more. She saw a squirrel skitter up a hemlock. A blue jay started screaming from a ways off.

"Yeah, I know. Crazy lady in the woods."

Shaken and frustrated, she headed back towards her truck. She had several other locations to check before it got dark. Maybe she'd be back tomorrow. Maybe not. Maybe she'd find some excuse to move the camera, send Sammy to gather up the equipment so she wouldn't even have to come back to Porcupine Hill. But as logical as it seemed to write it off to her own emotional state, she had a deep chilling feeling that something was wrong here. As she crunched off through the trees, the crying of a child played over and over in her mind.

TO HER GREAT RELIEF, Allison was able to gather SD cards and re-bait traps in three other locations without incident. By the time she was finished, it was almost dark. On the way back to the lab, she realized she was starving. She stopped and picked up a large pizza. When she got to the lab, she put the pizza box on one of the lab benches. She saw Sammy staring at her with a peculiar expression on his face.

"Why are you looking at me like that?"

"Uh, well, maybe because in the entire time you've been back not only have I never seen you eat, you certainly have never brought pizza."

"It's veggie with sausage."

"That doesn't make any sense."

Allison grabbed a piece of pizza. "What do you mean?"

"It can't be veggie if there's sausage."

Sammy got up and took a piece for himself.

Allison headed for her work table. "The sausage never has enough veggies on it, so I get a veggie and just add sausage."

"Ah."

"Sammy, what's the strangest thing that's ever happened to you?"

"Besides you bringing pizza?"

"Bring me another slice, okay?"

Sammy took it to her. "What do you mean by strangest?"

"You know, something you couldn't explain."

"Hm. Okay, did I ever tell you how I got my cat, Oshi?"

Allison shook her head as she took another bite of pizza.

"I'd gone to Japan to visit my parents about four years ago. When I got home, I unlocked my front door, walked in, and he was sitting at the far end of the hall. Just sitting there, looking at me. Except there was no way, he could have gotten in. I had the house closed uptight, and no one else had a key except a friend in Ottawa. I left a key with him in case of emergency."

"So he went to the house, and the cat snuck in."

"Huh-uh. He never went near the place. No reason to. I never figured it out."

"There must have been some other way in."

"Um, it's my house. Think I'd know."

"Something happened out at Porcupine Hill today. Really weird. I heard this crying, like a little girl."

"Fisher."

"Right. That's what I figured. But then I heard something running, like, right at me, but there was nothing there."

"Huh, that's weird."

"Never mind. I've been, well, you know."

"Yeah, I get it," said Sammy.

"I think I'm going to relocate that camera."

"Sure, whatever. Thanks for the pizza. I'm outta here. I'm going to Ottawa tomorrow for that Ministry meeting, and I need to get some sleep for a change."

"Oh, right, I forgot. See if they have any more camera mounts. One of them broke today."

Sammy started packing up his stuff.

Allison took the SD card from the Porcupine Hill camera out of her pocket. Even though she'd decided to move the camera and not have to deal with that location anymore, she figured there was no harm in checking out the recording from last night. As many times as she'd seen this kind of footage, tonight the infrared image seemed otherworldly and unsettling, creepy. She was still rattled by the events of the day and feeling vulnerable. She considered just packing it in and going home but decided to get through it and just be done with Porcupine Hill. The first action was another porcupine. It was sniffing at the bait cage, trying to find a way to get to the apples. A fisher leapt out of the shadows and pounced on it. It startled her.

"Whoa! Holy crap! Sammy, check it out." She paused the video.

Sammy was almost out the door. He came back, and Allison started it from the beginning.

"Oh, man," he said. "Big guy."

They watched as the fisher tore furiously at the porcupine's face, flipped it, and killed it. It was brutal and fast.

"We should tag him," said Allison.

"Absolutely," said Sammy. "Where is this?"

"Porcupine Hill."

"And you wanted to relocate that camera? We need to nab this dude and tag him. Probably oughta re-bait the trap with meat. "

"Yeah. Okay."

Sammy left. Allison was pissed at herself for loading the video. She really didn't want to go back there, but now she was committed. There was nothing for it. It was her job. She'd decided that all the stuff she experienced at Porcupine Hill was probably a combination of drug side-effects and some form of PTSD from the trauma of Linny's death. She told herself to shake it off and get back to reality.

She let the video play out. The fisher stood triumphantly on the porcupine for a minute, licking its bloody muzzle. Then it grabbed the spiny rodent by the snout and dragged the carcass off into the darkness. Fishers often haul their victims up into a tree where they can more easily defend their spoils if another predator happens by and challenges them.

She thought the video would automatically stop since the fisher was gone. It didn't.

Something flashed across the screen. An image moving fast from right to left.

"What was that?" She glanced quickly at Sammy's desk, forgetting for a moment that he was gone. She looked back at the monitor.

A ghastly, terrifying face filled the screen.

Allison screamed and pushed her chair back from the desk, almost falling over. She bolted for the door. She threw it open and ran outside.

"Sammy! Sammy!"

It was too late. She could see his taillights fading off down the road.

Allison leaned against a porch railing, breathing hard. Her hands were shaking. She didn't know what to do. She didn't even want to go back inside. She just wanted to get in her car and drive to the nearest bar. But her bag, keys, all her stuff was inside at her desk. God, it was completely insane. What did she just see? It just didn't make any sense. She took a couple of deep breaths and went back in.

When she got back inside, she could see from across the room that her computer screen had gone dark. The camera had shut off and the video ended. She went back to her desk. She grabbed her bag and her jacket and reached for the mouse to shut down the computer. She was emotionally wrung out. No more.

But she couldn't do it. She had to know if she really saw it. What if her mind was just playing tricks on her? She didn't want to spend a sleepless night alone, freaking out, wondering if she was completely losing it. She threw her bag down.

"Dammit." She clicked her mouse, and the computer screen came to life. She clicked on the video file to start it from the beginning. She watched the fisher attack the porcupine and drag it off. She paused the video. Her throat was dry. She had a bottle of water that was half full. She drained it. She started the video.

The strange shape flashed across the screen. There was a moment of nothing.

Then, wham! The dreadful face appeared.

Allison jumped again and hid her face in her trembling hands. She got up and backed across the room. Bumping into a lab table.

"Goddamn it!" She hit the table twice with her fist. "Shit! Come on, Allison, get it together."

She back at her computer. The screen was dark again. She took some deep breaths and went back to the desk. With a trembling hand, she grabbed her mouse and started the video once more. This time she fast-forwarded through the fisher attack. The shadowy shape flashed across again, then the face. She hit pause.

She stared. It stared back. Grotesque. Unreal. The eyes were lifeless and too large. The mouth was tiny and smiling oddly.

"Oh, my God. It's a doll!" It was filthy and scuffed, its synthetic hair was tangled and full of bits of twigs and leaves. It was frightening, definitely. But it was a child's doll. But if it was a doll, then someone had to be holding it up to the camera. So there was someone out there. In the middle of the night.

Allison went back to the part of the video where the odd shape flashed across the screen. She played it in slow motion. It had the vague shape of a shadow of a person. It was not exactly a shadow. It was kind of fuzzy, more like a mist. But these weren't the best infrared cameras, and they sometimes distorted moving images. It had to be a shadow. She tried to find some logic to explain it. If it was a shadow, then whoever it was had to be in between the camera and the space where the image appeared. This didn't make any sense. She'd simply be seeing the person, not their shadow. She played it a couple more times, but nothing became any clearer to her.

She shut the computer down and leaned back in her chair.

"I need a drink." She said it out loud just to hear the sound of her own voice, to make sure she was still functioning on some level connected to reality. She grabbed her bag and jacket, shut the lights off in the lab, locked the door, got in her car, and headed toward The Boat House. It was the only place she knew that would still be open at this hour.

It was their go-to bar. Her's and Craig's. Before Linny was born, they'd go there to meet up with friends, watch hockey or baseball. Driving faster than usual, she found herself surprised that anything would suddenly inspire her to consider going out in public, even a shock like she'd just had. After Linny died, she'd shut herself off from the social world. Several of her once-close friends had tried to keep in contact, but she stopped returning their calls and emails. Her new friend, nature, was the only friend in whose company she felt comfortable anymore. But today, her good buddy nature had really started messing with her.

She was halfway to the bar when she was suddenly overcome by grueling exhaustion. Every cell in her body was tingling with weariness so overwhelming that the idea of even lifting a beer to her lips sounded impossible. She turned her car toward home. She somehow managed to get herself to her bed, and without the aid of drugs collapsed into a deep, dreamless sleep.

When Allison awoke the next morning, it was after nine. It took her several minutes to focus on her bedside clock. She was disoriented and confused. The time didn't make any sense. She hadn't slept later than five a.m. in almost two years. Something was jabbing at her ribs. She reached under the blanket and felt one of the metal buttons of her jean jacket. She was fully clothed. The events of the previous day suddenly leapt into her consciousness. She threw the blanket off and jumped up.

"Oh, my God." She sat on the edge of the bed playing it back. Was it real? Did she dream it? No. It happened. Porcupine Hill, the doll's face on the computer, all of it. And she'd just had a nine-hour uninterrupted sleep. After a day like that. It didn't make any sense. She looked at the picture of Linny on her bedside table.

"Hi, sweetheart."

It was how she started every day. Then the tears would come. But they weren't there this morning. Why the hell not? The enormity of Linny's absence first thing upon waking was unbearable, and she would cry uncontrollably until she would somehow pull herself together and head for work. She picked up the framed photo and hugged it to her breast.

"What's going on, honey?" She had the feeling that Linny could tell her why the whole world felt so different.

Allison looked around her bedroom. Needs cleaning, big time. She put the picture of Linny back on the nightstand, got up, and went into her kitchen. This was her home. Home. The concept had been meaningless for so long. She drank some water. She opened the curtains above the sink. The sun was bright, the day spectacular. She went around the house, opening all the curtains. She'd been living in constant darkness. Now, all of a sudden, she had a pleasantly irresistible desire for light. She looked out into her front yard and saw a scraggly, weedy unkempt yard.

"Great, Allison. Get your act together."

She went to the bathroom, stripped off her clothes, and looked at her naked body in the mirror.

"Who the hell are you?"

She climbed into the shower. The hot water felt good. But that was crazy. Nothing felt good. She let it rain down on her. She had the sensation that her body was absorbing the water like a sponge that had been sitting dry for a long time. Her thoughts wandered back to Porcupine Hill. It was when she arrived there the day before that something changed. But what? Why? There was no answer within her grasp. She spent a long time scrubbing every inch of herself as if she were washing off a thick, grimy layer of sadness and self-loathing.

She remembered how she used to take a shower with Linny and how they used to have shampoo fights. She flashed on the time when, in midst of one of these joyous duels, she slipped and banged her knee hard on the edge of the tub. It hurt so much that she couldn't hold back the tears. And she remembered Linny saying to her, "It's okay, Mommy, it's only pain." Which is what Craig used to say to Linny whenever she hurt herself.

The memory led her to thinking about Craig. How much she loved seeing him interact with Linny when they didn't know she was watching. He always spoke to Linny as an equal, listening to what she had to say about things as if he could learn as much from her as she from him. And for the first time in many months, she missed him, consciously. She went into the kitchen intending to fix herself a bowl of cereal, but she stopped halfway there, listening to the emptiness. Alone wasn't feeling good anymore.

An hour later, Allison pulled up to Honker's Coffee Shop. The joint was on the outskirts of Sedgeham, and in spite of its fairly tacky Canada goose theme, it was pretty much the only place in the area that had halfway decent food. It was also where Craig took her on their first date, for lunch. She always teased him about how unromantic it was. But she knew he'd chosen it because he was nervous and at least they could laugh at the décor. Later, after Linny was born, it became their traditional destination for Sunday morning breakfast. Linny loved the Strawberry Belgian Waffles.

Allison walked through the door and paused, looking around. It was about half full. She half-expected the customers to all stop and look at her as if to say, "What are you doing here?" She sat down at the long counter, ordered some coffee, two eggs, scrambled with back bacon. Someone had left a newspaper on the stool next to her. She picked it up and looked at the headlines. It was the local Sedgeham paper, the one she and Craig always made fun of. They used to cut out their favorite absurd small-town stories and put them on the refrigerator: "Local Man Died of Natural Causes" "Goose Accused of Stealing Wedding Ring" "Rain Puts Damper on Jello Fest." The news was another thing that had become irrelevant to Allison's life since Linny died. There could have been a nuclear war, and she would have missed it. She glanced at the sports pages and saw that the Toronto Blue Jays were in first place. Wow, she thought, that's cool. She and Craig had been big Jays fans.

Her breakfast arrived. It came to her that she had no idea what she'd been eating for the last two years. She hadn't tasted a single bite. As she relished her perfect eggs and salty bacon, she started leafing through the paper. The new Prime Minister was taking a lot of flak from the opposition party for his plan to reverse health care cutbacks. So there'd been an election. She was browsing the local section when one particular story caught her eye. The headline read, "Friends Pay Respects on Third Anniversary of Girl's Disappearance." It was the accompanying photo that made her put down her bagel and stare, dumbfounded. The lovely girl with long blond hair was holding a doll. The doll's face looked eerily like the face Allison saw on her computer screen.

Allison tried to chalk it up as just a weird coincidence. There were surely lots of kids who had a similar doll, right? The story reported that a group of locals had gathered in the lakeside park in Sedgeham to place a wreath at a makeshift memorial someone had constructed. The memorial was dedicated to a girl named Gracie MacKenzie. The park was the last place anyone had seen her. There were no more details.

Allison knew the park well, of course. They'd taken Linny there many times. The swings were her favorite. With her beautiful hair blowing in the breeze, laughing and constantly asking to be pushed higher, she'd swing with pure joy. Back and forth. Back and forth.

The server came over to refill Allison's coffee cup. She put her hand over it.

"No, thanks. Hey, can I have the paper?"

"Be my guest."

Allison paid her bill and got back into her car. She sat for a moment, trying to decide what to do. She was already over two hours late for work. Nobody would notice or care. Sammy was in Ottawa, so she was the only one manning the lab. It was Friday, and she could always put some hours in on the weekend if she needed to. But she also wanted to get back out to Porcupine Hill and retrieve the SD card from the camera to see if anything new showed up from the previous night.

She glanced down at the picture of the sweet blond girl with the doll. She needed to know more.

A while later she pulled into the parking lot of the Sedgeham library. One of the librarians, Claire, had been a good friend, back when she was still in touch with people. Her husband, Ian, was Craig's number one fishing buddy. On the one hand, she sort of dreaded the whole reconnecting thing. On the other, she liked and trusted Claire, and it had to start somewhere.

"Allison?"

The voice came from the library parking lot and snapped her out of her thoughts. She looked out the window and saw

Claire walking toward her car. Allison got out of the car and went to meet her.

"Hey, Claire."

"Oh, my God. I can't believe it.

Claire hugged her, and Allison didn't resist. The friendly touch of another human being felt good.

Claire teared up. "I've missed you so much."

"Yeah. I'm sorry. It's been..."

"No. You don't have to apologize. Ever. And I'm not going to ask you any stupid questions, either."

"Thanks. But I think I'm okay with stupid questions."

"Can you come in for a minute? I gotta get back to the desk."

"Sure. I'm actually hoping you can help me with something."

"Name it."

Claire pulled up a chair next to her desk in the library, and they made small talk for a while. Claire started to tell her about her own kids but caught herself, thinking it was bad taste to talk about how they were doing. But Allison took her hand.

"It's okay. I want to know about them, honest."

Claire's lip started to quiver.

"Hey, come on. I'm not supposed to have to comfort you. That's just twisted."

They laughed together. Allison hadn't heard her own laugh for what seemed like a hundred years.

Claire asked her what she needed help with. Allison told her she was looking for a back issue of the local paper. She said it was a work thing. Claire took her to a computer and showed her how to access the archives.

"If you need to print anything out just hit the icon that says 'print this page.' It'll come out on the printer behind the counter."

It didn't take her long to find the issue. It happened to be a day when there was a huge fire at a famous old hotel in downtown Ottawa. The front section of the paper was dominated by the disaster and peripheral stories of heroism and personal tragedy. She found the story of Gracie McKenzie on page three. It was headlined simply "Local Girl Goes Missing." It was buried below a story with much larger headlines that read, "Police Officer Mauled by Bear." Allison remembered Craig's ranting about how so many really important stories got lost beneath all the sensationalist tripe about movie stars' marriages or UFO sightings.

The story of Gracie MacKenzie was fairly brief. This was the first report of her disappearance, and nobody knew, of course, that she would never be found. The paper explained that Gracie was a beautiful but mentally challenged girl. Although she was 14 years old, her emotional state was more like that of a five-year-old. She lived in a neighborhood on the edge of town. Her parents both worked and Gracie was cared for during the day by a nanny. On the day she disappeared, the nanny had been on the phone with a relative. There had been a sudden death in her family, and she was distracted. Gracie had slipped out of the house on her own. She evidently walked to a nearby park. Several people reported that they'd seen her playing on the swings and sitting at a table talking to her doll. The Nanny finished her call but thought that Gracie was simply playing in her room which was where she had left her when she got the call. So it was some time before she went to check on her. When she realized Gracie was gone, she immediately called the police. The local Constable was out on another call, but the Ontario Provincial Police responded quickly, and a search was launched.

Allison found follow-up stories in subsequent issues. Authorities combed the local woods for weeks using dogs, helicopters, even a psychic. From the reaction of the search dogs, her scent ended at the roadside near the park. The police were acting on the theory she'd gotten into someone's car. The search went national, even spreading into the States. Gracie MacKenzie was never found.

Allison printed out the articles and made plans with Claire to get together for lunch soon. She left the library and drove straight to the lab. She booted up her computer and started the video from Porcupine Hill. The appearance of the doll's face made her heart jump, but it wasn't as frightening as the night before. She paused the video on the doll and compared it to the photo in the newspaper. The paper's image was much smaller, but she was pretty sure it was the same doll.

Okay, now what? Her first instinct was to pick up the phone, call the police and tell them about the video. They could see for themselves. But was it Gracie MacKenzie's doll, or was Allison just assuming it was, because of a feeling? The police weren't too big on feelings. They were more into really solid evidence. But evidence of what? That a 14-year-old girl had been hiding out in the woods for three years? Yeah, right. But the doll didn't jump into the camera frame by itself. There was somebody out there. She had a new thought that made her shudder. If it was Gracie's doll, then what if whoever held the doll up to the lens was the person who kidnapped her?

But what the hell would they be doing out in the middle of nowhere, advertising themselves by messing with a wildlife camera? Nothing was making much sense. She grabbed her field bag and headed for Porcupine Hill.

Allison parked the Ministry pickup at the same turnout. The day had clouded over. The forest felt lonely and gloomy now. She suddenly had a pang of nerves. She unlocked the utility box in the back of the truck and grabbed the rifle that was kept on hand in case of an encounter with a threatening coyote or bear. Allison wasn't big on guns, but there was something about this whole thing that made her glad to have it. She headed into the woods with a queasy sense of foreboding.

By the time she got to the small clearing where the camera was set up, the temperature had dropped substantially, and she wished she'd worn a heavier jacket. She leaned the rifle against a tree, turned the camera off and replaced the SD card with a new one. Something landed in her hair. It was a piece of bark. She stepped back and looked up into the tree overhead. A porcupine was perched on a branch about ten feet up, looking down at her. Allison smiled.

"Hey, pal. Don't worry, not here to bother you."

She liked these spiky, often misunderstood rodents. She'd once helped nurse an injured baby porcupine into adulthood so it could be released into the wild. Most people didn't know they could be docile, friendly creatures.

Then she noticed another one, in another tree a few yards away. Then another. And another. She scanned the woods. There were about a dozen porcupines sitting in trees all around her. She'd never seen anything like it. It was completely bizarre.

"Okay. What's going on, you guys?"

She took her cell phone out of her pocket and started shooting a video. She couldn't wait to show this to Sammy.

As she was panning with her phone, she heard Linny's voice waft out of the woods behind her.

"You need to help her, Mommy."

Allison dropped her phone and spun around. Her heart stopped.

Standing amongst the brambles in the middle of the nearby marsh was Gracie MacKenzie.

She was pale and wispy. Her long hair hung flat against her head, as lifeless and colorless as her skin. She had on the same dress that was in the picture of her in the newspaper. But she wasn't smiling. There was a look of profound sadness on her ashen face. And she didn't have her doll. Her bare arms hung down, limp and deathly white. The fingertips of her right hand were bloodied.

Allison just stared, in shock, unable to comprehend what she was looking at. She was dizzy. Her focus faltered. The image of Gracie blurred. She closed her eyes. Her legs were giving out. She heard rustling sounds behind her. She opened her eyes and spun around awkwardly, almost falling. The porcupines were climbing down out of the trees and scrambling off into the woods. She looked back toward the marsh. The apparition was gone.

"Gracie?"

She scanned the woods. It was all peaceful and normal now. But she was cold and numb. She tried to suck in some air. She took a few shaky steps to the camera and grabbed the ironwood tree to steady herself. She was trembling. With a shaky hand, she turned the camera on, grabbed the rifle and, in a semi-conscious daze, made her way back to the pickup.

She set the rifle against the side of the truck, unlocked the door, and swung it open. She screamed and fell back, almost going down.

Sitting upright on the seat was Gracie's doll.

She grabbed the rifle and pointed it in all directions. She yelled at the woods.

"Who's there? Come on, Goddamnit, show yourself!"

She had no idea who she was talking to, but someone had put that doll on the seat of her truck. It was locked, though. The damn truck was locked. How the hell could someone put it there if it was locked? Nobody else had keys. No, Sammy had keys. But he was in Ottawa. Or was he? Was there some strange, seemingly impossible scenario where Sammy was responsible for all of this? Her thinking was all over the map. She realized the theory was ridiculous. No one can conjure up hallucinations for someone else. But still...

She grabbed her phone, walked about twenty feet away from the tuck, and dialed Sammy's number.

"Allison. What's up?"

"Where are you, Sammy."

"Uh, Ottawa."

"Prove it."

"Excuse me?"

"I'm not fucking around, Sammy. Prove to me you're in Ottawa."

"Jesus, Allison. What's going on?"

"Just do it, okay?"

"Okay. Umm. Okay. I'm taking a picture of myself in front of the ministry. Okay? I'll text it to you right now."

"Okay. Right now."

Allison hung up. And instantly knew she was insane to even think that Sammy was somehow involved. And, indeed, the text came through and there he was, outside the Ministry.

She immediately texted him back apologizing and saying she'd explain when he got back.

Allison walked back to the truck and looked into the cab, half expecting the doll to have disappeared. It was still there. She suddenly felt like that beetle on its back again, weak and helpless and completely out of control of her own life. It was as if some unknown force had taken hold of her and was thrashing her around inside a bizarre dream.

Then she remembered Linny's voice. It was Linny who had alerted her to Gracie MacKenzie's presence in the woods. "You have to help her, mommy."

"Linny. God, almighty." She looked toward Porcupine Hill. "Are you out there too, honey?" She could feel the fear melting away and her strength returning.

She put the rifle into the utility box in the back and climbed into the cab. She picked up the doll and studied it. It was a mess, just like she'd seen in the video. Twigs and leaves tangled in its hair, its face and clothing dirty and torn in parts. She sat for a long time just staring at it, trying to make sense of it. She'd seen Gracie. Or had she? She'd heard Linny's voice. Or had she?

Up until a little while ago, she was feeling like she'd regained a sense of herself as if the suffocating veil of grief had lifted and she was living in the world with others again. But now she was questioning all of it. She didn't trust her own ability to distinguish between fantasy and reality. But the doll was real. She was holding it in her hands. What about the porcupines? Were they really there.

She put the doll down, pulled out her cell phone, and played back the video she shot. Yes. Thank God. The porcupines were there. Over a dozen of them in the trees. They were real. The video went shaky as she'd lowered the camera, but there was a flash of what looked like the partial image of a human form. She played it back several times. It was fast, but it looked like a shoulder and arm. She'd have to take it back to the lab and upload it into her computer so she could play it in slow motion. All she wanted was something to hold onto that proved she wasn't going crazy. Then she realized what the implications of that actually were. Suppose her camera did record the apparition that presented itself as Gracie McKenzie? She knew, down deep, that it wasn't the living Gracie. It couldn't have been. Not what she saw. Not where she saw it. So how was she supposed to deal with the idea that she'd seen—it was difficult to even form the word in her mind—a ghost?

Allison didn't head back to the lab right away. Instead, she drove into Sedgeham and pulled into the parking lot of the park where Gracie was last seen. The park was on the shore of Sedgeham Lake and included a beach which, in summer months, was a very popular hangout for the locals. A chill wind was blowing off the water as Allison got out of the truck. She glanced over at the playground area. Memories of Linny running for her beloved swings flooded back at her, and her throat tightened. She spotted the makeshift memorial under a nearby tree and managed to shift her focus back to Gracie MacKenzie.

With the doll in hand, she studied the dilapidated and weather-worn tribute. Several bouquets of flowers had been added fairly recently, but were now drooping and looking sad. There was a corkboard on an easel that was covered with pieces of paper with messages and a number of faded photographs. It was draped with clear plastic to protect it from the weather. In almost all of the photos, Gracie was holding her doll. The only one where she didn't have it was a shot of her on the swings, laughing joyously. Just like Linny. Allison wished the two of them had known each other. She compared the doll in the photos to the one she was holding. She was sure it was the same doll. As she stared at the photos, Allison had an unsettling feeling that Gracie was looking, not at the camera, but rather right at her.

"What is it, little girl? What do you want me to do?"

She went over to a nearby picnic table and sat on the bench. It was time to talk to someone to report it. There was no doubt in her mind that Porcupine Hill had something to do with Gracie's disappearance. But could she just walk into a police station and tell them everything that had happened to her, all that she'd witnessed, and expect them to take her seriously? She was having a hard time trusting her own sanity, and wouldn't blame anyone else for thinking she was a nutcase. But she had the video and the doll. Tangible evidence. She got back in the truck and turned up the street toward city hall.

The police station was a small nondescript building next to the city administrative offices. A single police cruiser was parked in front. Allison grabbed the doll and walked through the front door to a desk where the receptionist, a middle-aged woman, sat filing her nails. She looked up and smiled, glad to have a chance to talk to someone.

"Hey there. Can I help you?

"Yeah. I need to talk to someone about Gracie McKenzie."

The woman at the desk wasn't smiling anymore.

"Gracie? What do you want to know?"

"No. I mean, I found this doll."

The woman stared silently for a minute.

"Oh. Okay. You think it's Gracie's."

"Um, I don't know for sure. But maybe."

At that moment the local constable, Raymond Morris, came out of a restroom and walked past them. The first thing anyone noticed about Constable Morris, besides a relaxed, pleasant demeanor, was that he had three distinct vertical scars running down his left cheek. He was focused on a newspaper in his hand.

The receptionist tried to get his attention.

"Excuse me, Raymond?"

He didn't look up from the newspaper.

"Guy out at Higgins Lake has a 3-stroke Honda 20 outboard for sale. I gotta make a quick call, and I'll be right back." He disappeared through another door, closing it behind him.

The receptionist noticed Allison staring after him.

"Bear."

"What?"

"His face. He surprised a young bear in a trash bin a couple of years ago."

"Oh. I wasn't..."

"It's okay. You want some coffee?"

"No thanks."

The receptionist seemed to almost enjoy telling the tale of the bear.

"Got him pretty good. He made it back here on his own. His shirt was torn up, and my goodness the blood. I drove him to the ER."

"Sounds awful. What happened to the bear?"

"Oh, nothing. He let it go. He said it wasn't the bear's fault. It was just scared."

"Wow, that's cool."

"Raymond doesn't even hunt. He loves animals."

Constable Morris re-emerged from his office. He smiled cordially at Allison and held out his hand.

"Hello, there. Ray Morris. How can I help you?"

They shook hands.

"Hi. I'm Allison Cote. I work for the M.N.R., Fish, and Wildlife. We're doing a study of the local fisher population. I was out at a location where we've got a motion-activated camera set up, and I found this doll. I've seen the memorial in the park, and I thought maybe it might have been Gracie McKenzie's."

The constable took the doll from her and studied it.

"Well, it looks like the same kind of doll, eh? Lois, you wanna pull the MacKenzie file?"

The receptionist swung her chair around and opened a file cabinet.

"As I remember, it was a popular doll back then," said the Constable. "Could have belonged to anyone."

"Yeah, sure. But I've also got some video that, well, maybe you should see it."

"Video? Of what?"

"It's from our camera out at that location, and it was recorded at night. But, someone held this doll up to the camera."

"Hang on. Someone held this doll up to your motion-activated camera at night out in the middle of nowhere."

"Yeah. I know. It sounds pretty crazy."

"Where have you got this video?"

"At the OPWS lab where I work. Over at the station on Tyler Lane."

"Sure, I know the place."

The receptionist handed a file to the Constable. She'd opened it to a photo of Gracie holding her doll.

"Thanks, Doris. Hm. Yeah, sure looks like it could have been Gracie's. Okay, how about if we go have a look at that video."

"Sure."

"We'll hang on to this doll. I'll have to send it to Ottawa and have it run for DNA, just in case."

"Oh, right." Allison realized that she didn't really want to give up the doll, which was curious, but she was relieved that the Constable was treating it seriously.

Constable Morris followed Allison in his cruiser. When they reached the lab, she booted up the video. He had her play it back several times.

"I've got to say, that's pretty strange, eh?"

"Yeah."

"And you found the doll out there?"

"Not exactly. When I got back to my pickup, someone had put it on the seat in the cab."

"Sounds to me like someone out there's messing with you. You made any enemies lately?"

"I thought about that, but no. I can't even imagine."

The Constable rubbed his scarred face.

"Tell you what. How about if I meet you out there tomorrow and we'll have a look around. Porcupine Hill, you say. That's out near Colby Lake, isn't it?"

Allison gave the Constable directions, and they agreed to meet there at two o'clock the next afternoon. She was relieved that finally someone else had at least partial knowledge of what was going on. It had all gotten so strangely twisted in her head that it was heartening to have an ally.

The events of the last two days suddenly caught up with her. She was beat. She went home, made herself a grilled cheese sandwich and tomato soup. Linny's favorite. She felt close to Linny tonight, not in a grieving way, but almost as if she was there with her.

When she finished eating, she went to Linny's room and pulled her copy of The Princess Bride off the shelf. It was her favorite book. They'd read it together at least twenty times. She took it to bed. She didn't even make it to page three.

She woke the next morning, made herself some coffee and toast, and set about cleaning the house. She'd planned to get some yard work in as well, but the weather had other ideas. The clouds had grown even thicker than the day before, and there was a light drizzle falling.

When she got to Linny's room, she realized she'd turned it into a kind of shrine, with Linny's stuffed animals and favorite knickknacks and books all arranged carefully. She remembered how she'd taught Linny that it was good to pass books, toys, and clothing on to others once you had outgrown them. Linny readily embraced the concept and loved taking her old stuff to one of the local charity thrift stores. She'd write little tags which said "I'm glad that you have this now," and attach them to toys. Allison packed up almost everything, except for Linny's artwork and a few other treasures, and put it all in the trunk of her car to be dropped off on Monday.

At about 1:15 she drove to the lab, got the Ministry pickup, and headed for Porcupine Hill to meet the Constable. She parked the truck in the turnout and started off through the woods to the camera site. Constable Morris hadn't arrived yet. The rain had stopped, but the sky was a deep threatening gray. As Allison stepped through the trees, she became aware that an unsettling silence had descended on the forest. Usually, before an impending storm, the birds and insects were more active. There'd be a cacophony of sounds filling the woods. But it was almost as if she'd gone deaf. There was no breeze at all. The air was heavy and dead.

Then she saw the porcupines. They were back in the trees just like the day before. There were, even more, this time, maybe twenty of them. They were just sitting there, perched on limbs, perfectly still. The last time Allison she saw them was when Gracie appeared in the marsh. She looked toward the brambly, swampy area but saw nothing. She couldn't help feeling that the porcupines' presence was more than some sort of natural phenomenon. Something just wasn't right. She was hoping the Constable would show up soon.

She knelt down to extract the SD card from the camera. Something sharp dug into her knee.

"Ouch. Dammit."

She shifted position and looked at her knee. Whatever it was she'd knelt on had drawn a little blood. She scratched in the dirt and saw the edge of something shiny and metallic poking up through the weeds. She dug further and uncovered a six pointed badge. She scraped the dirt off. CITY OF SEDGEHAM POLICE.

She heard the crunching of footsteps on the forest floor, getting louder and louder. She continued to stare at the badge, dazed. She didn't even look up as he approached. The footsteps stopped right next to her.

She knew. She saw it all. The truth was pressing on her temples, squeezing the blood out of her head. In her mind's eye, she saw the story in the paper of Gracie's disappearance. And from the same day another story. "Police Officer Mauled By Bear."

"I'll be damned. I looked all over for that badge."

She finally lifted her head and looked up at Constable Morris. He was holding Gracie's doll by the arm. It dangled sadly next to his leg. She stared at his calm, passive face. She thought evil should look different.

"She was just a helpless little girl."

"Not so helpless, really. She was a lot stronger than I expected. Raked those nails of hers across my face like a wildcat. I guess crazy people are like that, though."

"She wasn't the one who was crazy."

"I'll take that badge."

He started to move toward Allison. A bizarre ratcheting noise broke the ominous silence. It was coming from above, from the trees. The Constable stopped and looked up. The porcupines had all started a tooth chattering that was a warning to predators to stay away or else. It was a disturbing clatter, quickly growing in volume.

"What the hell?" Morris was momentarily distracted.

Allison leapt up and ran. She only got about three steps before he pounced on her, throwing her to the ground. He was big and fast. He pinned her hand under her and had a knee on her back. The air had been knocked out of her, and she couldn't move. As she gasped for breath the Constable reached under her and started to unbuckle her belt and pull at her pants.

"How about if we have some fun, huh? You're older than I usually like but waste not want not, eh? "

Allison struggled, but it was no use. Her face was pressed into the ground. As he started to wrench her pants down, she felt his body start to tremble. The cop was then suddenly and violently yanked off her by some unseen force. In the process, his knee hit her hard in the side, knocking the wind out of her. Gasping to catch her breath, she lifted her head enough to see him now lying on his back with his arms stretched back over his head. He struggled and screamed as something invisible dragged him across the ground. His shirt caught on some rocks and was almost completely ripped off of him. He was deposited in the shallow depression underneath the giant tree.

Allison pulled herself up onto an elbow. She watched in stunned wonder as several roots crawled up out of the earth and wound themselves around the Constable's arms and legs, pinning him to the ground. The pale specter that was Gracie MacKenzie manifested beside the oak and stared down at him, expressionless. When he saw the frightening apparition looming over him, he stopped struggling. He gasped, terrified.

"You're dead! You're dead! I buried you! Someone help me!"

Allison saw a blur of movement all around. The porcupines were scrambling down from the trees. When they reached the ground, they scurried toward the base of the oak.

The Constable saw them advancing on him.

"Oh God, no! No!"

He squirmed grotesquely, fighting to free himself.

The porcupines crawled onto his half-bare body. His screams were muffled by their combined mass.

As Allison watched, powerless to do anything about the horrific scene playing out a few feet away, she felt a comforting warmth envelope her. The sounds of horror faded into the distance. She had a soothing sensation that two tiny soft hands were gently lowering her head to the ground. She slipped off into unconsciousness.

When she woke, she was on her back. She lay still, blinking, trying to focus and reorient herself. She was staring up at the tree canopy. She heard the familiar chirping of birds and buzzing of insects. She felt something soft against her body. She lifted her head. Gracie's doll was tucked under her upper arm. It all came back to her, and she bolted upright. Her head throbbed with the movement.

She looked across at the old oak. The Constable's body was lying there, dead still. The roots that had entwined his arms and legs were gone. All that was recognizable as human was his lower half. The rest of him was a mass of thousands of porcupine quills.

The sky had cleared partially. A gentle breeze was blowing. Allison took the doll in her hands and looked at its poor weathered face. She pulled a burr out of its hair. She got to her feet and walked slowly over to the body under the oak. Flies were already buzzing around it. She took out her cell phone and called the Ontario Provincial Police.

When the police and paramedics arrived at Porcupine Hill, Allison told them everything. She left nothing out. They listened, incredulous, as she told them about Gracie's ghost, the way the Constable was yanked off her and dragged, the roots that bound his arms and hands to the ground, the porcupines. They started to question her about her state of mind, of course, asking if she'd been drinking or was on any medication. They were suggesting that she be taken to the hospital for "observation." She didn't argue. She simply walked over to the wildlife camera, extracted the SD card, and handed it to them.

Infrared works during daylight hours as well.

GRACIE MACKENZIE'S body was found buried under the shallow depression between the oak roots, beneath the very spot where her murderer had died.

The medical examiner determined that Constable Morris had succumbed to asphyxiation due to swelling of the mouth and pharynx as induced by the massive numbers of porcupine quills.

The police had no interest in releasing certain other details of his death to the public, however, which was why Allison had been called to a meeting with two high-ranking OPP officers as well as the Medical Examiner and a Superior Court Judge. It was explained to her that the investigation into Gracie MacKenzie's death had been re-opened and that Allison would need to be deposed to offer evidence in the case against Constable Raymond Morris. Information would eventually have to be released publicly. But, in order to protect the integrity of the law enforcement agencies, there were some peculiar aspects of the case that they would prefer be kept under seal. She assured them that she understood and they thanked her for her cooperation.

After leaving the meeting, Allison drove into Sedgeham to meet Claire for lunch. As she was passing the park, she glanced over at Gracie's memorial. She slammed on her brakes. There were two girls swinging on the swings, side by side. Linny and Gracie. They were laughing and smiling. They looked across the park at Allison and waved.

Allison's cell phone rang, startling her. She glanced down. It was Craig.

When she looked back at the park, the girls were gone. But the swings were still swinging. Back and forth, back and forth.

The Disappearance of Mrs. Kardos

Secrets have an unsettling life of their own. They lurk in dark corners of your mind, always watching, ever ready to jump out and remind you of the frightening power they have over you. It's as if once you make the pledge to yourself, or in a pact with others, to classify something a secret, it becomes an ominous protector of itself. Betray it, and it will leap out at you from the shadows and wreak havoc on your very soul.

But I think maybe there's some natural, or perhaps unnatural, human urge to defy the pledge and take back the power, regardless of the consequences. Maybe that's why I feel compelled to tell this story now, after all these years. Just to feel that little surge of ego you always feel when you're the one who comes up with the answer to a difficult question or you cleverly reveal something no one else knows.

I'm the only one alive now who might in any way be affected by the telling of the story, so I don't feel responsible for protecting anyone else. The two others who were closely connected to the event in question, my brother and our friend Leonard, are both dead now, so the only risk is that I will be judged, something that doesn't concern me anymore. My brother died many years ago, and an old friend emailed me recently to say that he'd read that Leonard had been killed in a car accident. I hadn't thought of Leonard or any of it for a long time. Even the dreams, which haunted my sleep for so many years, became a rarity. But when I heard of Leonard's death, I was compelled to search out the news myself. It didn't take long to find the story online. His car had plummeted over an embankment at high speed and struck a tree. It went on to say that he was pretty much all alone in the world, no family except for some distant relatives in West Virginia.

Oh, I will be judged, certainly. Because I don't expect anyone to believe any of it. I wouldn't. Except I was there. In fact, I was the one responsible for the event that became Mt. Pope's great unsolved mystery. I have no doubt that readers and even my closest friends will start thinking me either a flat out liar or someone in need of psychiatric help. Or perhaps they will be generous and regard this tale as a work of fiction. So be it. But I assure you, friends and others, as crazy as it may sound, this is what really happened that day.

It's been 35 years since Mrs. Kardos disappeared. Her house on Alwyn Avenue still sits there, the new occupants probably never having heard of Mrs. Kardos or the day when she vanished. In fact, the neat little white house with the tidy rose beds and cozy front porch looks pretty much the same. The only noticeable difference now is that the draperies in the large front window facing the street are open, revealing a bright and cheery living room. They were never open when Mrs. Kardos lived there. Never.

The neighborhood, like all the older neighborhoods in Mt. Pope, has been carefully preserved. It's just one of the small wine country towns that's become home to the affluent since the late 70's when the fruit of California's vines attained elite status and transformed the verdant valleys into destinations more popular than Disneyland.

My brother and I lived four houses up the street from Mrs. Kardos. We got to know her grandson, Leonard. Leonard lived in St. John, about twenty miles south, but stayed with his grandmother on most weekends. Leonard didn't talk much about his grandmother. His grandfather spent most of his time at their ranch, a few miles out of town. He was almost never around the house on Alwyn Avenue, and my brother and I wondered why that was, but it didn't seem to bother Leonard. I was 13, my brother and Leonard were both 15. We'd become good friends and spent many a weekend exploring the surrounding hills and creeks, riding our bikes anywhere and everywhere the terrain allowed. Sometimes we would get a ride from our parents out to the Kardos's ranch, where we could hunt birds and rabbits with our 22s.

The whole thing occurred on an early fall day. I remember because there were leaves all over the ground and the sulfurous fumes of recently crushed grapes wafted through the town from the fermenting rooms of nearby wineries. It was around noon, bright and sunny. My brother and Leonard and I were riding our bikes over the piles of rubble at the old gravel pit down by Hot Springs Creek. Our dog, Sammy, was bounding alongside us as if the whole thing were a game invented just for his enjoyment. He was a large miniature poodle and went everywhere with my brother and me. Just to be clear, miniature poodles aren't the little tiny ones. They're medium-sized dogs, about the size of a spaniel.

It was lunchtime, and our appetites interrupted our adventure. Leonard announced that his grandmother had made sandwiches for us so we could eat at his house. This was a surprise. Every once in a while, Mrs. Kardos had made cookies for us but never lunch. Truth be told, her cookies were virtually inedible, but we choked them down anyway to be polite. We almost always ate at our house. As a cook and baker, my mother was a magician, and Leonard loved to come up and indulge in whatever special treat she would conjure up for us. So my brother and I were not too optimistic about lunch that day. But Leonard seemed kind of proud to be able to invite us to his grandmother's house for a change, so there was really no way to get out of it.

We rode our bikes back across the creek, up Harlin Street and finally up Alwyn. Sammy bounded on ahead, leading the way. He was constantly looking back at us as he ran to make sure we were still with him. But we could never trust that, in his dog-brained excitement, he would avoid oncoming cars. So, whenever we saw a car coming, we'd stop and call him to us and make him sit until the car passed. He was smart and well trained and would always mind.

We turned into Mrs. Kardos's gravel driveway at high speed and skidded to a stop in the back yard. The rule was we had to use the back door. There were rules at Mrs. Kardos's house. Leonard was always very careful to remind us of the do's and don'ts before we went inside. He never seemed to be bothered by them, or find it peculiar that his grandmother was so strict about people being in her house. But there were a number of things about the place that my brother and I thought were pretty weird and creepy. Maybe the strangest one was that in all the years we'd lived there, we never saw a single soul go in or out of Mrs. Kardos's front door.

We left Sammy sitting by our bikes. As long as he knew where we were, he would mind and stay put.

The back door opened into a kind of mud room where we were required to leave any stuff we were carrying: baseball gloves, fishing poles, raincoats, whatever. Leonard, who always wore a baseball cap, would stash it in a utility closet. Hats weren't allowed on the coat rack. The mud room had several windows, but they were covered with heavy curtains, so it was pretty dark. There was also a refrigerator, which would have been no big deal, except that this one has a clasp and padlock on it. We asked Leonard about it once, and he said he wasn't sure, but thought it had his grandfather's winemaking supplies in it.

There was a door from the mud room that opened into the kitchen. This is where the real creepy began. Inside Mrs. Kardos's house, heavy curtains and drapes hung over every single window, blocking out all direct daylight. They weren't blackout curtains, so some small amount of diffuse light managed to creep through the heavy dark red fabric. The light that did penetrate turned the pale green walls an unpleasant gray. There were always a few lamps on, but they must have been very low wattage bulbs because they hardly had any effect on the gloom that pervaded the house. Even Leonard's room, where we'd usually hang out and play board games, was subject to the absence of light. Leonard explained, casually and without question that his grandmother had a rule that none of the curtains were ever to be opened. He didn't know why.

Then there was the smell. The predominant odor was some sort of rose potpourri. I knew that smell from the apartment of our Auntie Maude, an ancient relative in San Francisco whom we'd visit every now and then. But there was another smell in Mrs. Kardos's house. It reminded me of the odor of Hot Springs Creek in late summer when it had all but dried up, and the few remaining pools were clogged with rotting algae. Of course, we never said anything about the smell to Leonard. He always seemed to take the strangeness of his grandmother's house in stride, as if there was really nothing out of the ordinary about it at all.

Past the kitchen was a short hallway that went toward the front of the house and the living room. There were two bedrooms off the hallway and a small bathroom between them. One bedroom was Leonard's. The other, closer to the front, was Mrs. Kardos's room. We had only been into the living room once. About a year previously, we were given permission to watch a World Series baseball game on Mrs. Kardos's old television.

The furniture in the living room was all antiques, brocade upholstery on the couch and easy chairs. There was a fireplace that looked like it had never been used. Over it hung a painting of what looked like night in some tiny ancient village in a foreign land, dark mountains looming in the background. Leonard said he thought it was somewhere in Hungary.

As soon as we walked into the kitchen, the same thing always happened. Leonard would tell us to wait there, and he would go down the dark hallway and knock on his grandmother's bedroom door. We would hear a short bit of very quiet conversation, and then Leonard would return, followed by his grandmother.

Mrs. Kardos was short and obviously pretty old, but she didn't move like the other old people I'd come to know back then. She moved slowly, but with a certain strength that didn't seem right for her size and age. Her gray hair was always in a bun in the back, and she always wore a high-collared long-sleeved dress that stopped at her mid-calf. Below the dress were black stockings and what I would have called old fashioned lace-up shoes. In my youth, the faces of old people always looked the same to me. This applied to Mrs. Kardos. If you had asked me back then to describe her face, I would have said she looked like an old woman. Except for her skin. It wasn't exactly pale or gray but more like the color of dirt. Her face absorbed the dull maroon filtered light through the curtains the same way as the pale green paint. It seemed as though, like a chameleon, when she stood against a wall, her face would almost disappear, and all you could see was her clothing.

When she followed Leonard into the kitchen, she greeted us, as she did every time, by simply saying, "Hello, boys." "Hi, Mrs. Kardos" and "Thank you, Mrs. Kardos" for the cookies or, in this case, sandwiches, was all we ever said to her. She never really looked at us either, which seemed strange. But what was even stranger was that I don't think Leonard ever really looked at her. We'd been there enough times that I think my brother and I adopted Leonard's habit of avoiding making eye contact with Mrs. Kardos.

I remember even the smallest details of that fall day really well. You'll soon understand why. I remember how Mrs. Kardos took the plate of sandwiches out of the fridge - the kitchen fridge, not the padlocked one - and placed them on the table. Then she poured us each a big glass of lemonade. I was so thirsty. I drank it down fast. She left the pitcher on the table, and I poured myself another glass. She turned to go back to her room, but suddenly she paused for just a moment, turned slightly and looked right at me. That moment was the first time I actually saw her eyes. I got a kind of chill because the iris was maroon. and so small that all you could really see was the white around it. I looked away fast. My heart was suddenly racing. By the time I looked back, she was gone. Neither my brother nor Leonard noticed. I had no idea what had just happened. It really shook me up.

Leonard suggested that we take the sandwiches into his room and play Battleship, our favorite board game back then. All the time we were playing, I couldn't get that moment when Mrs. Kardos looked at me out of my mind. I kept wondering why she would do that, just stare at me like that with those weird eyes. Should I not have poured myself more lemonade? But she'd left the pitcher, so that didn't make any sense. I couldn't figure out any reason that she would look at me on purpose. Me and nobody else. I was just sitting there. But I had an awful feeling that something wasn't right. I couldn't concentrate on Battleship, and I remember I played really badly. My brother asked me at one point what was wrong. Of course, I lied and said, "Nothing."

All I wanted was to get out of that house. But I couldn't just say so. While we played, I tried to think of some excuse to leave. Then I remembered that our neighbor up the street had told us he saw a steelhead in one of the pools on Hot Springs Creek up near the cemetery, probably spawning. I reminded my brother and Leonard about it, and we decided when we finished this round of the game we would ride our bikes down there and see if we could find it.

I was feeling slightly more relaxed knowing we'd be leaving soon. I tried to concentrate hard on the game, so it would end as fast as possible. When we were done, we put it back in the box and headed out of Leonard's room. Two glasses of lemonade had caught up to me, and I badly needed to go to the bathroom. When I told Leonard, he hesitated for a moment but then just said hurry up and reminded me to be careful to close the kitchen and back door securely on my way out. He and my brother headed for the back yard to get their bikes. While I was peeing, I heard Sammy barking excitedly as they peddled down the driveway toward the street. I finished. I washed my hands. I was careful to arrange the towel neatly on the rack. That was another one of the rules at Mrs. Kardos's house. I grabbed the doorknob and opened the bathroom door.

Please understand that everything I am about to describe happened in a matter of seconds.

As I stepped out of the bathroom into the shadowy hallway, I suddenly heard the screech of brakes on the street. I heard my brother yell, "Sammy!" Without even thinking, I rushed into the living room, to the front window. More shouts came from the street. I grabbed onto the heavy fabric and pulled hard, yanking it open to see what had happened. There was an awful, chilling cry behind me.

As I was in the motion of pulling on the drapes, I spun around to see Mrs. Kardos standing there, a look of excruciating terror on her face. The combination of twisting my body so fast and the frightening sight of Mrs. Kardos caused me to lose my balance. I fell to the floor, pulling the drapes open even wider. The afternoon sun blazed through the window onto Leonard's grandmother. Her whole body instantly erupted in searing blue flames. They were not like normal flames from burning wood or a campfire. They were more like the flame produced by my father's welding torch, intense and forceful, with a low hissing noise.

All visceral connections to the rest of the world disappeared. I was stupefied, frozen, captured in time by a sight too unbelievable to process or comprehend on any level. It was as if my mind had simply shut off, and the only sense that was still functional was my sight. I stared. The flames that engulfed Mrs. Kardos intensified in seconds to the point that they lost form. They became simply an intense glowing mass of searing light. Mrs. Kardos had completely disappeared inside the fireball. There was a sudden powerful flash, so bright that my arms shot up to cover my eyes. Then silence.

I lowered my arm and looked. The strange fire was gone. So was Mrs. Kardos. A slight bit of smoke hung in the air but it, too, disappeared in seconds. I sat there slumped against the window sill, my heart pounding as though it would crash through my chest at any moment. I was breathing so hard and fast that my throat was making a dry rasping sound. A shout from outside spurred my mind back to a dazed awareness of where and who I was. I turned my head to look out the window. I saw a car stopped in the street. There were several people gathered. I saw my brother scoop Sammy up off the pavement and run down the sidewalk toward our house. Leonard was following him. Any other time, of course, I would have instantly bolted for the door and followed them. But the images

I was seeing were happening as if in a dream, or in some world I didn't seem, at the moment, to be a part of.

I turned my head back and stared at the spot where Mrs. Kardos has been engulfed by fire. Logic started to creep back into my thought process. It didn't make sense that a fire such as I had witnessed hadn't set the entire house aflame. I pulled myself up and took a few steps to the spot where she was standing. I looked down at the rug and saw a thin pile of ash about the size of a dart board. It was then that it hit me. I just killed Mrs. Kardos. I didn't mean to, but she was gone, burned up, and it was my fault.

Panic took over. The implications of what just happened were unthinkable. My 13-year-old mind could only imagine a nightmare of consequences in store for me. I spun around and threw the heavy drapes closed. I raced to the back of the house, to the utility closet on the back porch. I grabbed the vacuum cleaner and rushed back to the living room. I plugged it in and vacuumed up Mrs. Kardos. I stopped for just a second to gaze at the spot I had just cleaned. The fine white ash was gone, the rug was perfectly intact, there was no burn spot, nothing. I quickly returned the vacuum cleaner to the closet. I ran back to the living room once more, just to make sure I hadn't dropped anything or left any sign that I had been there. Everything looked normal. Absurdly normal. I sprinted for the back door.

I paused for a moment as I got to the kitchen. I realized that something was different. It was the smell. The strange rotting algae smell was gone. I moved on quickly and, as I got outside and closed the back door, I called back into the house, "Thank you, Mrs. Kardos." I figured that if any of the neighbors happened to see me leave this would convince them that Mrs. Kardos was fine at the time I left.

I grabbed my bike peddled hard down the driveway. The car I'd seen stopped in the street was gone. But a couple of the other neighbors, Mr. Hunt and Mrs. Lapier were still there. I decided to pretend that I hadn't heard anything. I hit the brakes and asked what was going on. Mr. Hunt told me that Sammy had been hit. It didn't look good. Just then I saw my mother's car pull out of our driveway and start down the street. I left my bike on the curb and ran out into the street. I jumped into the back seat where my brother was cradling Sammy. My mother was driving. Leonard was next to her in the front.

It became quickly clear that nobody was in the least concerned about where I had been and what I had been doing. All focus was on Sammy, our beloved pooch. He was shaking and whining in my brother's arms. We petted him and talked to him in the fifteen or so minutes it took to get him to the vet.

This is where my memory goes a bit limp. Those next couple of hours and the next several days, for that matter, are all a blur. It turned out that Sammy was okay, except for a dislocated hip. The vet gave him an anesthetic and reset the bone. We could return the next day and take him home. The vet's office was on Hitchens Lane, about a mile from Leonard's grandfather's ranch. Leonard asked us to drop him off there, which was a huge relief. I was terrified that if he went right back to his grandmother's house, he would, of course, find that she was not there and...I didn't know what would happen, really, but it frightened me.

The fear of being found out haunted me as much as the recurring visions of those horrible moments in Mrs. Kardos's living room. I was trying to act as normal as possible, but it was pretty obvious that I was shaken up about something. Everybody just attributed it to the situation with Sammy. I loved animals of all kinds, probably more than most kids. So when I woke up in the middle of the night with a scream and in a cold sweat, my mother soothed me and assured me that Sammy was going to be fine. There was nothing to worry about. God, how I wished there was nothing to worry about.

Four days after Mrs. Kardos...after, it happened...an officer from the Mt. Pope police department came to the door. I saw him pull up from my bedroom window. I stopped breathing. Did they know? I immediately started thinking furiously about what to say. Should I deny it? What could I say? I had the bizarre thought of what it must feel like for a prisoner, to be walking down a hallway on his way to the gas chamber.

Hiding behind the shades on the bedroom window, I watched, nauseous, as the policeman walked to the front door. My brother, an avid reader, was in one of his books and not paying any attention. I didn't want to tip him to my panic, so as casually as possible I went out into the hallway and stopped, out of sight of the front door, and listened as my mother answered the doorbell.

The officer explained that Mrs. Kardos, our neighbor, had disappeared. They thought it was possible that my brother and I and Leonard were the last people to see her. Would it be possible to ask us a few questions? They just wanted to see if we had any information that might help.

He didn't say, "We've come to arrest your son." They just wanted our help.

My mother, being my mother, invited him into the kitchen, offered him a piece of strawberry-rhubarb pie, and seated him at the breakfast table. He enthusiastically accepted the pie and a cup of coffee. My mother immediately connected his name to a local family she knew, and small talk ensued for a good twenty minutes. My brother and I sat at the table and also had a piece of pie. I was so terrified I could hardly swallow. But I forced myself to eat it. I thought if I didn't, he might suspect something.

The officer waxed on about how good the pie was, then got down to business. He

related the story that Leonard had told him about Sammy getting hit and all of us rushing to the vet. He asked us if that was how we remembered it. We told him it was.

The policeman shifted in his chair and looked right at me. He said Leonard had told him that I was still in his grandmother's house when Sammy was hit. He understood I had to go to the bathroom. I said, yeah, that was right. He asked me if I saw Mrs. Kardos as I was leaving. This was the moment. I could feel it. Instantly I knew what I had to do. My only hope was to be perceived as doing the right thing, even if it was four days after it happened. I was a nice kid. They had to give me a break, didn't they? Before he even asked me anything else, I had to tell him what happened. Right now.

I said nope. I didn't see Mrs. Kardos.

He thanked us all for our time, told my mother again how great her pie was and left. It was as simple as that. I'd survived. As far as the rest of the world was concerned, I was just another kid who just happened to live on the same block as Mrs. Kardos and was a friend of her grandson.

Small towns always like to keep news of unusual or disturbing events as quiet as possible, fearing that mention of any such occurrence might unravel the very fabric of the community. That's the way it was in Mt. Pope. A single, brief article was published in the local paper a couple of months later. All it said was that an investigation of Mrs. Kardos's disappearance was ongoing and that Mr. Kardos was putting the Alwyn Avenue house up for sale.

As time went on, I pretty much lived my days like I always had. I hung out with my friends, explored the wilds of the valley with my brother, went to school, all of it. Mr. Kardos had sold the house fairly quickly and, after that, we didn't see much of Leonard anymore. But I avoided walking past Mrs. Kardos's house. And nighttimes were never the same. The dreams wouldn't leave me alone. It was always some variation of this same dream. I'd be standing on Mrs. Kardos's porch, looking into her living room. But instead of her on fire, it was me. I'd wake up with a start, frightened, gasping for breath. From his bed, on the other side of the dark room, my brother would ask if I was okay. I never told him what the dreams were, of course. But if he hadn't been in the room, I don't know if I would have ever slept again.

The guilt has shadowed me for all these years. And it's taken its toll. But there was one thing that I held onto, that always helped me keep going. It was the hope that in her last moment of life, Mrs. Kardos understood that it wasn't really my fault. That I just happened to be a kid in the wrong place at the wrong time. But I couldn't know that any more than I could find an acceptable explanation for what I saw happen to her. Mrs. Kardos didn't have long pointy teeth and people in Mt.

Pope weren't being found dead with holes in their necks. And yet.

So, in finally revealing the truth of what happened all those years ago, I've taken back the power. I've flushed the sinister secret out into the daylight. Will it simply change form now, turn into a different kind of monster, one that shows itself in the skeptical grins of strangers and maybe even friends? No matter. As haunting as my own secret has been for all these years, it pales in the fiery blue light of whatever the unacceptable secret was that Mrs. Kardos had carried with her until that perfect, terrible autumn day.

Also, I wanted to know what was in the locked refrigerator.

Site 19

Flat Rock campground sat on the banks of an enchanting mountain stream, flanked by lush virgin stands of white fir and sugar pine. It was one of the more remote campgrounds in the area, a good hour plus from the nearest town. Its name derived from the giant shelf-like stone that stood sentinel over the picturesque canyon below. Local lore claimed that Native Americans who first inhabited the region had called it Spirit Rock but, for whatever reason, the US Forest Service settled on the less romantic and decidedly unimaginative moniker of Flat Rock. Like most National Forest campgrounds, it was a minimalist experience. Circular concrete fire pits, picnic tables, and one centrally located outhouse structure were the only amenities offered to adventurous campers who craved a bit more rustic experience.

On the face of it, Flat Rock was simply an unassuming but perfect jumping-off point from which one could launch hunting or fishing expeditions, or simply explore the wonders of the mountains. There was, however, one somewhat curious aspect of the campground, which was the strange and seemingly illogical abandonment of campsite number 19. It had been many years since anyone had pitched a tent or built a campfire at this particular site. Permits were no longer issued for its use and, if asked, Forest Rangers who were charged with issuing said permits couldn't, or wouldn't, tell you why. A weathered 4x4 post with the number 19 carved onto it still remained, but the fire pit and picnic table had long since been removed. A small "No Camping" sign had been pounded onto the old post.

The appeal of Site 19 was obvious. The giant boulders that were stacked by cataclysmic subterranean forces of nature some millennia ago, and topped by the flat boulder that gave the campground its name, hovered directly above the site. The trail that led to the top of the rock, where a magnificent view of the surrounding wilderness could be relished, began only about 20 feet away and a magnificent, ancient live oak tree stood majestically dead center of the site. It must have caused many a camper to wonder why the most desirable location in the campground was off-limits. But whatever it was that relegated Site 19 to its status as a forbidden zone remained a mystery.

IT WAS EARLY NOVEMBER when the sound of a vehicle disrupted the natural calm of a late autumn evening at Flat Rock. The timing, in itself, was odd. It was almost guaranteed that the last camper would pull up stakes at any of the campgrounds in the region somewhere near the middle of October. Typically, this would be a deer hunter trying his luck at the end of the season when the absence of competitors might increase his odds of sighting-in a buck who'd managed to survive the early season onslaught. So, to an owl or a chipmunk, who called Flat Rock home, the sight and sound of an SUV pulling into the campground at this time of year might have seemed surprising, if not downright bizarre. And if the two baffled creatures had conversed about it, they might have speculated that perhaps the unusually late Indian summer had inspired some hard-core nature-lover to get one final bit of communing in. They would have been wrong.

The SUV moved slowly along the one-way dirt track that snaked its way through the deserted campground and finally stopped. The owl and chipmunk might have been even more baffled to observe that it stopped at site 19. The engine continued to run for a few minutes, the driver evidently contemplating his arrival in some private manner. He didn't get out of the vehicle for a while, even after he had turned off the engine. It was a good seven or eight minutes before the door opened, and he emerged. The car door closing sent a jarring, unnatural echo rippling through the peaceful canyon.

The driver was a pleasant-looking man of about 50, dressed in jeans and wearing a grey sweatshirt. He walked slowly into the lonely campsite. He stopped and looked up at the rocks above. His heart jumped. He took in a cold, strangled breath. Mason Osbourne had been here before. The memory of his first visit to site 19 pummeled him like a boulder loosed from the ragged rock ledge above.

HE WAS ELEVEN. HE CONSIDERED himself an old hand at camping. It was the family's annual summer activity, exploring a different woodland destination each year. Mason loved it and was proud of his wilderness skills. His mother and father had come to trust Mason to be smart and careful in unfamiliar terrain. He'd proved himself capable of using good judgment and usually making, if not always the smartest choices, at least less than disastrous ones. And so permission for him to climb to the top of the rocks that evening was given without extraordinary concern. That's not to say it was granted frivolously. His mother doled out strict instructions to go slow and stay well away from the edge, once he had reached the top. She had the knack of making everything sound unquestionably sensible.

His sister, Emmy, however, was far less understanding of her parents' authority. An intensely emotional four-year-old, she had no tolerance for their protective instincts. Which was why, when Mason started out on the trail to the top of the rocks, he left behind a wailing, angry little sister who wasn't allowed to go along. Mason had requested, privately, that he be permitted to climb the rock alone. As much as his parents relied on him to be generous with his little sister, they understood that he deserved at least some adventure time to himself. Emmy was distraught and furious. She retreated into the tent to kick and scream and vent her rage on some innocent stuffed animal or maybe an air mattress that might not survive one of her relentless fits of anger.

The trail to the top of the rocks was steep but not dangerous. It was very well engineered to provide solid footing and handholds on the rock face that bordered the inside of the path. The whole family had hiked up some different rocks before arriving at Flat Rock and setting up camp at site 19. Mason had led the way with a bold, frontier spirit. Emmy was close behind doing her best to follow exactly in her brother's footsteps. As usual, Emmy's need to mimic and keep up with Mason took precedence over all else. Mason had always been reasonably patient with her idolatry, but he was trying to establish much broader boundaries now. He was more involved with his group of friends from school and was becoming more easily irritated by Emmy's continuing insistence that she be included in his every endeavor. He'd mostly enjoyed his sister's company, and the role of teacher and guide made him feel important. But lately, he was finding her intrusions more and more annoying. This led to shouting matches and, ultimately, to tears and out of control fits of rage. To Emmy, Mason's need for autonomy was insulting and hurtful.

Mason climbed the trail that evening with a self-satisfied sense of freedom. He reached the top of the rocks, exhilarated. A cool, pine-scented breeze whispered primeval secrets in his ear as he gazed across the great expanse of mountains and verdant forests. He was on top of the world. The sun was just setting, and the western sky was a fiery orange glow. He imagined himself an adventurer from long ago, looking out over an unexplored territory full of mystery. The real world disappeared. His eyes scanned the horizon, and he picked out a route through a distant mountain pass for his fantastical quest.

The breeze stiffened on top of the rock. Mason heard a scuffling noise behind him. He turned to see Emmy standing about ten feet away. He could tell she'd deliberately positioned herself so as not to be seen from the campground below. Mason wasn't going to cut her a break this time. She'd interrupted his private reverie, and he was angry.

"Mom told you you couldn't come. Go back down, or I'm telling."

But Emmy was as intransigent as always. "I don't have to."

Mason went to the edge and called down to his mother. "Mom! Emmy came up here!"

His mother dropped the bag of utensils she was holding and stiffened. "Bring her back down here, Mason. Immediately!"

Emmy rushed at him and hit him on the back. "I hate you!"

Their mother witnessed the attack from below with sudden dread. They were way too close to the edge of the rock. "Emmy! Take your brother's hand and get back down here now at once. Both of you get away from the edge."

Their father was just returning from the car with some more camping provisions. He dropped the bags and called out with that peculiar mixture of fear and anger that alters a parent's usual voice. "Take her hand, Mason, and get down here. You hear me!"

Mason grabbed Emmy's hand as he was told and started to pull her in the direction of the trail.

Emmy was having none of it. "No! I don't have to go!"

She yanked herself away with such force that her momentum propelled her uncontrollably backward. Mason watched in horror as his little sister disappeared over the edge.

NOW, YEARS LATER, MASON stared up at the rock. He remembered how it all seemed to happen in slow motion. How he just stood there, frozen, staring out at nothing. How...

No.

No. He looked away from the rock and pulled himself back to the present. He hadn't come here to relive the events of that evening. He had replayed it all in his mind and in his dreams over and over through the years. In a way, he had never really left site 19. But he was determined not to encumber this particular evening with nightmarish visions or morose images of Emmy's death.

The arrival of an extremely vocal blue jay helped him shake off the morbid flashback. The colorful creature landed on a lower branch of the huge oak tree and squawked loudly and unceasingly as if berating this intruder for even being here. Mason assured the noisy jay that there would soon be snacks available.

Mason was unaware that site 19 had been abandoned as an official campsite. His very emotional connection to the site had distracted him, and he hadn't seen the "No Camping" sign. Not that he would have paid any attention to it if he had. But he was surprised and annoyed to find that it lacked both a picnic table and a fire pit.

He decided to remedy the situation by borrowing a table from an adjoining site. The tables, however, were large and very heavy. Hauling one across the rough terrain wasn't going to be easy. After some careful consideration he concluded that if he flipped the table over onto its top, he could lash a rope around the legs at one end and simply drag it like a sled. As heavy as it was, the scheme worked, for a distance. He came to a shallow depression about 15 feet across, evidently a natural drainage. The table embedded itself into some softer dirt and refused to budge. This brought a few cackles from the blue jay. Mason took the bird's taunting as a gauntlet being thrown.

Mason had never been a physical fitness junkie, like so many of his friends, but he was stocky and strong. He never shied away from physical challenges if they seemed warranted. Given his plans for the evening, not to mention the blue jay's attitude, some serious use of muscle was more than warranted. He wrenched one end of the table up and flipped it over. He repeated this maneuver a number of times until he had it solidly situated under the branches of the enormous oak.

The blue jay lighted on the branch overhead and squawked its approval, knowing from his experience as a keen observer of campground activity that the combination of human and table would eventually produce something edible.

Mason went to the SUV and grabbed a bottle of water, guzzled half of it and took a few minutes to catch his breath. He opened the hatchback and grabbed a whisk broom and a couple of bags. As he turned to head back into the site, he saw the “No Camping” sign. This struck him as curious, but he didn’t consider it an issue since the likelihood of a ranger making an appearance at Flat Rock in late autumn was pretty much nil. Besides, he had far more important matters to deal with.

He cleaned off the tabletop with the whisk broom. From one of the bags, he grabbed a small cream-colored ceramic vase and a pair of scissors. The vase had belonged to a grandmother. He couldn't remember which one. It had been one of Emmy's favorite family treasures. The vase was always a centerpiece when Emmy served tea with her toy tea set. Mason once asked her why she never put flowers in it, and she said because it ruined it. Mason liked flowers, however. He spotted a cluster of bright blue bellflowers, still blooming due to the late warm spell. Mason cut a few sprigs for the vase, added some water, and placed it in the middle of the table. The blue jay squawked its impatience, reminding Mason in no uncertain terms that its own appetite was the priority here.

Mason made another trip to the car for a box of food. He had a nice baguette he was more than happy to divvy up with his feathered friend. As he was carrying the box back to the table, he was surprised to see the blue jay flying away. It seemed somehow to be in a hurry as if something had startled it. Mason stopped and watched it as it disappeared into some far-off trees. He shrugged, a bit disappointed to lose his crotchety companion. As he was about to put the box on the table, he noticed that the vase of flowers was lying on its side, the water spilled onto the tabletop. He set the box down on one of the attached benches and righted the vase. It was obvious that the jay had lost patience, landed on the table and knocked it over, scaring itself off. He righted the vase and filled it with more water.

The autumn air was beginning to take on a chill. Given the season, Mason had expected a cold night. He'd brought a down jacket as well as his ancient navy blue lamb's wool sweater, the last gift his mother had given him before her sad, untimely death. Whenever he put on that sweater, he could feel his blood pressure drop.

He unloaded some more gear from the car. He laid out a small tarp under the spreading limbs of the oak tree. On top of it, he arranged a foam rubber pad, his sleeping bag, and a pillow. There was a slight rise where the ground met the trunk of the oak. This would keep his head a bit elevated, Mason's preferred sleeping position.

He lay down on his camp bed and gazed up into the oak tree. The thick gnarly branches crisscrossed in every direction. He wondered what strange forces of nature caused them to twist and turn in so random a fashion and yet end up forming such beauty. Mason fell into a kind of peaceful trance, feeling in perfect harmony with this magical mountain world. He knew he'd made the right choice coming here.

As he was lying there in his reverie, the sun dipped below the western mountains, and the fading twilight transformed Flat Rock campground into a somber palette of dark mottled greys. Darkness was coming on fast, and the temperature was falling. Mason got up, went back to the table and started his preparations for the night.

His family had never been camping again, not since Emmy died. Nor had he, as an adult, ever had the urge to revisit the wilds. So, of course, he didn't have any camping gear. On the way to Flat Rock he'd stopped at a large outdoors supply store and purchased the sleeping bag, a cooler and a lantern. Mason pumped pressure into the brand new Coleman and opened the valve. Gas hissed into the chamber. He struck a wooden match and slipped it through a vent under the chimney. A puff of flame shot out through the vent, making Mason jump. But within a few seconds, the mantle was blazing hot, and site 19 was bathed in a long-forgotten glow. The surrounding area came alive with shadows. The enormous stack of giant rocks lit up in such a way that gave them more depth and contour. They looked like the petrified remains of some gargantuan prehistoric life form.

In the other direction, the lantern light pierced the night, went just so far, then seemed to run into a wall of darkness. Mason gazed up into the cosmos and had the thought that site 19 was just like one of the stars in the night sky, a tiny spot of luminescence in a vast sea of nothingness. For the first time since he'd arrived at the campground, he felt very far away and very alone. But then that was the idea.

The crickets had begun their soothing symphonic nighttime ritual. Mason looked around at the campsite and realized that he'd forgotten a key element of his plan. As much as he appreciated the lantern's efficiency, he was, after all, camping. He needed a campfire.

He went to the SUV and unloaded some split wood and kindling he'd brought from home. He gathered up some large stones and made his own fire ring. He took his time building a picture-perfect fire. The flames added a new dimension as the shadows now danced beguilingly on the rocks and trees, and the comforting smell of wood smoke tempered the chill of the night air.

Mason had stopped at his favorite gourmet grocery store on his way out of town and purchased a sixty dollar bottle of Bordeaux, some mini toasts, Beluga Caviar, Greek olives, a couple of his favorite cheeses, a pre-roasted mustard-glazed chicken, some German potato salad and some marinated white asparagus. He opened the wine and poured a large glass. He looked over at the lovely crackling fire and made a toast to it. Then he tasted the wine. He closed his eyes and succumbed to the wave of pleasure as the soft, luscious nectar warmed his soul.

He opened the caviar, the mini toasts, and the olives. He noshed as he set his table, putting his place-setting at the corner closest to the fire. He unwrapped the chicken and put it onto another plate with a carving knife. He spooned out some potato salad and white asparagus and sat down. He poured another glass of wine and proceeded to feast heartily on his favorite foods. The wonderful flavors were somehow intensified by the loneliness of the secluded campsite. There were none of the distractions that usually accompanied Mason's normal meal routine. Phone calls, traffic, television. He remembered hearing something about a religion where people didn't speak at all during meals. It seemed ridiculous at the time, but now he realized that they might have been onto something.

The crackling of the fire and the orchestra of crickets serenaded Mason while he ate. He pulled put a book he'd brought along, a collection of Carl Sandburg poems called Cornhuskers. He'd always loved Sandburg, although he hadn't read him in years. When he looked through his bookshelves for something appropriate to take with him to Site 19 and saw the Sandburg, he grabbed it immediately. He was interested to discover that he'd left a bookmark on a certain page. It was a short poem called Haunts.

THERE ARE PLACES I go when I am strong.
One is a marsh pool where I used to go
With a long-ear hound-dog.
One is a wild crab-apple tree; I was there
A moonlight night with a girl.
The dog is gone; the girl is gone; I go to these
Places when there is no other place to go.

MASON DIDN'T REMEMBER the poem, but it stirred him to some unexpected emotion. He washed the lump in his throat away with a large dose of wine. It was then he noticed the bookmark, a narrow yellow piece of craft paper with a child's crayon stick-figure drawing of a girl, the sun, and the words "This is me." A school project of Emmy's. He was sad that he didn't remember the exact moment she'd given it to him. He put it in his pocket.

Mason noticed the fire was dying down. He closed the book, got up, and put another couple of logs on. He was caught for some time in the hypnotic dance of flames as the new wood quickly re-invigorated the fire. An air pocket in one of the logs popped and threw some sparks, jolting him out of the spell. He went back to the table and poured himself another glass of Bordeaux.

He finished his dinner slowly, savoring every bite. He found himself more aware now of the night sounds, the crackle of the fire, a distant owl, the scurry of things in the brush. When he had finally finished his feast, he cleaned up carefully, put the remains in bags, and took it all back to the car. He couldn't remember if there were bears in this area or not, but it seemed likely. Dealing with a hungry carnivore three times his size wasn't part of his plan.

He pumped some new energy into the lantern and picked up the Sandburg again. He read another couple of poems, then put the book down. He realized that since he had finished reading, he really didn't need the lantern light anymore and, in fact, the intense glow had become annoying. He turned the gas valve off, and Site 19 was now bathed in the warm dancing flames of the fire.

He poured the last of the wine into his glass. He reached into his pocket and took out two little plastic bags. One of the bags had six pills in it, the other four. He opened them both and poured the pills out onto the table in two little portions.

There was a noise behind him. At the bottom of the wall of rocks he saw some small stones falling into the brush from above. He got up from the table, walked over to the spot, and looked up. The golden flickering reflection from the campfire made the stack of boulders look like they were glowing from within. The light stretched two-thirds of the way to the top, then faded quickly. Mason stared up at the top edge of the rock which was barely visible as a line of shadow that separated the earth from the starry night sky.

At that moment, the crickets stopped.

Mason turned to go back to the table and froze.

Some things betray all logic or rational thought and, regardless of circumstance, render the mind numb, as the normal world is bent into unimaginable shapes. At that moment, reality, as Mason perceived it, wasn't just suddenly twisted, it was sucked into oblivion.

Emmy was sitting there, at the other end of the table. She was wearing the party dress they buried her in. She seemed to be staring at the vase in the middle of the table. "Emmy." His own voice sounded as if it emanated from the bottom of a deep well.

The phantasm that presented itself as his four-year-old sister looked over at him. Her dark eyes should have reflected the fire. They didn't. "I've been waiting for you, Mason."

Mason fell to the ground. He crouched in a fetal position. He covered his face with his hands and started laughing. He laughed uncontrollably and desperately, shaking, tears streaming out of his eyes. The laughter turned to sobs then to anguished, strangulated sounds that Mason had no control over.

"Mason. Come here!" The words howled from her throat, took control of his body and jolted him up onto his knees.

Shaking uncontrollably, gasping for breath, he looked at her. She put her finger to her lips.

"Shhhhhhh."

The sound cut through the night like ice sliding down a metal roof. She did it again.

"Shhhhhhh. It's okay."

With a thin translucent hand, Emmy motioned for Mason to come closer. His whole body was trembling. His legs felt leaden. Somehow he managed to pull himself to his feet. He moved slowly toward the table, to the corner where he had been sitting previously. Emmy turned her hollow eyes on the two little piles of pills.

She shook her head slowly. "No, Mason."

"What? No, Emmy, listen. Please." He was breathless, struggling to get the words out. "I'm dying. I have cancer. A bad cancer.

"Wrong." It was the angry little girl voice he knew so well.

"No, Emmy. This isn't wrong. Wrong is dying with tubes sticking out of you and slowly suffocating while people you love stand by your bed and...and try to act brave. That's what the doctors want me to do. But I can't do that, Emmy. I can't let it happen like that. I need to go my way. Like this. Tonight."

"No!" She threw the word ferociously. The pills flew off the table and into the scrub brush and tall grass about ten feet away.

Mason leapt after them. "Emmy, for Christ's sake! What are you doing? Damn it! Goddamn it!"

He dropped to his knees and dug through in the weeds. "My God! I need those. You can't do this to me!" His search was in vain. It was too dark to see through the thick weeds.

He needed a flashlight. He got up and turned back toward the table.

She was gone.

"Emmy? Emmy, where are you?" He looked in every direction. He grabbed a flashlight out of a bag and shined it into the woods, all around. She was nowhere in sight.

"Where are you? Why'd you do that to me? Emmy!"

He took the flashlight and went back to where the pills landed. He scratched and clawed through the shrubs and grass, desperate. But they were too small to be found, and he realized he was making it even harder by trampling the grass down. He pulled himself to his feet again, gasping for air, overwhelmed with anguish.

"Damn it!" His extraordinary frustration turned to fury, and he yelled into the night. "Goddamn it, Emmy! You want me to suffer? Is that it? You blame me for what happened? You do, don't you? Mom told you not to follow me! So did Dad, so did I. But you climbed up there anyway. You had to do everything I did, didn't you? It wasn't my fault! It wasn't. You think I haven't hated myself all these years for not holding on tighter? You think I haven't suffered enough? Is that it? Goddamn it!" He threw the flashlight into the woods furiously.

He went to the fire and stood there, panting, the firelight flickering on his twisted, despondent face. He kicked some dirt into the fire and walked to the oak tree. He pounded his fist on its gnarly trunk. He leaned against it, his head on his arm, eyes closed. A suffocating confusion cloaked his whole being. He saw or felt no direction to move in, nothing substantial to give thought to. He was floating in a cold misty realm somewhere between life and death. He sobbed and sucked in deep tormented breaths. His head started to spin.

Then, like a curtain opening in a dark theater, he saw himself sitting at the little table in Emmy's room. She was serving him tea from her miniature tea set. The cream-colored vase was in the middle of the table. She sat down across from him and smiled. "I hope you like your tea." The image slowly faded, and Mason was once again in the moment. He felt himself leaning against the tree, the gnarly bark pressing into his arms. He heard his own labored breathing and felt the frigid night air.

The crickets started up again.

He lifted his head, opened his eyes, and stepped back from the tree trunk. An owl hooted overhead. He looked up into the vast expanse of twisting branches and thought he could see two glistening eyes.

He was still shaky. His legs felt rubbery. He stumbled back over to the table and sat down. He looked at the spot where Emmy had been sitting. He tried to fit it into some kind of logical mold. Maybe a waking dream or some kind of anxiety-induced hallucination. The effort was useless. She'd been sitting right there. She'd spoken to him. And the pills were gone, scattered and lost. She'd done that. There was nothing to hang onto. No explanation that could comfort him.

Emmy had decided his fate, and there was nothing for it. He got up, grabbed a bottle of water, walked to the fire, and poured. It knocked down the largest of the flames but left a small flickering few that still cast dim shadows into the woods.

He went to his car and yanked open the driver's side door. He looked up toward the top of the rock. Without the firelight or lantern, he was looking into a black void. He imagined her up there, staring down at him with ghostly sibling vengeance.

He climbed into the SUV. He turned on his headlights, which illuminated the old post that now had the "No Camping" sign on it. He saw something he hadn't noticed when he had arrived. Someone had used a knife to carve a word into the side of the post. The word was "HAUNTED."

His tires chewed at the gravel as he sped away from Flat Rock campground.

The last embers of the fire soon died out, and site 19 vanished into the deep lonely night.

MASON DROVE ALL NIGHT to get back home. His only stop was for gas, but he couldn't remember where. The wrenching encounter with Emmy had pushed him to the edge of his own emotional cliff. The dark storm howling through his psyche threatened to blow him over the edge. He cried. He pounded the steering wheel. The image of her pale unearthly face tortured him. He played it all over and over in his head. He turned the radio to a rock station and cranked it all the way, hoping to blast her visage from his mind.

He considered driving his car into the concrete embankment of an overpass and just ending it. But as he tried to will his hands to swerve toward instant death, he heard her voice again, cold and hard.

"No, Mason."

But he didn't want to hear it.

"Goddamn it, Emmy. Let go of me!"

He was damned if he would suffer like she wanted. He didn't deserve that. Getting another deadly cocktail of pills wouldn't be a problem. He'd just say he lost the first one. Simple.

It was about 10am the next day when he climbed the steps to his front door, completely exhausted. He fumbled for his keys but then noticed his front door was unlocked. He pushed it open and went in. He heard a voice coming from his office in the back of the house. As he warily approached the office door, he realized the voice belonged to his friend Tom. Tom and Mason had gone to college together and had been there for each other through all that life had thrown at them. Tom was a clinical psychiatrist and the one who'd acquired the lethal cocktail for Mason.

Tom was on the phone talking to his wife, Jen. His voice was distraught.

"I found his cell phone in the top drawer. God, Jen, what have I done?"

Mason stepped into the room. Tom's head whipped around. He stared at Mason in utter disbelief.

"Mason. Oh my God. Mason!"

He yelled, jubilantly, into the phone. "He's here, Jen. He's here. God, he's okay!" Then he jumped up and threw himself at Mason, grabbing him in a bear hug. He was laughing now, and tears rolled down his cheeks. It was entirely out of character.

"Jesus, Tom. What's going on?"

Tom released Mason from the hug held onto his shoulders.

"You're not dying, Mason. They messed it up. There's not a goddamn thing wrong with you. Okay, you got this thing, but it's totally benign. God almighty I thought I'd killed you."

"Whoa, slow down. What are you talking about?"

"Okay, sorry. I'm just so...God almighty. Remember how you gave your oncologist my number in case of emergency? Well, he called me last night. He was pretty rattled. He couldn't reach you. Anyway, they sent the CAT scans to Australia or Austria, or some godforsaken place, to be processed. Some moron technician screwed up and switched your results with somebody else's. You got some stupid benign something or other, but it's no big deal. There's nothing wrong with you. You're not gonna die."

It took a few moments for Tom's words to become real.

"Oh. Okay. Just, uh, give me a minute, okay?"

"Sure. Of course. Sure."

Mason went to the window and looked out at his back yard. He reached into his pocket for a handkerchief. He felt a piece of paper and pulled it out. It was Emmy's drawing he'd used for a bookmark. The crayon stick figure of a smiling girl and the words, "This is me." Tears welled up in his eyes as the truth washed over him.

She didn't want him to suffer. She wanted him to live.

Out loud he said, "She knew. She saved my life."

"What? Who?"

An anxious voice called from Tom's cell phone lying on the desk. It was Jen. The call was still live. Tom grabbed up the phone and reassured her that everything was fine now. He told Mason she was beside herself and on the way over.

Mason said, "No. I'm hungry, and I need some coffee. Tell her to meet us at Rudy's."

Tom relayed the message and hung up the phone.

"What did you mean 'She saved my life?' Who?"

"You drive. I'll tell you on the way."

As they made their way across town, Mason told Tom about site 19. He told it to him in detail and without emotional coloring. He had just finished the story when they parked at the diner. They got out of the car and crunched across the gravel toward the front door of the diner.

"So, Mr. Clinical Psychiatrist, tell me."

Tom thought for a moment and said, "We haven't even begun to understand what the human mind is capable of, Mason. It's possible that somewhere, buried deep down in your own psyche, you knew you weren't dying. But since the normal powers of logic and reason require us to believe what the doctors tell us, you had no way of accessing that knowledge. So, some kind of, I don't know, psychic survival instinct kicked in, and you created a scenario to save yourself."

"You mean I pretty much imagined the whole thing."

"Well, think of the things our subconscious creates in our dreams."

"But I was awake, Tom. I wasn't dreaming."

"A whole bottle of wine...maybe you weren't as fully conscious as you thought."

"Okay. What about the pills?"

Tom thought about that for a moment, then grabbed the Diner's door handle.

"Let's get some bacon and eggs."

THE FOLLOWING WEEK, Mason returned to site 19 to gather up all the stuff he'd left behind. He wasn't about to leave piles of his trash and camp gear to rot over the winter. A light snow had fallen in the night leaving about two powdery inches on the ground. He grabbed a couple of large black plastic bags and headed toward the campsite, the thin layer of snow silencing his footsteps.

He stopped for a moment and gazed up at the top of Flat Rock. It looked peaceful and magnificent in its white wintry cloak. He heard a loud squawk. The blue jay swooped in, lighted on a branch and demanded some treats. Mason was ready for him. He grabbed a handful of peanuts from his pocket and tossed them into the white powder. The vociferous jay swooped down, picked up a peanut in his beak, put it down, picked up another one. Decisions, decisions. Mason left him to his indecisiveness and headed into the campsite.

He got about ten feet from the picnic table and stopped.

In the middle of the table was Emmy's vase. It held several stems of lovely blue bellflowers.

There were no footprints in the snow.

What the Cat Saw

"Did you do the flea stuff on Mango?"

"Yep."

"He's really after something."

"He's just washing. I think that stuff kind of irritates him some."

"Tell him to wash on your side of the bed. I want to go to sleep."

"Mango, Lucy would like you to please move to my side of the bed."

"Funny."

"You asked."

"How can one cat take up so much room?"

"The great unsolved mystery of the universe."

"Did you close the patio door?"

"Uh, I don't think so. I thought you did."

"I wouldn't ask you if you did if I did."

"Makes sense."

"Go."

"Okay okay. Nag, nag, nag."

"And bring me a glass of water. Please."

"You have any laundry you need done while I'm at it?"

"No ice."

"Jesus."

"What?"

"It's freezing in here."

"It's 80 outside. How can it be freezing?"

"I don't know. But it's like a damn refrigerator."

"I turned the AC off hours ago."

"This is weird. You should feel it."

"I'll take your word for it. Was the door open?"

"Yeah. Closed now. What the fuck?"

"Now what?"

"The Swedish ivy by the door is totally wilted, like it's pretty much dead."

"What? That's impossible. It was fine."

"I know it was fine. Did you water it today?"

"Yeah, this morning. It wasn't even wilted."

"What did you use?"

"What did I use? Uh, gee, let's see. Oh, yeah, water."

"No, I mean what container did you use."

"The same pitcher we always use."

"There must have been something in it."

"Can we deal with this in the morning? I'd kinda like to sleep now, okay?"

"Yeah. It's just so weird. Maybe it's the cold."

"It's not cold."

"Not in here, but it is out there. Here."

"Thank you. Oh, god, I was thirsty. Could you turn your light away?"

"Sure. That okay?"

"Fine. Night"

"Night."

"WHAT?"

"Dammit, Jeremy. What what?"

"Sorry. I was talking to Mango. He just whipped his head around like he heard something."

"God, I was almost asleep."

"Sorry."

"Shit. Now I'm cold."

"Told you."

"Give me some more blanket."

"Mango won't allow it."

"Then get me my robe and throw it over me."

"Oh, I see. Doesn't matter if I freeze."

"Nope."

"Better?"

"Yes. How could it get so cold?"

"Right?

"WHAT THE HELL ARE YOU hearing, Mango?"

"Hello? Trying to sleep."

"I know, sorry again. But he's like...frozen in this one position and staring."

"He's a cat. They hear things."

"UM, LUCY? I GOTTA SAY, this is just a little too weird."

"Jesus, now what?"

"He just turned around, and he's in this hunch now, just staring toward the hall."

"Dammit, now you're creeping me out. Uh....okay, yeah, that's strange. Mango, what's up? What are you hearing?"

"I've never seen him do this before. Not for this long."

"You locked the door, right?"

"Of course."

"'Cause that lock sticks."

"I know. I locked it, honest."

"What about the front door?"

"I locked it when I came in from the garage."

Mrrrrrrrrrr

"Whoa. Shit."

"What the hell, Mango?"

"I've never heard him make that noise before. Have you ever heard him make that noise before?"

"Uh uh. There's gotta be something outside. He's totally freaked. I'm gonna go check."

"Be careful in the dark. Don't turn on any lights."

"Why not?"

"Because then people outside can see you, but you can't see them."

"Yeah, okay."

"See anything? Hello?"

"No. Nobody's out there. It's all quiet and normal. God, it's even colder. I can see my breath."

"Bring the throw from the couch."

"Is Mango still staring?"

"Yeah. And he's sorta panting."

"Doors are locked, and nobody's there. This is stupid."

"Yeah. Okay. But look at him."

"Forget it. He's just being a cat. God, I'm frozen now."

"Get back in bed, and get that throw on you."

"Damn, now I'm all hyped. And I have to get up early."

"Read for a while. You always fall asleep when you start to read."

"I won't be able to concentrate. Mango, could you please stop staring like that? Please?"

"He never listens."

"This isn't funny anymore."

"Sorry. But there's no way we can know what goes on in his cat mind or what he perceives or whatever. Let's just blow it off and go to sleep. You want a Xanax?"

"Yeah."

"I think they're in your drawer."

"No, I gave them to you a couple of nights ago."

"Um, oh, yeah. Here."

"Fuck, I'm out of water."

"Here, you can have mine."

mrrrrrrrrrrrrowwwwwww

"Shit. This is totally crazy. Something is not right with him."

"I think he's just messing with us."

"Stop. I'm serious.... Ah! Christ that scared me."

"Shit."

"Fuck, Jeremy. Why did the light go out?"

"Something must have blown a breaker."

"What could have done that? Nothing was on except your lamp."

"I don't know. It's an old house. Remember how the inspector said we might have to replace the wiring someday."

"What are you doing?"

"Getting a flashlight."

"There's one in the kitchen drawer."

"I've got one in my dresser, right here."

"Where are you going?"

"To check the breaker box."

"No. Don't leave me alone."

"Chill. I'll just be a minute. I've gotta get the lights back on. It's okay."

"Okay, okay. But hurry. "

mmmmmmrrrrrr.

"Hey, it's okay, Mango. There's no one there. It's okay, baby."

hhhhhhhhhst

"Ah, Jesus!"

"What happened?"

"I tried to pet Mango, and he hissed and spat at me, really mean."

"Don't try to touch him."

"What? I can't hear you."

"I said, don't try to touch him. Probably just freak him out more."

"Did you find anything?"

"Uh uh. None of the breakers are blown."

"Come back in here."

"I'm here. I'm here. It's okay. Holy crap, his eyes are just wild."

"Don't shine the flashlight right at his face like that."

"Okay, okay. Mango, come on. There's nobody there."

mmmmmmmmmmmmmrrrrrrrrrrrrrrrrr

"Crap. This isn't good, Jeremy. I think we need to get out of here."

"What? What are you talking about?"

"There's something wrong in here."

"Whoa, let's not get crazy. Besides, where would we go?"

"I don't know. Anywhere. Over to Charles and Mika's. Whatever."

"Oh, right. Call them at one o'clock in the morning and say our cat is freaking us out, can we come over and crash? Really?"

"But we don't have any lights."

"There must be something going on in the neighborhood."

"What about the cold?"

"I don't know. The weather just suddenly changed. It happens. The weather is fucking crazy these days."

"Go see if it's cold outside."

"Oh, come on."

"Go. I wanna know."

"Fuck. All right."

"And bring me another flashlight. I hate being alone in the dark."

"Got it."

"Well? Is it cold outside? Jeremy? Jeremy! Jesus, didn't you hear me?"

"I was outside. Take it easy."

"Is it cold?"

"No. It's really warm."

"Fuck.

"I know."

"Fuck, fuck, fuck. What about the lights? Were there other lights out?"

"The streetlights were on. But they might be on a different circuit."

"Flashlight?"

"Yes. Here."

"Thank you.

"Let's just..."

"I don't think it's a coincidence."

"Don't think what's a coincidence?"

"Mango, the cold, the lights going out."

"Okay, wait. Wait. Listen to us. This is getting absurd. We've gotta just chill. There's nobody in the house, obviously. We've been here all evening, and the doors are locked. And I looked outside and didn't see anything."

"Then what's wrong with Mango?"

"I have no idea. But, like you said, he's a cat. Cats do weird things. I'll get some candles. Let's play Scrabble or something. We'll figure the lights out in the morning. Okay?"

"Okay. Good idea."

"I'll be right back."

"There's a couple of big fat candles in the bottom drawer of the sideboard."

"Ow. Shit."

"What?"

"I just stubbed my toe. Where did you say?"

"The bottom drawer of the sideboard, on the right."

"I see them."

"Now I have to go to the bathroom. Excuse me, Mango...OW! Shit. Goddamnit, Mango...okay, okay. Let go. Jesus."

"What's going on?"

"I started to get out of bed, and Mango grabbed my leg with his claws. Like he was stopping me from getting up. Dammit, that hurts."

"Are you bleeding? Lemme see."

"Light the candles first. I need some more light in here."

"Okay."

mmmmmmmmrrrrrrr

"Jeremy, there is something fucking up with him, and it's not good."

"Maybe he's sick. Here, put this one over by you."

"I don't think he likes this house. He's been acting weird since we moved in."

"I haven't seen him acting weird."

"That's because you're not here as much."

"You never said anything about him acting weird."

"I just sort of wrote it off until now."

"I think he's sick."

"He's not sick. He ate a whole bowl of wet food. And he was playing with his catnip mouse just before we came to bed."

"Okay, so, maybe he's had a stroke or something."

"Oh, shit. I never thought of that."

"Remember how your parents' cat got all weird and started freaking out and they discovered he had a brain tumor?"

"Yeah, but he was really, really old. Like sixteen. Mango's only five."

"Six."

"No, he's five. We got him right after we got back from England."

"Yeah, but he was almost a year old."

"Whatever."

hhhhhhhhhhhhhhhhhhhhhh

"Christ. What the fuck is he hissing at? Goddamnit."

"Whoa. Holy crap. Mango?"

"What's he doing? Shit."

"Watch his head. He's seeing something. He was looking over by the door then it's like whatever he was seeing moved over there."

"Oh shit, why is he backing up like that? What's he...?"

"Oh, fuck!"

"Where'd he go?"

"Under the bed, I think."

"Okay, this isn't good. This is...something just scared the shit out of him."

"It was like something was coming toward him. Shit, Jeremy, I'm scared."

"Lucy, there's nothing there, okay? Mango? Hey, Mango, you under the bed?

hhhhhthwt

"Jesus, he just took a swipe at my face."

"Jeremy. Jeremy. Oh god, I just saw something."

"What? What do you mean?"

"When you leaned down to look for Mango. I saw a shadow or something over by the closet."

"Wait. Wait. I think our brains are messing with us now. We've gotta just....."

"Oh my god!"

"Fuck."

"What's going on. I'm really scared now."

"It's okay. It's okay."

"It's not okay. For Christ's sake, Jeremy, something just blew the fucking candles out!"

"I know, I know. Just try to stay calm."

"Ow. Goddamnit, let go of my foot."

"I'm not touching your foot."

"The hell you're....ahhhhh! Oh my God! Nooooo! Jeremy! Help me....!!"

"Lucy! Shit....I'm coming. God almighty! Let go of her! Let go of...."

"Jere......ulllgghhhh."

"No! Let her go! What the hell are you....? Get off....guhh-hhhh......"

meow

meow

meow

The Quantum Reality of Ghosts

"Many a trip continues long after movement in time and space has ceased."
- John Steinbeck

THE GHOST HUNTERS PACKED up their equipment and trudged out the door, mumbling to each other, bewildered and insulted. Barry Kaminsky didn't give a damn. He made himself a martini and sat at the tall breakfast table in his kitchen where he'd laid out some nice salty Roquefort cheese and baguette slices. He had no intention of letting these clowns interfere with his usual evening routine. Kelsey Laurents, the slender, attractive young woman who called herself the producer walked in, addressing him in a tone colder than his martini.

"We're all wrapped. Goodnight, Dr. Kaminsky."

"Goodnight." Barry hardly glanced at her.

She hesitated at the door. "Can I ask you a question?"

"Sure."

"What makes you so sure we're a bunch of fakes?"

"I didn't say you were a bunch of fakes."

"No, but you threw us out, implying that you didn't have any faith in our process."

"I'm a scientist, Ms. Laurents. I don't work with faith. I work with reasonable scientific processes."

"Question, hypothesize, predict, test, support, or refute hypothesis."

"That's right."

"Which part of our process didn't fit that model for you?"

"The part where your guys kept saying things like 'Did you hear that?' and 'Whoa, Dude, it just got really cold.'"

"It's a television show. We're selling soap."

Barry was caught a bit off guard. "Okay. I appreciate your honesty."

"Look, there's something in this house that defies logical explanation, right?"

"So they say."

"So, but isn't it logical, based on the number of reports about this house over the years, for one to hypothesize that there might be something here?"

"What's your point, Ms. Laurents?"

"My point is that you shut us down in the middle of our process, and with our equipment, we might have been able to support or refute that hypothesis."

"Can I ask you a question now?"

"Okay."

"Honestly, in all of your so-called investigations, have you ever actually been convinced that you found solid evidence of a ghost?"

"Our job is to entertain. It's a TV show."

"More honesty, again appreciated, but also an evasion. Care to try answering the question?"

Kelsey Laurents hesitated. "We were investigating an old abandoned mansion outside of Chicago last year. I got there early. The crew hadn't arrived yet. I was scoping out locations on one of the upper floors, and I heard what sounded like someone singing quietly. I went into the room where I was pretty sure it was coming from. It was a dusty mess. Broken furniture. It was really dim, but in one corner I saw this shape. It looked kind of like a small person hunched down, facing the corner. Then one of the crew called my name. I turned to the door for one second. When I looked back, the shape was gone. It rattled me. And I don't get rattled. I have no idea what I saw. But that's the point, isn't it?"

"What's the point?"

"That we don't know. So we try to find out if we really saw it or not."

"But you don't really care about that. You said your job is to entertain."

"Well, yeah, I did."

One of the crew guys poked his head in. "Hey, Kelsey, you coming?"

She gave him a quick wave. "You guys go ahead, Jess. I'll see you in the morning."

The crew guy left. Barry got up and carried his now empty martini glass across the room to a small bar.

"Would you like a martini, Ms. Laurents?"

"I thought you'd never ask."

"How come you're not more pissed off at me?"

"Oh, I'm really pissed. You just cost us a lot of time not to mention some substantial bucks, and we've got shit for a budget, to begin with. And I'm gonna get all kinds of grief from the network."

"Olives or twist."

"Olives, please."

Barry shook up a couple of martinis and handed one to her.

"So what did your investigation determine you saw in that room in the orphanage?"

"After researching the history of the place, we determined that it might be the ghost of a young servant who died during an influenza epidemic in the early 20th century."

Barry motioned her to one of the stools at the tall table.

"Have a seat. So, is that what you believe?"

"If I answer that you have to promise that it will not leave this room."

"That's intriguing."

"It's my job, you know, to make it all appear real."

"Right. Okay, I promise."

"I have a big problem with believing in anything. I'm pretty much a card-carrying skeptic. So I don't have any idea what I saw, or what I thought I saw. Maybe I had too much to drink the night before. Maybe the wind and shadows were playing tricks on my eyes. I haven't the faintest idea."

"Did your equipment record anything in that room?"

"Yeah. The thermal imaging camera picked up some stuff."

"Meaning?"

"Meaning it detected some kind of indefinable heat source. In real terms, it probably doesn't mean a goddamn thing. But you get to say it and let the audience decide it means something."

Barry took a sip of his martini and sat back in his chair, just looking at Kelsey, actually seeing her for the first time. He liked what he saw.

She noticed his new interest. It made her a bit uncomfortable. "What?"

"Nothing. I'm sorry I fucked up your show."

"I should have seen it coming. Full prof in the physics department at Caltech? Why did you let us in to begin with?"

"Community outreach, more or less. The department head's idea. After you guys called him, he talked me into giving you access. Everybody there has heard the stories. Not from me, incidentally. I haven't said a word to anyone about what I've..." Barry let the idea drop, but it was too late.

"Ah ha. So you've had experiences here, too. You lied to me earlier."

"Maybe a little lie of omission."

Kelsey's cell phone announced an incoming text. She pulled it from her pocket and dashed off a quick reply.

"Oh, joy. The network's already out for blood."

"Will they fire you?"

She laughed. "I'm delivering their number one show. They just get all crazy because the multi-national overlords that own their ass go ballistic at budget overruns."

Barry pointed out the door. "Let's go into the living room.

Noticing a suspicious look from Kelsey, he added, "No no, I have no ulterior motives, Ms. Laurents."

"What, I'm not your type? You can call me Kelsey. By the way, all that stuff the guys were saying, you know, the 'Did you hear that' and all? You were right. It's bullshit. I think."

"You think?"

"Sometimes I think they really believe they hear or see things that aren't even there. They've been doing it so long I think their brains conjure up sounds and images to fit the situation. Not on purpose, just some sort of post-hypnotic suggestion."

"Who hypnotized them?"

"Black Mirror, Stranger Things."

Barry led her into a charming classic craftsman style living room. Built-in bookcases, lots of dark varnished oak, and a Batchelder tile fireplace. On one wall, two glass-paneled doors led to another room. Barry settled himself in an old leather armchair that looked like it had been through the wars.

"Great chair."

"It came with the house. The University actually owns the property. I'm just squatting."

"So, what kind of physicist are you? Supersymmetry or multiverse?"

"Neither, actually. My world is nanoscience and ultra-low temperatures. I'm pretty much focused on quantum phenomena right now. Superfluidity and all that. It's not all that romantic to the outside world, but it's actually fun as hell."

Barry looked at his watch. He got up and crossed the room, turned off one of the floor lamps, leaving the room illuminated only by the table lamp next to his chair. He then took another chair from in front of a small secretary and moved it over next to his own chair.

"Would you mind sitting in this chair, please?"

Kelsey got up. "Uh, okay. What are we doing?"

Barry looked at his watch again. "Just waiting, another minute or two."

Kelsey sat down in the chair.

"You see, Kelsey, the real reason I threw your guys out is that, after watching all that bullshit they were engaged in, I decided they probably couldn't handle what you're about to experience."

"What I'm what?"

"Let's just say there's nothing entertaining about what happens in this house."

"Okay, now I'm really intrigued. And a little bit creeped out, to tell you the truth."

"I thought you didn't creep out easily."

"I don't. But I've never been set up for a supernatural experience by a Caltech physicist before. You have a bit more cred than our usual clients."

"Don't worry, I promise nothing will harm you. But in just a bit, you're going to hear a scream. At least I assume you will. You don't have to be frightened. It happens and then it's gone."

Kelsey pulled her phone out of her pocket. "You mind if I record it?"

"Go ahead. I've recorded it several times."

"And it played back?"

"Oh, yeah. It's fairly loud, so just be prepared."

Kelsey set her cell phone to record.

"Your neighbors are pretty close. Don't they hear it?"

"That's a curious thing. I've stood outside and listened, right at that window. And, unless I'm in the room, I don't hear or see—"

A loud anguished scream reverberated through the room. In spite of the warning, Kelsey jumped to her feet. The scream lasted a few seconds and then ended in a kind of soft choking sound.

"Jesus. I wasn't ready for—"

Barry held up his hand to silence her. He pointed to the double glass doors that led to the adjoining room.

A dim, hazy figure of a woman appeared in the darkness of the room on the other side of the glass door panes. She was small and thin, her hair falling partially out of a bun. She was wearing a long nightgown that had been ripped off her shoulder, revealing bloody scratch marks on a pale breast. She was staring through from the darkness on the other side of the glass doors, eyes wild and anguished. Her lips formed one word.

"Howard." The name was spoken in a faint cold voice.

The woman on the other side started to fall. Before she hit the floor, her image vanished.

Kelsey barely got the words out. "Oh my god." She was stunned. Her flesh was covered with goosebumps. She continued to stare at the door.

"You okay?"

"I...I'm...yeah. I think so."

"It's over," said Barry. "Come on." He got up and headed for the glass doors. Kelsey got up and followed him, a bit shaky.

Barry opened the doors, and they walked into the room. He switched on a light. It was designed to be a sitting room but he'd set it up as his office. There was a large drafting table, two computers, and two large chalkboards hung on the walls, both covered with equations. There was no one else in the room. Nor was there any other door.

Barry could see that Kelsey was still pretty shaken. "You sure you're okay?"

"No. I mean, I'm not sure of anything. Jesus, we just saw a ghost, didn't we? I mean a real ghost."

"Or something."

"I can't believe this is happening. How many times have you seen it?"

"Oh, maybe thirty or forty. It creeped me out at first, too. I didn't spend too many nights down here. But then I got more and more curious, and sort of got to think of her as, I don't know, kind of a roommate."

"Roommate. God almighty, that's some spooky ass roommate."

"In the television world it's all very entertaining, right? But in the real world, maybe not so much."

Kelsey felt woozy. She grabbed the back of a chair and sat quickly.

Barry was surprised. "Oh, hell. I'm sorry. I probably sprung that on you without enough preparation."

"No. It's okay. I'm just...I didn't realize...I mean, I guess I never expected to really see anything. At least, nothing like this. Jesus Christ, Barry."

Barry handed her a Kleenex. "Somehow I don't think he's got anything to do with it."

Kelsey took some deep breaths. "Okay. I'm okay now. That smell."

"Yeah, it's always here afterward. I don't know what it is."

"It's lavender."

"Is that what that is? It's kind of nice."

"Does the same thing happen when you're in this room?"

"Never. You have to be in the living room. You know, there's something really sad about it."

"Yeah. Yeah, I felt that. The woman...okay, if you'd let us stay and really got into it, we would have done some research to see if there was a history that could tell us who she..."

Barry interrupted her. "Melinda Tischman. Her husband, Howard, shoved a knife into her back in this room in 1933. The next morning, his mother, Martha, who lived with them, found Howard slumped in his chair out there and his wife's body on the floor in here. Howard confessed. He was convicted of first-degree murder and sentenced to life in prison. He hung himself in jail a day after the trial."

"Wait. Howard Tischman. I know that name. He was a physicist, right?"

"Right. One of the big boys. Or would have been. He worked with Einstein and Schrodinger in the '30s. Those guys liked all the publicity, the notoriety. Not Howard. He pretty much worked in the shadows. But he published some major stuff on quantum theory."

"So this was his house?"

"Yeah. He willed it and everything in it to the University. A lot of professors and their families have lived here over the years since none for very long. Seems they heard strange sounds and such."

"No shit. So the stories didn't bother you?"

"I thought it was all pretty silly. But it was kind of novel to live in a house belonging to Tischman. Most of the furniture was his."

"So that's Howard Tischman's chair out there?"

"Yep. Pretty cool, huh?"

"Pretty cool until dead people start showing up."

Kelsey moved to one of the chalkboards and stared at the equations. "The double-slit experiment."

"I'm impressed."

"I was a psych major with a physics minor. I really got into it. I was thinking about changing my major when I met this producer who seduced me into this world. I have my regrets."

"The producer still in the picture, if you don't mind my asking?"

"I don't mind, and no, he's not." She studied one of the chalkboards. "You're trying to figure it out, aren't you? You think there's a way to explain it in quantum terms?"

Howard shrugged. "Well, like I said, this is not my field, so I'm really just flailing away. But why not? As I guess you know, the double-slit experiment shows that, basically, a particle in the quantum world can exist in two places at the same time. So, how about if we flip that? Why not in the same place at different times?"

"Ouch. That's way out of my reach."

"I'm just taking some wild stabs, throwing stuff at the chalkboard to see if anything sticks. I'm sure if I pitched any of this to the theory guys I'd be laughed out of the university. How about a glass of wine?"

"Oh, hell yes."

Barry led her back to the kitchen where he uncorked a bottle of Stag's Leap Cabernet.

"Oh, yeah. Yum."

"Not bad, huh?"

"So, lemme see. You're hypothesizing that, in some parallel universe or something, Melinda Tischman's murder is happening over and over somehow?"

"Not sure about the parallel universe thing, but look, every thought we have is energy. So think of the intense energy that's generated by an extreme emotional event like a murder. Einstein's theory proves that energy can't be created or destroyed, so then what happens to the energy of emotion after it's initially created?"

"More wine, please. This might take the whole bottle."

"Indeed." Barry poured her another glass and continued.

"In wave theory, normal destructive interference causes the wave energy to dissipate, right? But suppose that, as a result of an extreme traumatic event, there was a constructive interference that resulted in a kind of amplification that left some of the emotional energy lingering? And instead of dissipating as heat, like we would normally expect, it stuck around in some way that nobody has ever understood?"

"Wait wait wait. We just heard and saw some sort of replay of something that happened in nineteen freaking thirty-three. I mean, something is lingering for sure. So...?"

"So what if the particle is fixed and time is the wave? And what we call a ghost is some kind of quantum echo in time of an emotional experience."

"Works for me."

It was Barry's turn to laugh. "Well, there's an explanation for everything, even in the metaphysical world. We may never figure it out, but it exists. Hell, we haven't really even scratched the surface of quantum reality. What if whole life forms, us, for example, could interfere with ourselves and, in some form, stay alive years beyond our death?"

"This sounds like something you could spend the rest of your life working on."

"Yeah. And probably be banished to the fringes."

"If everyone saw what we just saw they'd have a pretty hard time just writing it off." Kelsey took a sip of wine and glanced toward the living room. "But why? Why Melinda Tischman? Why does she appear like that? I mean, there's the old thing that ghosts are trying to tell us something, but that just seems like a cliché movie idea."

"Well, let's think about it like this; If someone were actually trying to communicate, what's the source of the images we're seeing?"

"You lost me."

"I mean if there's intention, who's in control? What creates objective reality? What we see. The sounds we hear. Our own minds. If there's some sort of quantum echo of emotion that we're connecting to and its source is the victim, Melinda, wouldn't the images we're seeing be from her perspective? But if we're seeing her, maybe we're picking up on someone else's experience."

Kelsey poured them each more wine. "Okay, I see where you're going here. You're saying the ghost is Melinda Tischman, but the image of her is someone else's perspective. We're talking about someone who witnessed the murder."

"The observer."

"And they want us to see what they saw."

"Maybe. But, if so, it couldn't be Howard Tischman. He was, evidently, in the room stabbing his wife. I'd rather not see his perspective, thanks. And the mom was upstairs sleeping."

"Then, who?"

"Who, indeed?" Barry yawned. "I think the wine just caught up to me. I'm afraid I'm going to have to throw you out again, Kelsey. But this time I regret it."

"Me, too. Look, would you mind if I sort of did some more work on this? Just a little investigating?"

"You mean you want to bring your guys back? I don't think..."

"No, no. Not with the Ghost Hunters. Just on my own. You've got the closet physicist in me all buzzed again."

"You sure it's not the wine?"

"No. Can I call you in a few days, after I grovel for the network and straighten up the mess you've inflicted on me?"

"Sure. You ever been to the Athenaeum?" Barry was referring to the magnificent old club at Caltech with its ornate dining rooms and gardens.

"Huh uh. But I've always wanted to see it."

"Then how about if I take you to dinner?"

"Hell yes. God, I have this feeling I'm going to wake up in the morning, and I'll have dreamed this whole evening."

"You have my number if you need verification."

Barry showed her out and went back into his study, the murder room. He stared at his equations. It was late. He had an early class in the morning. Thermodynamics and Stats. He could teach it in his sleep. He picked up a piece of chalk.

KELSEY SPENT THE NEXT day on the phone putting out fires and calming network executives, finally coming to an agreement that they would shoot two episodes in the same week to make up for lost time. She was able to sell them a couple of backup locations that didn't require travel. When she got off the phone she dove into her computer to research the murder of Melinda Tischman in 1933. The online details were pretty basic. There seemed to be no specific motive for the murder. Howard Tischman signed a written confession the day he was arrested but offered no explanation as to why he wanted his wife dead. He refused to speak to police or testify at the trial in his own defense. The trial only lasted two days, with the guilty verdict arrived at in less than an hour.

Kelsey needed more information. She knew her best bet would be to read the actual transcripts of the trial. After a few calls to the county courthouse she found that, if it still existed, it would be in the Archives and Records Center.

She got lucky. Criminal trial transcripts went back as far as the year before the Tischman trial. The bored and lonely archivist sat at an ancient grey metal desk in a colorless basement wing that felt like a crypt. When Kelsey told her what she was looking for the archivist brightened up. The chance to dig so far back into history was exciting. After a lengthy search through stacks of records she proudly produced a roll of microfilm, apologizing that it hadn't yet been uploaded to their computer archives. Kelsey thanked her and took it to a fairly ancient microfilm reader in a stuffy windowless room with a few dusty tables and cold steel chairs.

To Kelsey's disappointment, the transcript wasn't proving to be very helpful. The prosecution's main witness was the lead detective, who didn't offer much except a straightforward description of the physical evidence in the case. He confirmed the ID of the knife used to murder Melinda Tischman, which had Howard Tischman's fingerprints on it. It was entered into evidence. The detective then described the actual act of the murder, based on the position of the body and the state of the furniture and objects in the room, some having been broken or knocked over during the attack. Then, of course, there was Howard Tischman's confession. When the police arrived at his house the morning after the murder, Howard presented them with a signed document that stated simply that he had killed his wife. That was it. From the moment he presented the confession to the police he did not utter another word related to the event. He wouldn't even converse with the court-appointed attorney assigned to his case. As a result, the attorney, who was actually very clever and who went on to be a famous trial lawyer, filed a plea of not guilty by reason of temporary insanity.

The defense called several of Howard Tischman's colleagues who all spoke of him in glowing terms and expressed their disbelief that he could be a murderer. They had all attended many social events with the Tischmans and had never witnessed anything but obvious affection between Howard and Melinda Tischman. Even their housekeeper, a Mrs. Edna Hinde, testified that the couple seemed to live in "very noticeable harmony."

The only minor squabble she'd ever overheard was an incident when Mrs. Tischman complained to Howard about his mother's overuse of her lavender perfume.

AT ABOUT 9:30 THAT night Barry Kaminsky was sitting at the tall table in his kitchen, sipping on a glass of gin and reading some student papers. There was a loud knock at his door. He carried his drink to the foyer and opened it. Kelsey grabbed his hand without saying a word and pulled him into the living room.

"Whoa, easy. This is expensive gin. What's going on?"

Kelsey looked at him with victorious eyes. "Howard Tischman was sitting in this chair when his wife was killed. He's here. He's the observer. It's his experience you've been reliving every night."

"What?"

"He didn't kill his wife. His mother killed her. Look."

She handed him a hard copy of the page of the trial transcript on which she had highlighted the housekeeper's testimony mentioning Estelle Tischman's lavender perfume.

"It's the smell in the room. His mother was in the room with Melinda, stabbing her to death. Howard was covering up for his mother."

Barry quickly read the bit of transcript.

"Wow." He put the drink down on a side table and sat on the arm of the leather chair, considering what Kelsey just laid out. "Yeah, okay. Makes sense. But why would his mom want her daughter-in-law dead?"

"She was a total whack job. I mean clinically insane. I did some more digging and found records of her being incarcerated in an asylum in upstate New York before Howard got the gig at Caltech and moved out here. She'd gone after his father with a garden hoe, cut him up pretty bad. Then she tried to burn a neighbor's house down."

"Holy crap."

"Howard sprung her and brought her out here with him. Maybe he thought she'd gotten better or something. God, it's so sad. His life was over. His wife was dead, and his crazy mother the murderer. And he watched her jam that knife into Melinda's back. But in spite of what she did, he couldn't send his mother to the electric chair. So he took the rap and then killed himself."

"Wow. I think you might have nailed it. Poor bastard."

"Yeah."

Barry was standing with his back to the double glass doors, facing Kelsey. She saw something behind him. The expression on her face changed from excitement to shock. Her eyes got wide. She took in a quick gasp.

He turned to see what she was looking at.

Standing behind the double glass doors was Estelle, Howard's mother. Her raven black hair and black floor-length dressing gown were barely visible in the darkness of the room so that her pallid face and hands seemed to be floating in the air. She was clutching a bloody knife and looking toward the doorway, not at them, but at some unseen presence on their side of the glass. There was a ghastly madness in her eyes.

The doors flew open. A blast of frigid air tinged with the smell of lavender whooshed into the room and almost knocked

Barry and Kelsey down. They regained their balance and stood there shivering, staring in rapt wonder at the grotesque apparition. Estelle lowered her hand and dropped the knife. She started to back up into the darkness of the room.

The doors then swung closed, hitting the door jams with a loud slam that echoed through the house. Barry and Kelsey jumped. The image of Estelle Tischman was gone. There was only empty darkness now beyond the glass panes. The smell of lavender dissipated, and it was quiet again. They both just stood there, not speaking, absorbing the fantastic experience.

Kelsey broke the silence.

"I'm kind of....woozy. You think Howard would mind if I sat in his chair?"

"I don't think so. My head's spinning a bit, too."

Kelsey sat. Barry took a chair nearby.

"My god, Barry. She was terrifying."

"Those eyes." He picked up his glass of gin, took a slug, and handed it to Kelsey.

She drained the glass. "Thanks. So, what just happened? Why was it...different? Why did we suddenly see Estelle like that? Before, it was only the image of Melinda. What made it change?"

"Yeah. I've been wondering that myself. Maybe, okay, so knowledge is thought, and thought is energy. Maybe our own knowledge of the truth is what changed it, somehow allowed us to connect to another part of the observer's experience. I don't know. We could probably make ourselves crazy, trying to figure it out."

Kelsey took a deep breath.

"I'm quitting the show."

"You serious?"

"I'm done. I could never consider it entertainment again. Not after this."

"The equation has been changed?"

"Exactly."

"I get it. I just hope I never have to see Estelle Tischman again. I'm going to shut down my computer, and then I suggest we head over to the Athenaeum and have some dinner."

"They have a bar, right?"

"Oh, yes, a very nice bar."

Barry went to the double doors, opened them, and walked into his office. He switched the light on. Kelsey joined him. As Barry headed to the desk with his computer, her gaze fell on the chalkboards.

"Wow. Speaking of the equation being changed, you've been busy."

Barry turned and looked at the boards. The math had been significantly modified. Symbols were scratched out and new ones written in their place.

Kelsey noticed that Barry had suddenly turned pale. "What the hell, Barry?"

He walked slowly across the room toward one of the boards and stopped. He studied it.

"Barry? Hello? What is it?"

He didn't answer right away. He moved to the next board, staring. He put his hands behind his head, locking his fingers.

"Barry? You're freaking me out here. What?"

"I didn't do this."

Kelsey looked at the boards again. This time she could see that, indeed, all the corrections were in a different hand. "Oh. Right. Then who did?"

Barry looked at her for a moment, then walked over to a bookcase. He removed an old leather-bound journal, laid it on a work table, and opened it to a page of notes and equations.

"This is one of Howard Tischman's original notebooks."

The script and form of Dr. Tischman's equations were exactly like the new symbols that graced Barry's chalkboards. Barry went back to the second board and focused on the end of the equation.

Kelsey examined the books and the boards. "God almighty. It's his writing. It's exactly the same."

She turned away from the journal and moved next to Barry. She studied the equation. She didn't have a clue what it meant. She recognized some of the symbols. Time. Distance. Energy. But there were some she had never encountered.

She looked at Barry. He was staring at the symbols with a look on his face somewhere between fear and wonder.

"What is it?"

"Not exactly sure yet. But I'd say there's a distinct possibility that our whole concept of reality just changed, big time."

They both stared at the chalkboard. Kelsey put her arm around Barry. He reciprocated.

"Dr. Kaminsky?"

"Yes, Ms. Laurents?"

"Take me to that very nice bar."

Origins

A sprig of Indian paintbrush, crimson and vibrant, protruded from the rocky soil like a small flame. An artistic eye might think that it had been the brush used to paint the rugged red desert mountains, rather than the long light of the summer sun just dipping over the ridge to the west.

The creature paid no heed to the delicate flower, crushing it with an ancient withered hand as it crept to the edge of the cliff. Something had stirred it from the shadow world, a scent in the wind, a sense of something long missing. It hunched beside a large rock and stared down at the trail below.

A group of ten school kids, on their way down the mountain from a nature hike, were stopped on the narrow trail, focused on one of their party. Sarah Llewelyn, a girl about nine, had fallen and skinned her knee on a sharp chunk of granite. Her skin was ripped enough that a fair amount of blood flowed, leaving a glistening deep red splotch on the rock. She was being tended to by a counselor, who produced a bandage from a kit and soon had the wound covered. Sarah winced from the pain, but she wasn't about to let the others see her cry. She was up quickly and back on track with the rest of the group. They continued down the mountain toward the trailhead.

Moments later, the creature was hovering over the rock that inflicted the damage to Sarah's knee. It sniffed like a hungry animal at the freshly spilled blood. Its pale dying human eyes lit up with a demonic glow. The sense of new life, renewed power, surged through the decrepit phantasm. It stared down the trail, watching the children disappear over a ridge.

AMELIA LLEWELYN WAS standing in a deep canyon, shivering, wrapped in a cloak of cold darkness. Her eyes were focused on a hillside in the distance. She was watching a small glowing form that was moving slowly upward, along a high ridge on the southern slope. Saguaro cacti grew in profusion on both sides of the canyon. The night sky was filled with large dark birds that were only visible as indistinct shapes fluttering against a starless void. They dove menacingly at her head, screaming at her like airborne banshees. She heard her daughter's desperate cry, echoing down through the canyon from far above.

"Mommy. Mommy."

She wanted to call out to her, but the words wouldn't form.

"Amelia! Amelia! Wake up!"

Ben was holding her shoulders, firmly, and gazing at her with a soothing smile.

"Hey. You're okay. It's me. You were dreaming."

Amelia looked around. She was standing by the front door to their New York brownstone on 65th Street.

"Where's Sarah?"

"She's in Arizona, honey. Remember? Science camp?

"Oh, shit. It happened again."

"Same dream?"

"Jesus, Ben, what the hell is going on with me?"

It was the third time it had happened. Three times in three nights. This was the furthest she'd gotten. The first two times Ben caught up to her in the hallway right outside their bedroom. These sudden somnambulistic events were bizarre, to say the least. Amelia was a woman of exceptional health, sound of mind, and not prone in any way to unusual behavior, psychological or physical. She was a staff hematologist at Mt. Sinai Hospital in New York City. Her husband, Ben, a district health liaison with the CDC, was just as surprised at these inexplicable occurrences as Amelia. They lived comparatively stress-free lives, had two healthy children, a twelve-year-old son, Zachary, and a nine-year-old daughter, Sarah.

Amelia looked down at the table next to the front door. On it lay a necklace of beads, what looked like turquoise interspersed with some kind of hard dried, shriveled berry. Amelia found it in the pocket of her hospital coat earlier that day. She had no idea where it came from. She picked it up.

"You think there's a connection?" Ben asked.

"What? No. Of course not."

"It is kind of weird, though. You have to admit."

"I think I'll have a glass of wine."

"Uh, at two o'clock in the morning?"

"I don't have to work tomorrow. Come on, where's your sense of adventure?"

"You may not have to work tomorrow, but I do."

"Call in drunk."

Ben laughed. They went into the kitchen and opened a bottle of prosecco.

Amelia took her glass and walked over to the window, gazing down on the street two floors below.

"Hey. Ben. Come here. Look. See that guy there, across the street?"

There was a tall man standing under a streetlight, staring up at their window. He was quite old, with long gray hair, a ragged sport coat, and a beat-up fedora.

"Yeah. He's looking up here."

"I've seen him before."

"Really. When?"

"A couple of times. Once on a subway platform. And another time on 8th Avenue. Both times I was sure he was staring at me."

"That's...weird. I'll go down and talk to him."

Amelia turned to him and grabbed him. "Wait. Maybe we should call the police."

Ben chuckled. "Come on. He looks ancient. I'll be fine."

Amelia looked back out the window. "Hold it. He's gone."

Ben joined her again. "Huh."

Just then a large black raven flew up to the window and hovered for a moment, staring in at them. Its sudden appearance caused them both to jump back. It screamed a hard, angry caw that rattled the window glass and flew off.

"Holy crap, Ben."

The phone rang, which startled them yet again.

"Jesus, what the hell is this?"

Amelia grabbed the phone.

"Hello. Yes it is."

"Hospital?" They were used to midnight calls from Mt. Sinai.

Amelia waved a hand for him to be quiet. "What? When? Oh my god. Well, is she okay?"

"What? Is it Sarah?"

Their son Zach walked in, sleepy. "What's going on? I heard a big noise."

Amelia put the phone against her chest for a moment.

"Hang on, Zach." She looked at Ben. "Yeah, it's Sarah. She's in the hospital in Tucson. But they say she's fine."

"Well if she's fine why is she in the hospital?"

Amelia heard a voice come back on and put the phone to her ear. "Okay. Yes. We'll be there as soon as we can. No, we'll take the first plane out in the morning. Can I talk to her? No, I want to talk to her, right now."

Ben was getting frantic. "Amelia, what the hell's going on? What happened to her?"

Zach was concerned for his sister. "Is Sarah sick?"

Amelia shook her head. "I don't know. They...they said they don't know. She...Sarah? Hi, baby. I know, I know. It's okay. Daddy and I are coming there. We'll be there tomorrow. Okay? I know honey. We love you. You're going to be fine. How do you feel? Well, see? If there was something bad wrong with you, you wouldn't feel fine, would you? That's right. So you just sleep tight and do what the doctors tell you, okay? Okay, honey. We'll be there tomorrow. We will. As soon as we can. I promise. We love you, baby. Okay, bye. We love you. Bye."

Amelia hung up the phone and looked at Ben.

Ben just held his hands up. What?

"They can't find anything wrong. But she's...glowing."

THE NEXT AFTERNOON they were standing next to Sarah's bed at the University of Arizona Hospital. Also, there was Dr. Wendy Martinez, a staff pediatrician, and Megan Willis, the program director for the Arizona Science Foundation summer science camp. Sarah had been at camp for a week, with one more week to go. She and sixty other kids were exploring the natural wonders of the high desert, learning about the flora and fauna, and studying astronomy at one of the wonderful observatories close by.

Amelia and Ben were avid outdoor types and had taken their kids into the wilderness numerous times. Sarah was particularly drawn to the desert and had found the science camp in Arizona on her own.

Sarah lay in the hospital bed, obviously uncomfortable with having so many people focused on her. She was, indeed, glowing. It was a subtle aura of light emanating from her pale skin. It was at once beautiful and alarming.

"I wanna go. Can I go now? You said I'm fine."

Amelia looked at Dr. Martinez, who shrugged. "I have no problem with releasing her. We've done a complete blood workup, and there's just nothing there, no red flags of any kind. We haven't got the PE back yet, but I doubt if it will show anything.

"What's a PE?" Ben asked.

Amelia fielded it. "Protein electrophoresis. It'll show up certain diseases." Amelia noticed the band-aid on Sarah's knee. "What happened to your knee, honey?"

"I fell and skinned it on a rock. It's okay."

Ben asked, "Could she have picked something up from that?"

Dr. Martinez shrugged. “That was over a week ago. It would have shown on the blood work. As far as I can tell, she’s perfectly healthy.”

“Okay, honey. The doctor has to do some paperwork, and then we'll take you to our hotel. Just be patient a little longer, okay?”

“You're not going to go away, are you?”

“No, we'll stay right here until you're ready.”

Sarah looked at Ms. Willis. “Can I go back to camp?”

Ms. Willis put her hand on Sarah's shoulder. “I hope so, Sarah.”

Ben and Zach stayed with Sarah while Amelia, the camp director, and the doctor went into the hallway to talk.

Amelia wanted some answers. She addressed Ms. Willis. “Okay, what happened to her?”

Ms. Willis shook her head. “I honestly don't have any idea. Sarah woke up in the middle of the night and went to Meredith's room—that’s her counselor. She woke her up and, well, Meredith was startled when she saw that Sarah was glowing like that. Sarah told her that there was a funny light in her room and a dog outside her window. The counselor took her back to her room. Her roommate, Emily, was pretty upset. Well, there was no light in Sarah's room other than the desk lamp they'd turned on.”

Dr. Martinez turned to Amelia. “Is Sarah prone to unusual dreams?”

“No. Never. And even if she was dreaming, how does that explain the glow?”

Nobody had an answer. Amelia went on. “What about the dog?”

"Yeah. The counselor asked her if the dog was on the lawn outside. Sarah said no, it was right outside the window." Ms. Willis paused, seemingly unsure of how to continue.

Amelia could see there was some sort of issue. "What?"

"Her room was on the third floor."

Dr. Martinez suggested that they don't travel right away or put Sarah through anything stressful since they didn't yet know what was causing the strange condition. She thought it would be best if they stayed on Tucson for a few days so they could monitor her.

Amelia agreed to the strategy and asked for a copy of the blood work they'd done so far that she could take with her.

Dr. Martinez offered that if they wanted to look at further medical options, they could consider a spinal.

The thought of putting her daughter through that made Amelia shudder. She said they'd just keep that option on the table for the time being.

A couple of hours later the family was settled into a suite at the Arizona Inn, a classic old hotel in downtown Tucson. They ordered a late lunch from room service and asked Sarah about science camp, trying to keep the conversation light and casual. They decided that downplaying Sarah's unusual problem was the best tack. But Sarah was well aware of the elephant in the room and was especially sensitive to Zach's reaction.

"Stop staring at me."

"Dude, you're glowing. How am I supposed to not stare at you?"

Amelia and Ben had discussed the possibility of sending Zach back home to stay with his grandparents. Ben's mother and father lived on New York's Upper Eastside and would be happy to take Zach. But they were scheduled to leave on a European vacation in a couple of days and upsetting their plans seemed extreme at this point.

"Hey, Zach," said Ben, "how about coming with me to the grocery store? I want to get some stuff for tonight."

After the two of them had left, Sarah asked, "What's wrong with me, Mom?"

"Don't know yet, honey. But nothing really bad, I'm sure. You know how it's my business to know when people are sick, right? Well, we can tell almost anything by looking at a person's blood, and your blood is fine. So don't worry, okay?"

"But the doctor said there's more tests they're doing. What if one of those is bad?"

"Hey, did you know that everyone glows?"

"No, they don't."

"Yeah, actually they do. The thing is, it's such a low-level glow, such a very very faint amount of light that we can't perceive it. So maybe there's some reason that your natural glow has suddenly just gotten brighter. You want something to drink? We've got some lemonade."

"Wish I was old enough to go to a rave. People would be totally freaked."

Amelia went to the small kitchenette and poured them each a glass. When she turned around, she saw that Sarah had fallen asleep on the couch. She got a blanket from the bedroom and covered her daughter. She sat for a while, just starring at her. There was something nagging at her. What is this? Why are you glowing, Sarah? She had an odd feeling that she should know the answer.

Later that evening, after they'd all eaten a dinner of take-out chicken and the kids were in their bedroom watching TV, Amelia stood at the window staring at the nearby mountains. It was sunset. The jagged peaks of the Santa Catalina range were bathed in amber light.

"Beautiful, isn't it?" Ben asked.

"I don't like this place."

"Really? Why?"

"I don't know. I was here once before, summer break from college. A bunch of us decided to go to L.A."

"The trip when you tried to surf and almost drowned?"

"Yeah. I got a creepy feeling driving through the desert back then. It was weird. It felt, I don't know, familiar, but not in a good way. And I feel it again now."

Just then, Amelia's phone rang. It was Dr. Martinez. The PE blood tests had come back. They showed no abnormalities. Amelia thanked the doctor for calling and told her she would get in touch if anything about Sarah's condition changed. She told Ben the results. She started pacing.

Ben poured them each a glass of wine. "Okay, what? That was good news, right?"

"I just wish it made me feel better."

"Look, if there's nothing showing up...maybe this is just one of those things we'll never be able to answer. There's just stuff in the world, you know? Mystery conditions. Didn't you say that you had some guy once who had a blood type you couldn't even identify?"

"Yeah, but I have a feeling there's something more to this, Ben. I wish I could explain what I mean. But I don't like it."

Ben went to the kitchen to pour a glass of wine and noticed that Amelia had emptied her purse of some of its contents. One of the items on the counter was the necklace of beads she'd found in her hospital gown.

"You brought the beads. How come?"

"I don't really know. We were leaving and I just grabbed them. I kind of think they're cool. Aren't they kind of cool?"

"Yeah. They're kind of cool."

Amelia went to the kids' room and peeked in. They were both sleeping soundly. The glow from Sarah's face cast faint eerie shadows on the walls. Sarah had fallen asleep reading. Amelia carefully moved the book to the bedside table. As she did so, she noticed that the glow was almost bright enough to read by.

Sarah's eyes flickered open. "Zach called me a night-light."

"Shhh. Go to sleep." She bent down and kissed Sarah on her forehead. When she did so, she felt an odd tingling sensation in her lips. It startled her. She quickly but quietly left the room and told Ben what just happened.

"Go kiss her. I want to know if you feel it."

Ben went into the bedroom. He came back out and shook his head.

"I didn't feel anything."

"Christ, this is starting to make me crazy. I'm going to go for a walk."

Ben didn't make a big deal of it, but it was unusual to see Amelia rattled like this. Walking was a good idea. It was her meditation. She'd often go for long walks in New York, even late at night. Neither one of them had ever felt that New York was as frightening as the media like to paint it. But they weren't careless, either. Amelia had taken several self-defense courses just in case.

"Okay. If you see a liquor store, get us another bottle of wine."

"Good idea." She grabbed a light jacket, gave him a quick kiss and headed out.

Walking the streets of Tucson was like being on another planet. There was nobody out, only the occasional car passing by, and a disconcerting quiet. She was used to a vibrant, noisy city, even late at night. She walked about six or seven blocks and found herself at the edge of the University of Arizona. She headed into the campus, following an attractive row of lights lining a path through the quad. She stopped. Perched on top of one of the lights was a large raven. It was staring down at her. The huge blackbird was perfectly still, its glistening dark eyes focused right on her. Without a sound, it spread its wings, leaped off the pole, swooped low and flew past Amelia and down a dim pathway between two buildings. Two strange encounters with a raven. One in New York and, now, one here. Amelia's brain was trying hard to perceive it as just a coincidence. It wasn't working. She followed the mysterious blackbird.

The path opened up again on the other side of the buildings, becoming a circular walk around a stand of trees. Once again, she stopped in her tracks. There was a man standing in the middle of the trees. Very old, long gray hair, weathered fedora hat, and a raggedy sport coat. He took his hat off and made a little bow to her.

Amelia walked up to him. "Who are you?"

The old man stared into her eyes. She felt as if he was looking right through her. He spoke in a soft, nonthreatening voice that had the distinctive sound of a Native American.

"She is coming for your daughter."

"What? How do you know about my daughter?"

"She waits for the new moon. Then she will call her."

Amelia felt like she'd just fallen down a rabbit hole.

"What are you talking about?"

"The yee naaldlooshiii. Your daughter's blood will revive her powers, make her strong again."

"I have no idea what you're talking about."

"You and your daughter have the blood of the old ones."

"The old ones?"

"Your ancestors. The Sazi."

"This is crazy. I don't know who you are, but I don't have any Sazi ancestors, whatever those are. You're wrong."

Just then, a college couple entwined in each other's arms and laughing with alcohol-induced attitude burst out of a dorm behind Amelia. They startled her, and she spun around to look. The hammered couple saw her and waved, semi-apologetically. When she turned back, the old man was gone. She didn't see him anywhere. She called to the students.

"Hey, did you guys see where the old man went?"

"Uh, old man? Sorry, didn't see him."

"She's drunker than we are." Their laughter faded into the night.

Amelia now stood alone on the shadowy campus, her mind reeling with questions. She felt like she was lost in some ghostly dreamscape where any direction she looked was another mystery. What happened to Sarah? Why did she feel so strange about being here in Arizona? Who was the old man? How did he know about Sarah? What did he mean she had the blood of the Sazi?

She needed to get back to Ben. She started jogging, re-tracing her path back to the main streets of Tucson. As she ran, she passed a Native American art gallery. She stopped to look at a print in the window that was labeled Anasazi Ruins, Mesa Verde. Sazi. Of course. She remembered enough of her American history to know of the ancient tribe. She realized it must be what the old man was referring to. But she still didn't have any idea what it had to do with her.

When she got back to the hotel room, she plopped a grocery bag down on the counter and pulled out a bottle of Irish Whiskey.

"Irish? Uh oh. Something happened."

"Yes."

Ben grabbed two glasses, led her to the couch, and poured two shots.

"Okay, what's up, Doc?"

And so she told him. They spun scenarios for the next three hours before deciding to stick with what they knew.

Amelia had been adopted. It was not something that played any kind of emotional role in her life. Her adoptive parents were her heroes. They were both doctors and had each worked extensively for Doctors Without Borders. It was how they met. They were attending a conference at the World Trade Center on 9-11 when Amelia was in college. Their deaths were a crushing blow.

Unlike a lot of people, Amelia didn't care about her birth parents, or what that history was all about. She felt strongly that you are the child of those who raise you. What her parents did tell her was that records had shown that her mother was Portuguese, hence her black hair and dark complexion. But now a strange old Native American man was telling her she has Anasazi blood. And that fact, if it were a fact, was somehow connected to what happened to Sarah. Amelia wanted some answers.

The next morning she walked into the Arizona State Museum on the UA campus, the largest anthropology museum in the American Southwest, and asked if she could speak with someone familiar with the Anasazi. She was directed to the office of a curator, Becky Natani. Ms. Natani was about ten years older than Amelia, with long black hair and the beautiful dark almond-shaped eyes of the Navajo. What startled Amelia was how alike they looked. But she thought that, given how rattled she was by all that was happening, her mind could be playing tricks on her. Being this kind of shaken was an entirely new feeling for her, so she didn't know whether she could trust her own judgment.

After friendly introductions, Becky asked, "So, Amelia, you're Navajo, right?"

"Uh, no. I'm actually Portuguese."

Becky seemed taken aback. "Really. That's interesting. Okay. Please, sit. Well, how can I help you?"

"I was speaking to an older man, a Native American, yesterday who mentioned the Anasazi. And he spoke about something...I may not get this exactly right...called the ay nalooshi or something? Does that mean anything to you?"

"The yee naaldlooshii. Skinwalkers. A Navajo legend. Skinwalkers are supernatural beings, sort of like witches. They're shapeshifters. It's said they can assume animal form and take over another human's body. Pretty powerful stuff in the old world of Navajo beliefs. Who was this old man?"

"I don't know. We just sort of struck up a conversation in a park." Amelia wasn't going to get into the story of Sarah and how she really encountered the old man. Not just yet. "What do these skinwalkers do?"

"The usual witch things. Put curses on people. Gain power over others and have them do their bidding."

"Right. Okay, thanks. Sorry to have taken up your time. Nice meeting you."

Amelia started to get up, but Becky put her hand gently on Amelia's arm.

"Look, Amelia, I'm not sure why you're in denial about your ancestry, or what's going on with this old man. That's your business. But I'll tell you, I can see very clearly that you're Navajo, and I can tell you're upset about something. If you ever want to confide in someone, I won't judge you. Here's my card. Don't hesitate to call. The skinwalker thing, well, it's generally thought of as superstition, of course. But just be careful."

Becky's words left Amelia rattled. On her way out of the museum, she saw a photograph of some sort of Navajo ceremony. Standing next to a fire, there was a man wearing a sport coat and a fedora. She went back to the office and asked Becky if she'd come look at the photo.

"Do you know who that man is?"

"No. But I know someone who probably would. You want me to find out?"

"Would you mind?"

"Is it the old man you spoke to?"

"I think maybe it is, yeah."

"No problem. Call the museum tomorrow, and I let you know if I've got anything."

When Amelia got back outside, she sat on the steps of the museum, caught her breath and called Dr. Martinez.

"Amelia, hi. How's Sarah doing?"

"She seems fine, so far. Look, I need a favor."

"What can I do?"

"The University has a lab that does genetic ancestry testing, doesn't it?"

"Yeah, one of the best in the world."

"Can you get me in there today?"

"Okay, that's maybe the most mysterious request I've ever had."

"I know. Sorry. I'll explain, I promise. But I really need to get some info asap."

"Okay. Let me put you on hold for a minute while I make a call."

Two hours later, Amelia was having blood drawn by Dr. Jung, a gregarious young researcher in the human origins genetic lab at the University.

"Dr. Martinez says you're a hematologist."

"Yeah. I work in New York."

"Hey, we're gonna be neighbors. I just took a research job at NYU. Can't wait to get out of the desert."

"I don't blame you. Not my favorite climate. How long will it take to run the test?"

"I'll need four or five hours. We usually do a cheek swab, but with a blood sample, I can do it faster and a lot more accurately. Dr. Martinez said you were in a hurry. Can I ask what the rush is? I mean, I have a feeling you're not looking to snag a reservation card."

"No. There's a chance it's relevant to a medical condition my daughter has."

"Any particular tribe?"

"Anasazi."

"Whoa. Didn't see that coming. I don't think there are any bloodlines left from the Anasazi."

"Really. I didn't know it was...how close can you get to a particular tribe?"

"We can get pretty accurate. The autosomal test will break it down into one of five different canonical haplogroups. We'll run 25 markers and look for a single nucleotide in your DNA sequence. We can match that up to a pretty specific geographic origin."

"Is there any chance you wouldn't recognize the marker?"

"No. Even if it shows up as a previously unknown, we'll see it as indigenous. Leave your number, and I'll call you as soon as I can."

It was lunchtime when she got out of the genetics lab. She called Ben and met him and the kids at a big, busy Mexican food restaurant. Sarah was nervous about being out in public, so she wore a hoodie, keeping her gaze down and her face as hidden as possible. She wanted to know why her mom had been gone so long.

"I was doing some research to see if I could find out what might have happened to you."

"Did you find out anything?"

"Not yet. But don't worry, honey. We'll figure it out."

Zach chimed in. "I wish I glowed."

Sarah looked up for the first time.

"No, you don't."

"Yeah. I do. I think it's cool. Seriously."

Amelia and Ben glanced at each other. They'd never been so proud of their son.

"Okay," said Ben, "Let's have us a big old Mexican feast. Who wants chips and guacamole?"

"Two orders," said Sarah.

A little while later, Amelia glanced over at a window. The old Navajo man was standing outside at the edge of the parking lot. Her heart jumped. She didn't want to let on anything was up. She excused herself and slipped out of the restaurant. Fortunately, the kids were focused on the chips and guac.

As Amelia approached him she saw that he was holding a small leather packet and a knife in a beaded scabbard.

"It's the new moon. She'll come for your daughter tonight. You will need these."

He handed her the packet and the knife.

"Who'll come for her? The skinwalker?"

"You will have to face her. This is ash from the bones of your tribe. The knife dipped into the ash is your only weapon. And the necklace. You should wear it."

"Why my daughter? Why doesn't she come for me?"

"Young blood is more powerful."

Amelia heard a commotion from the restaurant. She saw that something was happening at their table.

"Oh my god." She ran for the restaurant.

When she got inside, she found Ben clutching onto Sarah, who was crying profusely. Two police officers, whom they'd seen at a nearby table when they came in, were trying to calm a wild-eyed old Native American woman.

Zach was on his feet, yelling at her. “Leave my sister alone!”

Amelia pulled him back. “Zach! Ben, what’s going on?”

“That old woman was walking by and suddenly just stopped and pointed at Sarah and started sort of railing in some language. No idea what she was saying.”

“Let's get out of here.” The old woman continued to rant as Amelia hustled her family out of the restaurant.

As they got in their car, Amelia scanned the parking lot. The old man had vanished. Again.

Back at the hotel, they ordered an enormous meal from room service. Sarah was still shaken, but Ben started making growling animal noises and tearing into the food like a hyena. This got both of the kids laughing and pulled Sarah out of her upset from the restaurant event. When they had finished with the main course, he declared this a national family holiday and called down for a sampling of six different desserts. An hour later, both kids were slumped in front of the TV in their bedroom, their stomachs bulging.

Amelia told Ben about her encounter with the old man outside the restaurant. She showed him the knife and the sack of white bone ash.

Ben shook his head. “Weirder and weirder.”

“I'll say. Look, he said that this skinwalker was going to come for her tonight.”

“You believe him?”

“No, of course not. It's all superstition. But it still worries me. I'm thinking, let's just get back home. I'm not worried about Sarah getting on a plane.”

"You mean now? Tonight?"

"Yeah."

"Okay. I'll see if we can get a flight."

Ben spent the next hour and a half on the computer trying to book them back to New York that evening. No good. The best he could do was a noon flight the next day. Amelia's phone rang. It was Dr. Jung from the genetics lab.

"You're an Indian. Came up with a positive for haplogroup B4'5, which we identify directly with Native American DNA. I did some more research and found some studies on Anasazi bones I didn't know about. You're a match. The B4'5 group is also shared by Hopi and Navajo, but it's pretty likely you can consider yourself a descendant of the Anasazi."

Amelia thanked him and hung up. It was what she was expecting, but it still seemed so odd.

"Jesus, Ben. I'm a freaking hematologist, and now I discover I don't even know my own blood."

"You think your parents knew?"

"I kind of doubt it. I don't think they would have covered up something like that. It's not who they were. I think they just believed what they were told."

"So someone falsified your birth papers. Maybe they were trying to protect you."

"From what?"

"Skinwalkers?"

"I need to talk to the woman from the museum again. You okay here with the kids for a while?"

"Sure. You go. I've got a bunch of work to do."

Amelia called Becky Natani, who suggested they meet at six at her favorite wine bar.

On her way out of the hotel room she saw the bead necklace lying on the counter. She put it on.

As they sipped on a couple of glasses of very tasty Oregon pinot noir, Amelia filled Becky in on everything that had happened.

"This is serious business, Amelia. I know that you...well, all of us in the scientific world...we consider things in rational scientific ways. We just chalk stuff like this up to superstition. But, trust me, you can't take any of this lightly. There's a lot of power in these ancient beliefs. They have a way of...I don't even know quite how to say it...sort of creating their own reality. Where did you get that necklace?"

"I found it in my gown at the hospital in New York. No idea how it got there. But the old man told me to wear it. You know what it is?"

"They're called ghost beads. Dried juniper berries, actually. A ghost bead necklace is said to provide protection from evil spirits."

"Ghost beads. Jesus, Becky. I feel like we stepped into some kind of parallel universe the minute we got here. There's something else. The old man gave me a knife and a bag of what he said was ash from the bones of the Anasazi." She started to pull them from her purse, but Becky stopped her.

"No. Leave them. I don't want to see. I mean, it's probably best if I don't. If it ends up being actually useful, better that it doesn't have any other energies attached to it."

"What kind of energies? What do you mean?"

"To tell you the truth, it frightens me. The old man who gave that to you? I tracked him down. He's a Navajo medicine man. From everything you've told me, it looks like he's trying to help you, to protect you and your daughter."

"From the skinwalker."

"Yes. I know this is hard to get your head around, but for the knife and the ash to be useful to you, you need to believe in it, just as he does. If anyone else were to pass judgment on it, it could weaken your belief, and that might be harmful."

"Harmful how? What am I supposed to use the ash and the knife for?"

"I have no idea. Look, I've known of people in our culture who took their own lives because they believed they'd been cursed. Like I said, these beliefs create their own very powerful reality. There have been many sightings, even by non-Native Americans, of what fit the description of skinwalkers."

"Okay, wait. Actual skinwalkers? What did they look like?"

"Coyotes, some other animals, like sheep. They are described as animals, but sometimes walking upright like humans, with human eyes."

"You believe that?"

"I don't know. But there's something else. When I was a kid, we heard a story about a baby that had been taken away from one of the tribes up north. They said her mother was descended from the original peoples. The Anasazi. They say the curse of the skinwalker originated with the Sazi. The story was that the child's mother had died when it was born. Not long after, a skinwalker entered the home of the mother's aunt, who was caring for the baby. It was the middle of the night. The creature tried to kidnap it. A neighbor's dog alerted her to the intruder, and the skinwalker fled. But the aunt was so frightened by the experience that she took the child a long way away and gave it up for adoption."

"You think that I'm that child."

"Maybe. You're the right age."

The bartender came over to their table. "Can I get you ladies anything else? It's last call."

Amelia was perplexed. "Excuse me? Last call? But it's what...seven?"

It was the bartender's turn to be perplexed. "Uh, well, actually it's midnight."

Amelia noticed Becky had a strange look on her face. She was staring out a window. Amelia looked. It was dark out. A large raven was perched on top of a fence railing, staring in at them.

"What the hell?"

Becky took Amelia's hand. "It's okay. We can deal."

Amelia's phone rang. It was Ben.

"Jesus, Amelia, what's going on? I've been calling you."

"What? I don't know Ben, something..."

"Sarah's gone."

Amelia just sat silently for a few seconds, trying to process what she heard.

"Hello? Amelia?"

"What do you mean she's gone?"

"I went to check on her about an hour ago, and she was just gone. The door to the suite was unlocked."

"Shit, Ben! Where were you? How could she have left?"

"I wasn't anywhere. I mean, I was here. I have no idea. I was working and somehow time just...I don't know. It was like it was suddenly three hours later. I've checked with the hotel, nobody saw her."

"I'm on my way."

By the time she hung up, Becky had laid money out for the tab. She looked at Amelia with a serious resolve.

"Let's go. I'll drive. And I'll stay with you. You're going to need help with this."

When Amelia and Becky got back to the hotel room, there were two uniformed Tucson police officers talking to Ben. Amelia was trembling. Ben grabbed her and held her.

"I'm so sorry. I can't believe I let this happen."

"It's not your fault, Ben. The time thing...it happened to us in the bar."

SEVERAL MILES AWAY, on the northeast edge of town, John Cardona was pulling into his driveway. John was a lawyer. He'd been at his office late, prepping for a big court date in the morning. His house was in a fairly exclusive area at the base of Crooked Stick Canyon. He had a spectacular view of Tucson to the south and west and a gorgeous view of the mountains to the north and east. The majestic saguaro cacti that made the Sonoran Desert unique started at the back edge of his property and spread up the hills behind his house. He parked his car in the carport and happened to glance up the hill to the north. He stopped when he saw a strange light on the side of the mountain. From his calculations, it seemed to be coming from the trail on the north edge of Crooked Stick Creek. The light was moving slowly up the edge of the canyon. He thought at first it must be a night hiker with a flashlight. But the light was wrong.

It wasn't a beam. It was a glow. He wasn't sure what he was looking at. He went into the house and got a pair of night vision binoculars he and his wife used to watch wildlife in the dark. His wife, Tessa, came back out with him. He focused on the strange glow.

"Holy cow. I think that's a person. So weird. Take a look."

Tessa took the glasses. "Oh shit, John. It's the girl."

"What girl?"

"They just interrupted the Late Show. The police are looking for a nine-year-old girl who disappeared from The Inn earlier tonight. Her name was Sarah something. They said she had this glow."

"Seriously?"

"I know. It's weird, huh."

"God almighty. If that's a kid, she's in big trouble up there. The coyotes and pigs will...I gotta get up there. You call the cops."

Tessa ran inside to call. Cardona quickly threw on some trail shoes he had in the garage and a field jacket. He grabbed a high powered flashlight and started running for the trail head. He was in very good shape and an avid hiker. He knew Crooked Stick. It was his back yard. He'd hiked these trails scores of times. He could move as fast as the terrain allowed. But it was a new moon and the night was exceptionally dark. The canyon path was fraught with twists and turns and dangerous drop-offs.

John moved as quickly as he could. The saguaro cacti loomed over the trail, dark giant ghosts, their arms raised like strange aliens paying homage to the starry sky. As he ran, he heard emergency sirens in the distance. He started calling

Sarah's name, not just in hopes that she would answer but also to scare off any predators that might be stalking her. He came to a precarious part of the trail where it took a sharp drop. It required some nimble moves to climb down a stack of large jagged boulders. He grabbed onto a rock ledge and was about to lower himself to the next foothold when two coyotes suddenly jumped into view on the trail below him. They were snarling viciously. He froze.

The eyes.

He'd seen coyote eyes at night before, many times. These were different. He couldn't figure out what he was looking at. He kept his light shining on their faces, hoping it would keep them somewhat blinded. If they couldn't focus clearly on him, they might not make a move. He backed off slowly, backtracking on the trail. He looked for something to defend himself with and found a stout broken branch.

He knew that it was rare for coyotes to attack humans, but there were two of them, and maybe more he couldn't see. In packs, they were unpredictable and frightening. He backed up a few more yards. The snarling stopped. He kept the flashlight focused on the spot where the trail disappeared over the boulders.

Any other time he'd just get the hell back home as fast as possible. But he couldn't leave the girl out there alone. He weighed his options. Trying to go forward again wouldn't be at all smart. Even if the coyotes weren't on the trail anymore, they certainly weren't far away. They knew he was here. Then he had a thought that turned his stomach. He wondered, since they didn't come after him, if they were protecting a kill. If they knew he was here, they certainly knew Sarah was out here as well. He felt nauseous. He heard voices some distance behind him and saw the beams of several flashlights. His cell phone rang.

"Mr. Cardona, this is Matt Ferris, Tucson Fire, and Rescue. Can you tell us your position?"

"I'm on the East Crooked Stick Canyon trail, about a half-mile up. I was just stopped in my tracks by a couple of coyotes."

"Do you have a weapon?"

"No."

"Okay, stay put, we'll be there asap."

"I can see your lights."

"Any sign of the girl?"

"No. I've been calling, but there's been no answer."

" Try to find a high spot to protect yourself."

"Okay."

The whole time he was on the phone, John kept shining his flashlight all around, looking for the coyotes. But they didn't show. He thought it was strange, almost as if their intention was just to prevent him from going forward along the trail. And he kept thinking about those eyes.

He was looking around for a high point to climb to when he saw the glow again. But it was on the other side of the canyon now, higher up the mountain. It seemed impossible. A nine-year-old girl couldn't possibly have gone from his side of the canyon, across the creek, and all the way to that position in that amount of time. There weren't any trails or bridges across the creek. It was completely crazy. He grabbed his phone and immediately called Matt Ferris.

"Look up the hill across the creek, about two o'clock."

There was a pause. "Good god. How the hell did she get up there? Are you sure you saw her on your side?"

"Positive. I know these trails."

The sound of a helicopter approaching filled the night.

"Mr. Cardona, it looks like we're going to have to change course. But I'm sending a couple of guys to assist you getting back down."

"Okay, thanks."

John watched the helicopter as it headed up the far side of the canyon. The glowing figure was now moving up the Mesa Cave trail, a steep trail that branched off of the main track. The copter turned on its brilliant Nightsun spotlight. The beam made a bright golden circle on the mountain side. It was getting close to Sarah. Then, suddenly, the light went out. John wondered why they would turn it off.

A couple of minutes later two Fire and Rescue guys showed up. They introduced themselves as Reyes and Garman. Cardona asked them why the copter turned off its spotlight.

"They didn't," answered Reyes. "It just went out. Some sort of malfunction."

"There's some bad timing."

"Copy that. Come on, let's get outta here before those coyotes show up again."

It took about ten minutes to get back down. Reyes took Cardona to the Fire Chief who was standing with Amelia and Ben. Becky Natani had volunteered to stay at the hotel with Zach while they went after Sarah.

"I'm Chief Fallon, Mr. Cardona. These are the girl's parent, Dr. and Mr. Llewellyn."

Ben reached out and shook Cardona's hand. "We can't thank you enough, Mr. Cardona. You may have saved our daughter's life."

Amelia jumped in. "Did you see Sarah? Did you talk to her?"

"I'm sorry, no. Where's she going?"

"I wish we knew."

"I kept calling her name. I thought I was catching up to her, but a couple of coyotes blocked my path, and I had to stop. Then I saw her on the other side of the canyon, so the coyotes obviously didn't know she was there."

Amelia said, "They know."

Ben looked at her. "Amelia? Talk to me."

Amelia didn't answer. She just stared up the canyon at the distant glow that was moving further and further away.

Just then the helicopter passed overhead. The Nightsun was back on. They watched as it headed back up the canyon. A Fireman in rescue gear approached the chief.

"The point squad is about a third of the way up the trail."

"Good."

"Not really, sir. They've been stopped."

"Stopped? By what?"

"Coyotes. About twenty of them, they estimate."

"Jesus H. Christ. What the hell is going on?"

"Sorry to interrupt, Chief," said John, "but those coyotes who stopped me...well, I had the weird feeling they were intentionally preventing me from moving forward. Soon as I backed off, they disappeared."

"I have no idea what to make of that, sir."

The Fireman added, "The crew has a couple of rifles, but there's a lot of coyotes, and they don't want to start shooting and scare the girl."

"Right. Well, tell them to back off while we figure something out."

"Yes, sir."

Amelia pulled her gaze away from the canyon and looked at John Cardona. "You know these trails, right?"

"Yes, real well."

"What's up there? Where could our daughter be going?"

"That trail she's on now leads to Mesa Cave, about three-quarters of the way up the ridge. It's sort of an unofficial monument. It's kind of famous for some ancient Native American relics they found there a long time ago."

Amelia looked back up the canyon. "Oh, God."

Ben was rattled. "What is it, honey?"

She ignored him and moved her gaze back to Cardona. "Was there anything else strange about the coyotes?"

Cardona hesitated.

"Please. It's our daughter."

"Well, yeah. Their eyes were...different. I mean, they didn't exactly look like coyote eyes."

"Did they look human?"

He didn't answer right away. The conversation had taken a turn into an area he wasn't comfortable with at all. Amelia was staring at him as if she already knew the answer.

"It was a pretty tense situation. I couldn't swear."

Ben looked at his wife. "Amelia? What the hell is it?"

"Skinwalkers."

The Fire Chief, who wasn't far away, overheard and glanced at her.

"Honey, come on. Just because some crazy old Indian man..."

"One of them has taken Sarah, or has her under a spell or something."

A couple of hours ago she'd written this kind of stuff off as obvious superstition. Ben was irritated by his wife's sudden reversal.

"Oh, come on, Amelia."

"Listen to me, Ben. Just put it all together. Sarah's glowing. No medical explanation. She said she saw a big dog outside her window. On the third floor. Sarah doesn't lie, you know that. And she wasn't lying. What she saw was a skinwalker. Like the coyotes, Mr. Cardona just saw. And tonight's the new moon, just like the old man said. Believe me, I've tried to write it off, too. But I feel it, Ben. I know it's the truth."

"Okay, look, say for a minute you're right. Why do they want Sarah?"

"I'm not sure. But Sarah has the blood of the original people. Like me. We're Anasazi. And, according to Becky, the skinwalker curse originally comes from our people."

Just then the helicopter came flying back over them, heading out of the area. The fire chief came up to them.

"The Nightsun went out on the copter again. They're gonna try to get another one down here from Phoenix."

Amelia addressed the fire chief. "Don't bother. It's not going to work. I have to get up there. I'm the only one who has any chance of saving my daughter."

Ben was having none of it.

"No way, Amelia. You can't go..."

"Stop, Ben. Please. You have to trust me. I know what I'm doing."

"There's a huge pack of coyotes ready to..."

"They won't stop me."

The Fire Chief interrupted. "Sorry, ma'am, but I can't allow you to go up there. It's way too dangerous. I don't know what's going on, and I guess you have some ideas yourself, but..."

"Listen to me. All of you. You think our nine-year-old daughter just decided to sneak out of the hotel and go climb a mountain in the middle of the night? Somebody is doing this to her, and they're up on that mountain, and unless I get up there, there's a good chance she won't survive."

The Chief tried to calm her. "Mrs. Llewelyn, I'm gonna send some men up there with more rifles, and we'll get through those coyotes."

"No, you won't. Chief, get on your radio and tell your men to shoot one of the coyotes. Right now."

"What is this about...?"

"Just do it."

"Please don't be offended, ma'am, but since there's some potential serious risk to your daughter, I'm gonna need both her parents to sign off on this." He looked at Ben.

Ben realized that his wife was deadly serious. Amelia was the most reasonable, rational person he knew. If she felt this strongly about what she was saying, as hard as it was to believe, he had to trust that there was something in it. He nodded to the chief.

The Chief shook his head, and reluctantly pulled out his radio.

"You there, Sean?"

A voice came over the radio. "Yeah, I'm here, Chief."

"You the best shot up there?"

"DM in Iraq, sir."

"Shoot one of those coyotes."

"Uh, there's about twenty of them up here, Chief."

"Yeah, I know. Just go ahead and shoot one of them."

Half a mile up the mountain, Fire, and Rescue Lieutenant Sean Cavenaugh was trying to figure out the peculiar nature of the order from the Chief. It didn't make sense to him, but an order was an order. "Okay, Chief."

Cavenaugh and seven of his fellow fire and rescue guys were hunkered down along the side of the trail in a cluster of boulders and saguaros. Above them, where the trail made sharp switchback as it wound up the mountain, about twenty coyotes glared down at them.

Cavenaugh moved to one of the guys who was holding a rifle. "Gimme that, Donny."

"Focus your beams on that coyote down the end there."

They focused their lights on the one coyote. Cavenaugh sighted it in with the rifle and fired. The shot echoed through the night and down the canyon like thunder.

The coyote didn't flinch.

"What the hell." He aimed and fired again. Still, the coyote was unharmed. It raised its snout to the night sky and let out some chilling high-pitched yelps. The other coyotes joined it, as if they were mocking the humans below.

Cavenaugh got on the radio. "Chief. Yeah, I, uh, I shot him twice, but nothing happened. I mean, I don't know how I could have missed, but...hell, I don't get it."

Back at the base camp, the Chief listened to the message from Cavenaugh and looked at Amelia.

She simply said, "It has to be me, Chief."

He spoke into the radio. "Okay, Mac. Just sit tight." Then, to Amelia, he said, "I have a whole lot of questions I'd like to ask you, Mrs. Llewelyn, but there's obviously not enough time. And I'm not sure I want to know the answers anyway. You know that trail?"

"No."

"I do," said Cardona. "I'll take her."

"That all right with you, ma'am?" asked the Chief.

"Yes."

"I'm going, too," said Ben.

Amelia took her husband's hands in hers. "You can't. I have to know you'll be here for Zach, in case..."

"In case what? I'm not just staying here while you..."

"Sarah's life depends on this, Ben. You have to trust me."

"Okay. I know. Just...bring both of you back."

She kissed him. She opened her bag and took out the knife and sack of white ash the old man had given her. She nodded to Cardona, and they headed up the trail.

The Chief looked at Sarah's father. "You sure you're good with this, Mr. Llewelyn?"

Ben shook his head. "I'm not good with any of this, Chief."

On their way up the south trail, Amelia pushed Cardona to move fast. He was being careful for her sake, but when he saw how nimble and strong she was, he doubled their pace. When they arrived at the point where the Fire and Rescue guys were gathered, Lieutenant Cavenaugh handed her his radio. "The

Chief wants to talk to you. Just push this to talk, let go to listen."

Amelia took the radio. "Hello?"

"Mrs. Llewelyn, keep a radio with you. Lieutenant Cavenaugh will show you how to set it so it's open for two-way com. Just keep it on the whole time so we can follow you."

"All right."

"Your husband wants to talk to you."

"Amelia? I just...I love you."

"I love you, Ben."

Amelia handed to radio to Cavenaugh. He adjusted it then clipped it to her belt. "Okay, you're all set."

"Where are the coyotes?"

"Up on that switchback. As soon as you make a move out there, you'll see them. You should take a rifle with you." He turned to one of the other firemen who handed him the gun. He turned back to hand it to Amelia, but she was gone.

It was pitch black on the side of the canyon. Amelia's flashlight barely made a dent, as if its beam were being smothered by some dark force. She climbed up a short embankment onto the trail. Twenty pairs of glowing, demonic eyes appeared above and in front of her. Human eyes, on the faces of coyotes. Murderous sharp white teeth seemed to reflect more light than was available. The snarling turned to a cacophony of different cries: yipping, howling, and yelps that grew louder and louder. It was a terrifying, unearthly clamor.

Amelia knew this was only the beginning. It was going to get much worse. Fear, hesitation, disbelief, she knew she had to bury it all right at the start. She made it to the top of the switchback and, as Cardona described, this section of the trail was fairly flat. The flashlight went out. She wasn't surprised. Her eyes had adjusted to the darkness, and the trail wasn't hard to follow. She considered holding onto the flashlight and using it as a weapon if necessary. But if bullets didn't even work...she tossed it aside and pushed forward. Her brain struggled to ignore the relentless, preternatural din of the skinwalkers.

She forced herself to focus on Sarah, keeping the image of her daughter at the front of her mind. After about fifty feet, the coyotes descended fast and closed in on her. They didn't attack. But they ran circles around her, leaping from rocks in front of and behind her. She was in the middle of a nightmarish maelstrom of savage sound and frenzied movement. She kept seeing glimpses of human forms mixed in with the coyotes, people wearing coyote skins. She was dizzy. It was a wrenching mind battle to concentrate and keep moving. Sarah, Sarah, Sarah.

The coyotes suddenly disappeared into the rocks and brush of the mountain. She stopped for just a moment. The relief from the onslaught was unbelievable. And she didn't believe it. Not for a second. She had to take this opportunity to get as far up the trail as she could. She increased her pace.

She got another several hundred feet when she felt a hot sticky wind kick up. Her head started to spin. Her vision blurred, and her whole body went numb. She staggered, thinking she might pass out. She stooped over with her hands on her knees, taking deep breaths. The air she was sucking in was sour and wet. She finally managed to regain her balance. The world came slowly back into focus.

But it was a different world. Everything had changed. The saguaros had come alive. The giant armed cacti were writhing, undulating monsters. Their spines were wriggling needles with what might have been venom dripping from their tips. They reached out for her, forcing her to dodge and weave across the rocks and ground that were now covered with a layer of roiling, dripping slime. She pushed forward. Her feet still found solid footing, proving to her that the illusion was only attacking her mind. But the grotesque hallucination was powerful, and she felt herself wearing down. Sarah, Sarah, Sarah. Repeating her daughter's name was her only source of strength now.

She rounded a tight corner and found herself staring at a writhing giant serpent. The hideous snake was coiled in the path in front of her. Its body was black and shimmering. Its head, stretching up eight feet off the ground, was that of a horned viper and seemed too large for its body. It spread its massive jaws, revealing two enormous dripping fangs. It struck at her. She jumped back and fell, hurting her back.

She was writhing on the ground in intense pain. She could see, beyond the snake, the switchbacks that led to the final ascent to the cave. She was close. She had to keep going. She forced herself up to her knees, took out the knife and the bag of bone ash. The snake was rearing back as if to strike again. She dipped the blade of the knife into the powder.

Exactly as the snake sprang forward, she leapt and met it, plunging the knife into its body. The snake and the rest of the illusion instantly vanished. Her momentum caused her to fall forward, hitting the ground hard. The knife flew out of her hand and over the edge of the trail. She scrambled to find it, but it was too dark. Her one weapon was gone. She pulled herself up off the ground and started running up the trail with furious determination.

"You don't get to have her. I'm coming, and I will fight you!"

Just then a bolt of lightning struck near her, knocking her against some rocks. Her face was scratched badly and bleeding.

"Not good enough!" She kept running. A vicious bombardment of lightning strikes blasted the night. They exploded on the ground all around, close to her. She could feel the earth shake with every strike. They rocked the entire mountain, causing her to stumble with each step. But she fought through them, muscling her way up the last of the switchbacks.

Her legs were screaming in agony with the effort. Sarah. Sarah. Sarah. She could see the looming shadow of the opening to the cave above her. A lightning bolt hit right in front of her, blinding her. She collapsed onto her knees. Her eyes were burning from the heat of the flash. She knelt motionless, hands on her face. The lightning stopped. It was silent again.

It took her some time to be able to open her eyes. When she did, all she could see for a while was the intense afterglow of the lightning. It gradually faded and the night came back into focus. She saw what she thought was a coyote, walking down the trail toward her. The sight of it made her nauseous. It had no skin. It had been completely flayed. Its tongue was hanging out of its mouth to one side. It was a mass of musculature and blood. Its eyes were bulging from its bloody, skinned skull. They were not the human-like eyes of the skinwalkers. This was a real coyote. It was an awful, gut-wrenching sight. She had never seen a sadder thing in her life. The tortured animal collapsed about five feet from her and died. The coyote was a sacred animal to those she now knew as her people. She felt an overwhelming, primordial sorrow at seeing it treated with such contempt and cruelty. She knew why the skinwalkers are so reviled. Their evil goes beyond a lust for power, it violates the tribe's sacred connection to the natural world.

Amelia got to her feet, stepped over the poor animal and started to climb the last leg of the trail to the cave. As she climbed, she saw that the sides of the trail were littered with more skinless bodies of coyotes. They were being devoured by insects and rats. She knew that this wasn't another illusion. It was real and heartbreaking.

A crackle from the radio on her hip startled her. It was her husband.

"Amelia? Can you hear me? Are you there?"

She'd forgotten about the radio and the rest of the world. She grabbed it.

"Ben? Yes, I'm here. I'm almost at the cave."

"Are you all right?"

"Ben, there's...ahhh!!"

The radio burst into flames. She dropped it. Her hand was burnt. She looked up at the cave, her eyes full of rage.

"Damn you."

The momentary contact with Ben and the pain in her hand snapped her back to life. She looked at the carnage around her. The skinwalker had made a mistake. The awfulness of the coyote carcasses had become a sudden source of new energy and strength. Seeing the unimaginable savagery of the demon, the unconscionable evil it was capable of, made her realize the horrors that might await her daughter. Amelia bolted up the last stretch of trail to the cave, a fierce primal anger surging through her Anasazi blood.

The opening of the cave was over twenty feet high, just as wide and twice as deep. Sarah was standing in the middle of the cavern dressed only in the long white T-shirt she always wore to sleep in. The light from her glowing skin illuminated the space around her. No skinwalkers anywhere. Sarah was staring blankly at nothing.

"Sarah. It's mommy. Can you hear me, honey?"

Sarah didn't answer. She just stood there, in some sort of trance. Her mother started toward her, but movement caught her eye, and she stopped. The walls and roof of the mine were a solid, writhing mass of scorpions. One of the creatures dropped down onto Sarah's head. Amelia rushed toward her daughter but stopped cold, as she saw the pattern of bones arranged on the ground. They formed a pathway leading to a circle of more bones, in the middle of which Sarah was standing. At the top of the circle was a dog-like skull.

It was a trap, she could feel it. More scorpions fell onto Sarah, who simply stood there, not reacting to them at all. Amelia was shaking with fury and horror. Scorpions fell in mass and completely covered Sarah, crawling all over her body. Her mother stood her ground, terrified that she was making a mistake, that she could be witnessing the death of her daughter. But she had to gamble that this was another illusion, another trick of the skinwalker. If she took the bait, she had no chance of saving her.

"Get off my daughter." Her voice was deep and powerful, as if it were coming from another part of her being.

The scorpions crawled off of Sarah's body and vanished into the ground.

The bones that had been laid out on the floor of the cavern started to move. They skittered across the earth and pulled slowly together into a mass that rose up into a skeletal form. Before Amelia's eyes, it grew flesh and transformed into the yee naaldlooshiii herself.

The skinwalker stood upright, a coyote with human eyes, but diseased, covered with sores and missing patches of hair. She was bent over, a ridge of spine protruding from her back. Her eyes were burning with unmistakable evil. They also betrayed deep misery. The mouth was open, revealing ugly rotting teeth and a black tongue. There was a brownish slime dripping out of it. A dead raven hung from a braided cord around her neck.

Amelia faced the repulsive vision without fear. "Give me back my daughter."

The yee naaldlooshiii thrust her wicked cadaverous snout close to Amelia's face and sniffed. She spoke in a raspy, high-pitched voice that echoed through the mine.

"I sense another child. Good. Once I've used your daughter, he'll be next."

Amelia could smell the morbid stench of her breath. "Let her go."

"Those ghost beads can't protect you in my presence."

The skinwalker ripped the necklace off Amelia's neck and threw them. They incinerated in the air.

"You're nothing but a harmless mouse to me."

She grabbed the dead raven from around her neck and threw it onto the ground. It burst into raging scarlet flames that shot almost to the roof of the cavern. The yee naaldlooshiii walked into the flames and was consumed instantly. Thick black smoke rose out of the inferno and took the form of a huge raven with wings of fire. Its eyes glowed a deep blood red. The shapeshifter, now in raven spirit form, glared down at Amelia and screeched with a deafening power that knocked Amelia to the ground.

Amelia's ears were ringing and her head pounding. She managed to twist her body to look back at her daughter.

The fire had formed a ring around Sarah. It was moving in toward her. The evil raven had turned its attention to Sarah, hovering over her.

Sarah suddenly came out of her trance and saw herself surrounded by flames. She saw her mother lying on the ground.

"Mom?"

"Don't move, baby." Amelia saw the bag of powdered bones the old man had given her. It had fallen out of her pocket.

She rolled her body away from the vile fiery bird spirit so it couldn't see her empty the white ash into her hand. When the ground bones touched her skin, a sudden powerful energy pulsed through her body, a blood connection to thousands of long-forgotten souls. She felt a surge of desperately needed strength.

Acting now not just as Amelia, but as an entire people, she rose to her feet. She called out in a voice from ancient times.

"Yee Naaldlooshii!"

The demon bird whipped its head toward her. Amelia threw the ash into its face. The creature screamed hideously, flapped its fiery wings and flailed, out of control, tumbling over and over in the air. Amelia leapt through the fire and grabbed Sarah. She threw her to the ground and shielded her with her own body. Ghastly ear-splitting shrieks made the whole mountain shake. Rocks were falling from the roof of the cave. The smoke turned to a deathly yellow color and started to swirl in a powerful funnel-like inferno. Amelia could just make out the shape of the raven, which transformed into an old woman grabbing in agony at her own hair. The shapeshifter was sucked into the hellfire.

Amelia felt intense heat on her skin as a sudden flash of blazing white light consumed the whole of the cavern.

Then it was gone. All of it. The cave was still.

Amelia pulled herself up onto an elbow. "Sarah? Honey? Are you with me? Sarah?"

Sarah Llewelyn lifted her head and looked into her mother's face, then around at the cave.

"Where are we?"

"We're in a cave way up on a mountain, honey."

"Why are we here?"

"Well, you were sleepwalking. But I found you. Everything's okay now."

"Am I still glowing?"

Amelia had forgotten about the glow. When she saw it was gone, she couldn't help but laugh with overwhelming relief.

"No, honey. You're not glowing anymore."

"Oh, good. Mom?"

"Yeah, honey?"

"I'm hungry."

Amelia hugged her daughter tight. She looked across the cavern. Lying on the ground were the remains of the old yee naaldlooshiii. The skinwalker was no more. All that remained was a human corpse, ancient and withered, skin dried and shrunken and barely clinging to the bones.

TWO DAYS LATER, THE Llewelyn family was heading for the Caribbean, having booked ten days at a resort with all the amenities. They'd quickly come to the conclusion that a complete change of scenery would be the best start to healing the psychological damage done by the entire ordeal.

Before they left, Amelia wanted to thank the old Navajo Medicine Man that Becky had tracked down. She paid another visit to the museum.

"His name is Jensen Henry," said Becky. "Turns out he's pretty well known."

"Where does he live?"

"He's in a care facility on the north edge of Tucson. Shouldn't take you more than twenty minutes to get there."

She wrote down the address. Amelia thanked her for all her help and for looking after Zach. They said goodbye, promising to keep in touch. Amelia wanted to know much more about her ancestry, her new culture.

Driving north, on her way to the care facility, Amelia gazed out at the vast Sonoran landscape. The desert no longer made her feel uneasy. Just the opposite. The red rock mesas and the craggy canyons adorned with saguaros were a part of her. They were in her blood.

She walked into the office of the assisted living facility and asked where she might find Mr. Henry.

"Are you a relative?"

When she heard the question, Amelia realized the receptionist had recognized, as Becky had, that she was of Native American decent. It made her feel good. "No," said Amelia,

"We just ran into each other a few times. He did me a huge favor, and I wanted to thank him."

"You ran into him? Really? Where?"

"Well, I first saw him back east. But we actually met here in Tucson."

The receptionist looked at her oddly. "You saw him back east?"

"Yeah, in New York, where I live."

"I'm sorry," replied the receptionist, "but that's impossible."

"What do you mean?"

The receptionist got up and said. "Come with me."

She led Amelia to a grassy courtyard with lovely gardens, tables and chairs and a small fountain. A number of elderly people were playing cards, or just sitting out in the sunshine, some alone, some in conversation.

She pointed out at the lawn. "That's Jensen, over there."

It was him, definitely. He was wearing his old fedora and sport coat. He saw Amelia. He smiled and nodded his head.

"Jensen hasn't left our home here for over two years, and I doubt if he's ever been to New York. Maybe you're mixing him up with someone else."

He was sitting in a wheelchair. Both of his legs had been amputated above the knees.

The Spring

from a story idea by Cynthia Carle

Residents of Henley lived at a quiet remove from the outside world, oddly proud of their isolation and irrelevance. Surrounded by the silent foggy mists of Redwood National Park, it was a town that seemed lost in time, several miles off Highway 101 in a picturesque valley north of the more vibrant communities of Eureka and Arcadia. Being enveloped by the park had spared Henley from the onslaught of loggers and ravenous developers who had chewed up countless acres of pristine wilderness beyond the park boundaries. The population of the town, hovering just under a thousand, hadn't changed substantially in many years.

The town's newest resident was Dean Morrison, an eighty-one-year-old widower who'd moved in with his daughter, Laurie, following the death of his wife the previous year. Dean and his wife, Uma, lived in San Francisco for over forty years. He'd been a tenured professor of environmental science at San Francisco State University. In his field, he was a celebrity. His seminal works on global warming, especially on the exchange of carbon between the atmosphere and biosphere, and how carbon stocks change in response to reforestation and deforestation had garnered him worldwide praise. He'd spent the bulk of his life trying to convince the world that forests were the lifeblood of our atmosphere and should be protected at all costs.

After Uma died, the big house in Pacific Heights had become unmanageable for Dean, and he reluctantly agreed to move up to Henley and live with Laurie. It was a hard move for Dean. He cherished his daughter and had nothing against Henley. But leaving San Francisco, and everything that represented the life he'd shared with Uma for so many years, was gut-wrenching.

The one consolation was that he was moving to the redwoods, a part of the earth for which he and Uma had developed a special fondness. Before she became ill, they'd made many a trip north to visit Laurie and take long walks through the park. Their favorite trek was a virtually untraveled canyon trail along the banks of a creek not far from Laurie's house. It was a lush, moist primeval world of huge ferns and moss-covered rocks and logs, unchanged for millennia. Hiking through this soft verdant realm was like stepping back in time. They often joked that one day they would round a bend in the trail and come face to face with a dinosaur munching on a huckleberry bush.

It was not always just the two of them. For the last years of their life together, they were accompanied on their adventures by Cinda, their black lab/border collie mix. They'd rescued her fourteen years ago from a pound in the city. Cinda favored the lab, except for the white streak between her eyes and two white back feet. She was the perfect dog, smart, devoted, and happy.

Since Uma died, Cinda stuck to Dean like glue, doing her best to make up for Uma's absence.

Cinda wore a faded red bandana that they'd tied around her neck years before. She was very proud of her bandana. Whenever they took it off to be washed, Cinda would sit by the laundry and wait until it was finally dry. If the dryer stopped and no one was paying attention, she would bark to alert them. When the bandana was finally tied back around her neck, she would jump for joy and run around the house in celebration.

These kinds of Cinda antics were one of the main things that still kept Dean going. But the old age thing pissed him off. He resented the creaky bones, the shortness of breath, the way young people looked at him now. He used to be treated with admiration from students, aspiring environmental activists who saw him as an inspiration and wanted to follow in his footsteps. "Will you sign your book for me, professor?" But now he was just another old man in America. He felt like an annoying broken-down car blocking the road to the future. Honk. Honk. For God's sake, get that old jalopy out of the way.

When Uma was alive, they defied the concept of age. Dean had kept himself in the best of shape, toned and strong and always ready for their next trip to the Amazon or the wilds of Alaska, often with a group of students who were surprised and intimidated that their professor was in better shape than they were. He pushed them as hard in the field as he did in the classroom. "How are you going to save the world if you can't even climb a mountain?"

Even as age started messing with ligaments and lung capacity, Dean and Uma laughed off the aches and pains and lived, at least in their minds, pretty much like they did when they were thirty. They were masters of their own world and fed off of each other's energy. Without Uma, however, Dean had lost interest in his own physical well-being, and his energy was fading fast.

When Uma had suddenly developed major heart issues six years earlier, Dean felt compelled to quit teaching and devote himself to caring for her. He hadn't intended to retire that soon, and Uma tried her best to talk him out of it. She insisted that she was perfectly fine with hiring a home health assistant to tend to her special needs. But Dean refused. He put his all into her care without an ounce of bitterness.

But sitting on the sidelines as the world spiraled toward environmental disaster ate at him. As he read headline after headline about droughts and floods and melting ice caps, he knew should be out there, on the front lines, helping develop the science that would pull humanity out of this death dive. He kept these feelings to himself, of course, never speaking of his frustrations to Uma, or anyone else for that matter. But she knew. And it upset her to see him reading his colleagues' work or magazine features, knowing how crushing it was to him not to see his own name there, not to be involved and productive.

When he first retired he did some bits of consulting work that he could handle from home and wrote a few papers for select publications. But what logically might have resulted in at least some satisfaction actually led to even further frustration. He felt like it was some sort of desperate, half-assed attempt to remain relevant. And he had always lived by the creed, that his father had pounded into him as a boy, that if you're going to do something half-assed don't bother doing it at all.

And so, steeling himself to his irrelevance, he'd passed the torch to the young. It was the way it worked, right? The future of the earth has always been and will always be in the hands of the young. Except he didn't believe a word of it, thought it was all a bunch of crap. He didn't trust the young. They didn't have the patience and experience to focus their idealism and energy on practical solutions. Where would South Africa be if they'd left it in the hands of the young? It was Nelson Mandela, an old man who'd been in prison for 26 years, who saved the country and changed the world. When was the last time someone 25 years old won a Nobel Prize?

Now, six years after his retirement, Dean felt pretty much like a footnote in history. Unless he wanted to sell memberships to Greenpeace at farmers' markets, there was no place for a forgotten eighty-one-year-old prof.

LAURIE'S HOUSE WAS on the edge of town on a street that dead-ended at the park border. There was an unofficial trailhead at the end of the road that was really only known by the locals, so the park personnel didn't go to any great lengths to limit its use. This was the trail that Dean and Uma had walked countless times.

Seven months ago, Dean, accompanied by Cinda, had carried Uma's ashes to their beloved woods and spread them amongst the ferns and soft redwood mulch. It was the second morning of his new life in Henley. Each day since, after Laurie had left for work, Dean and Cinda walked the same three-mile round trip through the canyon and back. Every so often, on their way to the trailhead, they would stop to chat with one of the locals. Over the months, Dean had gotten to know a few of the neighbors. They were quiet and friendly people, sometimes gathering for a neighborhood barbecue to swap stories of elk incursions into their vegetable gardens or the spotting of a banana slug of world-record proportions.

On this particular morning, Dean and Cinda met up with Aaron Boyle, a shy ten-year-old riding his bike to school. They frequently ran into Aaron on weekdays, as his school schedule usually timed out with their morning excursion. Aaron was crazy about Cinda, and Dean often let him take her for short walks on his own in the evening when Dean didn't have the energy himself.

Aaron skidded his bike to a stop, let it fall and kneeled to pet Cinda. She wagged her tail and licked his face copiously.

"Hi, Cinda."

It was hard to get much in the way of conversation out of Aaron, but Dean did his best. "Morning, Aaron. Get all your homework done last night?"

"Yeah."

"Big day at school?"

"Math test."

"You'll do fine."

"If I get a B, I get a puppy."

"A puppy?"

"It's my birthday next week."

"A puppy is a lot of responsibility, you know."

"That's what my dad keeps saying."

Dean knew that a puppy was in the plans for Aaron's birthday. He'd run into his mother a couple of days before, and she'd kiddingly blamed Dean, since Aaron's obsession with having a dog had begun when Dean and Cinda had moved to the neighborhood.

"Can I walk Cinda after school?"

"Sure."

"Okay. Bye, Cinda." Aaron climbed back onto his bike and rolled off down the road.

"Good luck with that math test, Aaron."

Cinda gave a quick bark and made for the trailhead. Her morning encounters with Aaron's youthful energy always gave a boost to her doggie spirit and put an extra bounce in her step. If it had any such effect on Dean, he didn't show it.

The path that led into the park wound through a small meadow for about a hundred feet before reaching the tree line and disappearing into thick woods. The trail was bordered by sword ferns, sorrel, huckleberry and a profusion of rhododendrons, which were in full Spring bloom. As many times as he'd been here, whenever Dean entered this primordial realm, he would stop and gaze up in fresh wonder at the majestic three hundred-foot giants.

Anyone entering an ancient redwood forest for the first time couldn't help but think they had stepped into a dream, or perhaps been transported into the fantastic world of a Tolkien novel. Uma once said that just standing there felt like a privilege, as if she and Dean were here only because the trees had allowed them to be. Such was the sublime majesty of the redwood forest.

A walk through the redwoods is a unique experience, not just for the awe-inspiring presence of the magnificent trees, but for the incomparable quietude. Within moments, one becomes aware of an almost unearthly silence. The mulch underfoot is a thick cushion of decomposing bark and needles, which completely dampens any sound a footstep might make. Contributing further to this transcendent peace is the peculiar absence of bird sounds. A few seabird species nests in groves near the seashore, but the inland redwood forest is distinctly lacking in feathered inhabitants, save for the occasional Steller's jay, whose sudden loud rawwwk can startle a visitor basking in the solitude of the woods.

In her own dog way, Cinda seemed to take as much pleasure in their walk as Dean did. She would dig and roll in the soft forest floor and every once in awhile root out a chipmunk or a wood rat. Then she'd tear through the underbrush, determined to make the kill, but never succeeding. Sometimes she would go so far that Dean would lose sight of her. But a whistle or call would bring her back to his side quickly and without fail.

Leaving their scant bit of civilization behind, Dean and Cinda made their way along the soft winding trail, down a gradual embankment toward a creek. Through the ages, the creek had cut a relatively deep canyon through the trees. A thick blanket of ferns festooned the vertical sides of the canyon. On the steeper sections of the path, steps had been dug into the hillside and a railing added to aid hikers. At the bottom of the steps the trail leveled out a few feet above the beautiful brook which spilled over moss-covered rocks and the remains of fallen trees, forming crystal clear pools in which tiny fish darted about.

Further down the track was a bench that was carved out of an enormous ancient fallen redwood. This was Dean and Uma's favorite spot. Across the creek was a fantastic stand of redwoods towering over a carpet of sword ferns. Dean thought of this particular stand as "Uma's trees." It was amongst these trees that he had sprinkled Uma's ashes. Dean would sit there on the bench, gazing at the arboreal beauty with Cinda at his feet. In her own way, she too somehow understood the meaningfulness of this spot.

Dean's mind often wandered back to the times when they would indulge in the silence, and soak in the ethereal wonder of the forest. Dean had once noticed a peculiar look on Uma's face. He asked her what she was thinking. She said she wasn't thinking, she was listening to the trees.

"Do you hear them?" she asked.

"I don't hear anything. What are they saying?"

"They're saying 'Tell him to listen closer.'"

Dean loved that Uma had access to realms he couldn't perceive. While he cherished the trees and the quiet of the forest as much as she did, his scientific mind was focused on carbon storage and oxygen conversion. Uma was in touch with something else, something magical, beyond science and his kind of logical thinking.

And it was here, on this bench that he would still sit and talk to her, let her in on his daily frustrations and challenges his life took on without her.

But what was once an easy jaunt had become harder and harder, not only testing his physical abilities but his patience. Today's hike had made him especially weary, his legs in particular complaining loudly. He winced, kicked at a piece of bark and unleashed his anger.

"Damn stupid useless old body! What's the point, keeping someone like me alive? Nothing to offer to anyone. Just a bunch of damn nonsense! Burdening our own daughter with this pathetic existence. Shameful! Shameful! You and I never had to deal with this crap when we hiked these trails. Oh, I know, I know. Deal with it old man, nobody said anything about fair. Huh. Easy for you to say. You got out when the getting was good."

Wearing himself out even more with his outburst, Dean began to drift off. In a dreamy alpha state he had a vague image of Uma sitting beside him, touching his leg. It seems she was speaking to him but her words sounded more like a high-pitched crying. He was startled awake to discover that the sound he was hearing was Cinda, who was standing a ways down the trail whining. Dean looked down at her and saw her focused intently on the grove across the creek, Uma's trees.

"What is it, girl?"

"Ciiindaaaa."

A voice was calling to his dog, a faraway voice that echoed through the forest. He gasped. A chill shot up his spine. His heart started racing. He knew the voice. He knew it like he knew the color of the sky. It was Uma's voice. But, of course, that was impossible, absurd.

Cinda whined once more, then jumped up and bounded across the creek and into the grove of trees.

"Cinda, come back here!" Dean pushed himself up off the bench and stared as Cinda ran through the ferns and disappeared into the forest. He heard the voice calling her again.

"Ciiindaaaa."

Good God. It was Uma's voice. He was sure of it. He thought he must be losing his mind. What the hell was going on? He thought maybe he'd had a small stroke when he nodded off.

He called out as loud and sternly as he could. "Cinda! Cinda!" Then he whistled. Nothing.

That Cinda didn't respond to his command was almost as startling as the voice he was hearing. There was only one person who ever had more authority over her than he did. Uma. But this was completely insane. It couldn't, of course, be Uma. He was trying and failing to get his mind around what was happening. He made his way to the creek, splashed across a shallow rocky section, and pulled himself awkwardly onto the opposite bank. His feet were now soaked, and he stumbled up a slippery embankment. He fell to a knee once but finally managed to get himself up onto the forest floor beneath Uma's trees. He heard Cinda barking.

"For Christ's sake. Dumb dog. Cinda!"

He headed in the general direction of her bark. The way the redwood forest dampened noise, it was impossible to tell how far off she might be. He was hoping she was closer than she sounded.

Dean knew that moving off-trail in a redwood forest was not the best idea. Young redwoods grow in crowded profusion in many areas, and huckleberry and rhododendrons can create an almost impenetrable thicket. But he couldn't leave Cinda out there. His adrenaline kept him going, as well as his extreme curiosity about who it was that was calling to her.

The effort served to clear his mind some and allow him to think more logically. This was a situation in which a scientific mind could, and probably should apply the principle of

Occam's razor. Always start by considering the phenomenon with the simplest hypothesis possible. Okay, someone was calling to Cinda. It sounded like Uma but, obviously, it wasn't Uma. It had to be someone who happened to have a voice very similar to hers. So, following the sound of Cinda's barking would eventually reveal the source of the voice and solve the mystery.

The problem, however, was that cutting a path through increasingly more difficult terrain was a slow and painful slog. But Dean was committed and not about to turn back. Every so often, he would hear her bark again. Sometimes she sounded close as if he was gaining ground, but then the next bark would seem even further away. He continued calling to her, knowing that if he could hear her, she could certainly hear him. But it was no use. Whoever was leading her off was in charge.

Dean pushed through a thick tangle of brush and stopped at the edge of a steep slope. Another small creek had cut a deep ravine through the forest. It extended a long way in both directions. There was no obvious way to get across it. The bank pitched steeply down about thirty feet to an abrupt edge that then dropped off to the creek fifteen feet below.

He was standing on the edge, pondering the next move when the earth suddenly gave out under his feet. He fell on his back and started sliding down the embankment. He was heading fast toward the drop-off. He grabbed at the ground, desperately trying to stop his momentum as he slid toward disaster. He was in no shape to survive a fifteen-foot drop onto a rocky creek bed. His feet slipped over the edge. At the last moment, his hand touched on a large root, and he managed to grab onto it and stop his slide. He held himself there, gasping with exhaustion and relief. He had come close to what would most likely have been the big goodbye. Even if the fall didn't kill him outright, lying in that creek bed injured would be curtains. He doubted that anyone ever ventured into this part of the park, so there'd be no one to hear a call for help.

He lay still for some moments and caught his breath. He was in a very precarious situation, to say the least. He had to get back up the hill, away from the drop-off. His legs were dangling over the cliff from the knees down so as he tried to push himself up with his feet he only managed to gouge the fragile rim of the shelf and push dirt and rocks over the edge. He finally managed to turn over onto his stomach and grab onto the root with his other hand as well. His strength was waning, and he used all of his reserves to gradually pull himself up, a few extra feet from disaster. He cursed his weak old-man arms.

He saw another root a little ways further up the slope. He managed to just grab it and hoist himself, somewhat painfully, into a sitting position. He braced his feet on the lower root.

He heard another bark. This time it seemed fairly close.

"Oh, shut up. Damn mongrel."

Dean glanced up to the top of the embankment. It was way too steep to try and climb back up. Nothing to hold onto, no footholds. He might get a few feet then find himself sliding back down, and this time he wouldn't have any strength left to resist. Only a couple of yards below him was the perilous drop into the creek bed. He let himself fall back onto the ground. He closed his eyes and listened to his heart pounding. He thought perhaps the old pump might just give out and relieve him of having to deal with anything more. He realized, oddly, that in spite of his exhaustion, he was surprisingly comfortable. The redwood mulch beneath him was cool and soft as a mattress. Okay, not a bad place to die.

As he was lying there, he remembered a winter hike he and Uma had taken in Denali Park in Alaska. They were on a steep snowy trail when they hit a patch of ice, lost their footing, and slid a good forty feet back down the hillside. They lay there laughing hysterically. Dean joked that he was just going to make an igloo and stay right there. He didn't have it in him to go any further. Uma called him a wimp and challenged him to a race back up the hill. Now, lying there on this far more threatening slope, he didn't have Uma to inspire him.

He heard a faint buzzing sound. He opened his eyes and sat up. A dragonfly zipped up in front of his face and hovered there. It was fairly startling, even though it wasn't really unusual behavior for a dragonfly. They seem to be curious creatures. He'd had the same experience a number of times in marshy areas near the coast where they're plentiful. What was strange was that it was happening here, in the middle of the woods. This was not a dragonfly habitat. Even odder was the dragonfly itself. It was almost completely transparent with a slight, shimmery golden glow to it. Dean stared, fascinated and, in spite of the circumstance, somewhat delighted. The vibration of its almost invisible wings created a soothing high-pitched hum. It was hypnotic.

The glassy dragonfly shot off to his right, flew about sixty feet down the edge of the embankment, hovered for a moment, then lighted on a large root that stuck out from the hillside. Dean leaned forward and noticed that it was part of an old tangled root system from an enormous redwood that extended over the embankment to the creek bed below. It had been exposed over the years by natural erosion. If he could get to it, he might be able to lower himself down the roots into the creek bed.

He thought it odd that this unusual insect might have accidentally provided a way out of his predicament. He smiled, thinking that Uma would undoubtedly laugh at his accident theory. She'd probably say the creature was some kind of woodland sprite sent to help him. The dragonfly lifted off the root, hovered for a moment then sped away, disappearing into the forest on the other side of the creek.

Accident or not, Dean still had the substantial challenge of getting across the slope to the roots. One false step and he'd go over the edge. But there was really no alternative.

Using some breathing techniques Uma had taught him, he got his heart rate back down to something approaching normal. He stood up slowly, steadied himself and made his move, planting one foot carefully in front of the other. Fortunately, the ground was soft enough to be able to dig in and make a bit of a foothold with each step. About halfway there, he slipped and almost lost his balance. But he had one foot well planted and managed to catch himself. He finally reached the root system. It was a more massive tangle than he even realized. He could see that if he wasn't careful climbing down, he could get trapped in the branches in such a way that he'd never be able to extricate himself. But he might not get out of this mess anyway, so what the hell.

He heard Cinda's bark again. It seemed further away than ever.

"Yeah, yeah," Dean called into the woods, "We're both too old for this, you crazy mutt!"

He sat on the edge of the bank, grabbed onto one of the stouter top roots and lowered himself over the edge. He dangled there, trying to get his feet to connect with something, but all of the larger roots were vertical, and there was nothing substantial to use as a foot brace. His arms were straining badly. His weight was too much and he slid down the root, burning and scraping the flesh of his palms. But he finally grabbed onto another root with his feet, as if he were climbing a rope, and stopped his fall. His hands felt like they were on fire, but he managed to hang on and lower himself a bit at a time.

He didn't look to see how far below the creek bed was. He knew that if he did, he'd be tempted to give up and just let go, come what may. It was an almost unbearable strain as he inched his way downward. He could feel the last bits of energy leaving him. His feet finally touched the gravel of the creek bed. His heart was beating so hard he thought he could hear it echo through the redwoods. He looked at his burnt raw palms.

He hobbled over to the creek, knelt down, and plunged his hands into a cold pool. The relief was palpable. But he knew it wouldn't last long. He cupped some water into his hands and drank. He splashed some over his face, and the back of his neck then sat on a moss-covered boulder. Every bone and muscle in his body was screaming.

Another bark. He pulled his aching body off the rock and headed down the creek. He'd gotten about a hundred feet when he heard a flurry of barks off to his left. Just ahead he saw a huge redwood tree that had fallen into the creek. Its roots were still embedded into the hillside above. He pulled himself up onto it and used the branches that were still protruding vertically to steady himself as he climbed up out of the creek bed and back onto the forest floor.

Dean found himself in a stand of redwoods the likes of which he'd never seen. They were beyond magnificent, so enormous that the canopy above was completely invisible. He moved beneath the arboreal behemoths, stopped and stared up, in awe. He'd seen some amazing stand of trees before but nothing ever like this. He had the feeling that, in spite of the pain he had endured getting here, something very sacred had been bestowed upon him. He wished that he could share this moment with Uma.

He heard Cinda bark again. She was closer now.

"Cinda!" His voice was tired. He wasn't sure she could even hear him now.

Moving reverently to the far edge of this glorious grove of giants, he came to another dense thicket of underbrush. But this one was different. He couldn't quite decipher what he was seeing. Deep into it, he saw a strange light, a twinkling luminescence, like the sun glistening off raindrops. He strode into the thicket, pushing aside branches and squeezing between young trees.

A new sound emerged from up ahead. A kind of high-pitched yipping. He couldn't tell if it was a sound of excitement or distress.

He made his way out of the thicket and stepped into a dream.

Before him was a glimmering pool of water, almost perfectly round, no more than forty feet in diameter. It was surrounded by tufts of deep green grasses and a round-leafed groundcover alight with bright purple flowers. Larger bushes were decked out with various shades of exotic blooms. On the far side of the spring was a stack of mossy boulders. Lacey ferns adorned the rocks and a small waterfall spilled from a crevice near the top and splashed into the pool below, creating a lovely fine mist. The air was filled with a profusion of glittering translucent golden dragonflies, just like the one that had visited Dean in the forest.

Dean gazed out at the enchanted world, transfixed with wonder.

Something in the pool caught his eye. About a foot from the shore, he saw a reddish form, floating just below the surface. He moved to the edge and reached into the water. He felt a slight tingling sensation in his hand. He grabbed the object and pulled it out of the pool. It was Cinda's red bandana.

His eyes scanned the spring. Was it possible? Cinda was always a very good swimmer. But she was old now, and she hadn't been in the water for a long time.

"Cinda! Cinda! Come on, girl."

He heard a splashing off to his right. Then a yip. A small puppy came bouncing along the shallow edge of the spring toward him. It was soaking wet. It stopped at his feet and stared up at him. It yipped several more times and jumped a little as if wanting to play. It ran back into the pool and splashed around the shallows at the edge, jumping and frolicking in the crystal clear water. It trotted back to Dean and started gnawing on his shoelaces.

Dean leaned over to pick up the dripping little pooch. The puppy grabbed the red bandana in its teeth and shook it playfully. Dean held it away from his face a bit.

"Where did you come from...oh, good lord."

The puppy was black with a white streak between its eyes and two little white back feet.

Puppy Cinda yipped again and licked Dean's face.

A soft ocean breeze wafted through the redwoods.

Dean stared out at the spring. He stared and stared.

THE EARLY EVENING SUN hadn't quite dipped beneath the tips of the western hills above Henley. Aaron Boyle was in his front yard, sticking flame decals onto his bicycle.

A dark shape loomed into view next to him. He looked up. Someone was standing there. But the figure was between him and the sun, and he couldn't make out who it was.

"Hello, Aaron. I have something for you."

Aaron stood up and shielded his eyes. He saw Dean, holding a little black and white puppy.

"Hey, where'd you get the puppy?"

"Well, I got her from an old friend. She needs a good home. You think you could take care of her?"

"You're giving her to me?"

"That's the idea."

Dean handed the puppy over to Aaron. He laughed as it slathered his face with licks. Dean had never heard Aaron laugh before.

"I hope my mom lets me keep her."

"I already talked to her, so I don't think you have to worry about that."

Dean wasn't twenty again, but he felt like it. When actually presented with the choice, he'd understood. The three-thousand-year-old redwood giants wouldn't exist had it not been for the ones who came before, that succumbed to age and fell, creating the rich earth that nourished new saplings. Against all the odds, they'd withstood eons of fires and floods and become the magnificent sentinels that Dean and Uma so cherished.

Uma led him to the spring and offered him a gift beyond imagining. He hadn't taken the dive back into youth, but from that extraordinary gesture of devotion, Dean felt reborn in a different way. The energy of life was flowing through him again with all the intensity of the love he felt for Uma the first time he saw her. He didn't know how long it would last. He didn't care. He'd touched the magic that Uma had known.

"Where's Cinda?" asked Aaron.

"Well, she's gone to live with someone who can take better care of her."

"Oh. I can bring my puppy to visit you. You can take her for walks when I'm at school if you want."

"That'll be nice, Aaron. Thank you."

The puppy wriggled and squirmed and licked Aaron's face.

"Hey. She has markings like Cinda."

"How about that."

Don't miss out!

Click the button below and you can sign up to receive emails whenever Christopher Reed publishes a new book. There's no charge and no obligation.

Sign Me Up![1]

https://books2read.com/r/B-A-TLIJ-BHXBB

BOOKS 2 READ

Connecting independent readers to independent writers.

1. https://books2read.com/r/B-A-TLIJ-BHXBB

About the Author

Christopher Reed is a screenwriter, novelist and playwright. His screenwriting credits include THE SIXTH MAN (Touchstone Pictures) and YOU WISH (Disney channel) for which he was a Humanitas Award finalist. He is the author of two novels, THE BIG SCRATCH (Ballantine Books/Bastei Lubbe) and THE BLACK CLAW. He has written screenplays for Disney Animation, Sony Pictures and Nickelodeon, often teaming with his wife and writing partner, Cynthia Carle. His plays have been performed in various cities across the country, and he recently wrote a feature animation screenplay for the Chinese company Mili Pictures Worldwide. He is also a screenwriting consultant and teaches screenwriting for The Writing Pad, Inc. in Los Angeles.

About the Publisher

Madness Heart Press is dedicated to bringing you quality horror from new and amazing authors. You can find more books, stories and even listen to the Madness Heart Radio Podcast at MadnessHeart.Press

Made in the USA
Middletown, DE
22 November 2019

79184861R00151